D0031275

BOOK THREE

THE BALANCE OF POWER

BOOK THREE

THE BALANCE OF POWER

WRITTEN BY
STAN LEE AND STUART MOORE

ART BY
ANDIE TONG

DISNEY PRESS
Los Angeles • New York

Printed in the United States of America

First Edition, March 2017

1 3 5 7 9 10 8 6 4 2

Library of Congress Control Number: 2016953974

FAC-020093-17020

ISBN 978-1-4847-1351-8

Visit disneybooks.com and disneyzodiac.com

THIS LABEL APPLIES TO TEXT STOCK

Stan Lee's
POW!
ENTERTAINMENT

PART ONE
THE MOUNTAIN OF FIRE

CHAPTER ONE

STEVEN LEE inched his way down the rocky wall, grabbing at one handhold after another. *Don't look down,* he told himself. *You're not gonna fall. There's a rope holding you up, a big thick cow-wrangler-type rope strapped to the harness on your back. You're not gonna fall.*

Just don't look down.

He looked down. The chamber was wide and dark, made of yellow-and-brown rock dotted with shiny mica deposits. Little streams of water trickled down the walls. The cavern floor was at least six meters below, with a surface almost as jagged as the walls. If he fell, he could really hurt himself.

Okay, he thought, reaching for an outcropping in the wall. *You looked down. That was a mistake. But it's okay. Just don't fall. Don't fall. Do. Not. Fall.*

He fell.

The rock wall whizzed by at a dizzying speed. His harness pulled tight against his waist, but the rope went slack. *Great,* he thought. *The rope's no good if it's not tied tight enough!*

He scrabbled and grabbed, slowing his fall, but his gloves kept slipping off the slick rocks. He twisted his body, willing the Tiger—his Zodiac avatar—to emerge, to take control of his reflexes. But the Tiger was silent.

Stupid, he thought. *The Zodiac powers are* gone, *remember? That's why we're here!*

A thick hand grabbed his arm, arresting his fall. Steven cried out; his shoulder felt like it was being pulled out of its socket. Another large hand grabbed his harness.

Steven looked over at his rescuer, a big man in paramilitary gear with a pack on his back. The man, Malik, had anchored himself against the side of the wall by digging a pair of mountain-climbing pitons into the rock and hooking them on to his own harness.

"Welcome to the volcano," Malik said.

Volcano. The word echoed in Steven's mind. He'd been trying not to think about that.

"You're all right," Malik continued. "Just flex that shoulder a few times."

Steven nodded, struggling to catch his breath.

CHAPTER ONE

Malik shifted his muscular body, depositing Steven easily onto a small outcropping. Like Steven, Malik had once wielded the Zodiac power; as the Ox, he'd been almost supernaturally strong. Now he was merely *very* strong.

"You two havin' fun up there?"

Steven squinted down, his eyes adjusting to the dim light. About a meter below, another big man was anchored to the wall, grinning up at Steven and Malik. A long scar ran from the man's thick blond hair down his face, through his missing left eye.

"I wouldn't call it fun, Nicky." Malik's voice echoed off the rock walls.

Nicky reached up. "Want a hand down, kid?"

Embarrassed, Steven shook his head. He turned toward the wall and grabbed for a handhold, then stepped off the ledge onto the next small outcropping. Slowly, hand over hand, he descended to the floor of the chamber.

When he reached the bottom, he shrugged off his harness. *With the Tiger's power,* he thought, *I could have made that descent in half the time. Being normal is overrated!*

Nicky and Malik made their way down the wall above him. When Nicky—Dog—had held the Zodiac power, he'd boasted a carpet of yellow fur over his entire body. Dog had been a fierce fighter. He was both heavier and stronger than Steven, but when they'd fought hand to hand, Steven's agility had made them an even match.

Nicky and Malik had both worked for Maxwell, the man the Zodiac team had been formed to stop. After

Maxwell turned against his own agents and stole all their powers, they joined Steven's team. Like Steven, they were just ordinary people now.

"Kid?" Nicky asked, jumping the last meter or so to the floor. "You still breathing?"

"I just fell twenty feet," Steven protested. "Give me a minute."

Nicky turned to Malik, laughing. "I don't think the kid's used to working with this team."

"We're all adjusting." Malik smiled. "I'm not used to taking orders from a fourteen-year-old, either."

"Fifteen," Steven said. "I'm fifteen."

Nicky and Malik were right. Steven was used to operating with his old team, the team he'd worked with so many times in the past. He missed having them by his side: Ram, Rooster, Pig, and especially Rabbit.

But those particular teammates were occupied elsewhere. And if Steven was to pull off this mission, he'd need the help of every ex-Zodiac he could find—even those, like Nicky and Malik, who'd been enemies in the past.

Nicky turned to stare up at the hole they'd entered through, a hundred meters above. It was barely visible in the dim light, a dark spot on the yellow rock ceiling.

"Josie!" Nicky yelled. "You comin', girl?"

A fourth figure dropped into view, descending in a perfectly straight line. She let out her support rope with even, expert movements. Like Malik and Nicky, she was a trained soldier with years of combat experience.

CHAPTER ONE

And I'm just a kid, Steven thought. *But I've got to lead them. Somehow.*

Josie touched down and shook off her harness. Her eyes were blank; her movements seemed unenthusiastic, almost robotic. She didn't look at any of them.

"Joze?" Nicky said. "You with us?"

She turned and walked away.

"We shouldn't have brought her," Malik said.

Nicky glared at him. "Maybe we shouldn'ta brought *you.*" He turned and followed Josie over to the far wall.

Steven frowned. When he'd worked with her before, Josie—Horse—had been a ball of energy, a determined fighter who never gave up, with or without her powers. She'd guided Nicky in their defection from Maxwell's Vanguard army, leading him and telling him what to do.

But something had changed. Josie seemed almost hollow now, a shell of her former self. And Nicky was taking care of *her,* instead of the other way around.

"We're not very deep yet," Malik said, running his eyes up and down the wall. "This volcano goes hundreds of feet farther down. How 'bout a scan, kid?"

Steven nodded. He reached into his pack, pulled out a thick headset, and fitted it over his eyes. A night-vision HUD schematic appeared, bright against the black background projected by the virtual-reality device.

Green lines sketched out the uneven cavern floor and the angled walls rising up all around. Three red dots, indicating Steven's teammates, shone within the chamber.

Readouts scrolled down the left side of his vision: SENSOR RANGE 3.2 KM. BATTERY LEVEL 94%. CHAMBER HEIGHT 24.7 METERS. WIDTH (MAX) 16.7 METERS. FLOOR PITCH 8.4°.

Along the right side, a menu of options presented itself. ZOOM. SEARCH. BRIGHTNESS/CONTRAST. INFRARED LEVEL. REFRESH/REBOOT. He selected ZOOM and panned the image down.

"You're right," he said. "There's another chamber below this one. I don't see any life signs down there."

"That doesn't necessarily mean anything," Malik replied. "If Maxwell's got Vanguard soldiers hiding in here, they'll be shielded from our scans."

The image zoomed out, revealing the volcano's entire shape: a mountain bisected by a large open mouth. Below the main caverns, a network of tunnels and corridors snaked through the earth. Steven zoomed in on one of those passageways, four or five levels beneath the ground. Three more red dots winked on, smaller ones this time.

The second team, he thought. Their objective was as important as his—more important, actually. He wanted to contact them, to make sure they were all right. But he had to maintain radio silence for now.

"Any Zodiac power signatures?" Malik asked.

Pain stabbed through Steven's forehead. The HUD-set was Vanguard tech, stolen by Malik when he'd made his exit. They'd managed to equip only one unit for the mission, and Steven had barely had any time to practice with it. It gave him a headache.

"What?" he asked.

"The *Zodiac tracker*," Malik said impatiently.

"Right, yeah." Steven reached into his pocket and pulled out a small device, the size of a thumb drive. He pressed it into a port on the HUDset, just above his ear. A large menu item appeared on the HUDset display, flashing blue: ZODIAC TRACKING.

"Is it scanning?" Malik's voice seemed far away. "That's your tech, not ours. I don't know how well the devices sync together."

"I think so." The entire display went black for a moment, then winked back on. "It's kinda buggy."

"Hurry up," Nicky called from the other side of the room. "I wanna get my powers back!"

Once again Steven zoomed the schematic view up through the chamber, to the volcano's mouth high above. He panned back down, past the three red dots indicating the positions of the second team, and plunged deeper into the subterranean labyrinth. The ZODIAC TRACKING text blinked blue the entire time. Steven waited for the device to detect something—anything—infused with Zodiac energy.

"Nothing," he said. "No Dragon, no artifact, no energy traces at all. No nothing."

"Again: not a surprise," Malik said. "Maxwell has wave

blockers, same as you, that can shield the Zodiac energy so it doesn't show up on scans. Doesn't mean the artifact's not here—but we're not gonna find it the easy way."

Steven glanced at the readout menus on the side of his display. The power level read 46 percent. That seemed low. "This thing's getting hot," he said, tapping the HUDset.

"Zodiac scanner's probably draining the battery. Better turn it off for now."

Relieved, Steven flipped the lenses up off his eyes.

Malik was already walking away, across the chamber. Steven followed him over to Nicky, who stood above Josie. She was down on one knee, staring at the floor.

"Joze?" Nicky said. "We gotta go. We gotta find the jee—the jin—the juju—"

"*Jiānyù*," Steven said softly.

"The thing," Nicky said, "the artifact, the old brass widget that's got all our powers in it. You wanna get your powers back, don't you?"

Josie turned halfway around. There was hardly any expression in her eyes.

"We don't even know if that 'widget' is here," she said.

"We'll find it!" Nicky turned to Steven and Malik, his eyes pleading for help. "What's this jye-annie thing look like, anyway? Is it a *boring* artifact like a pot or an urn, or a cool one with skulls all over it?"

"The *jiānyù* is a sphere," Malik explained, "a little bigger than a softball. It's built to absorb and contain the

Zodiac powers. When it's holding them, it's been known to morph into the shapes of those powers: an exaggerated ram or tiger. I dunno how it does that . . . something to do with the tech inside it."

"The tech enhances it," Steven said. "But the *jiānyù* was built centuries ago . . . during the Shang dynasty in China."

"And what do we do when we find this medieval basketball trophy?" Nicky asked. "Blast it to pieces? Lay our hands on it and chant like monks?"

Steven and Malik exchanged glances.

"Unclear," Malik said.

Josie snorted. Nicky glanced at her with concern, then ushered Malik and Steven away, out of her earshot.

"What if she's right?" Nicky whispered. "Maybe it's not here. The Jay-Z—the jazz hands—"

"*Please* stop trying to say *jiānyù*," Malik growled.

"I'm just sayin'. Maybe Vanguard ain't stationed here at all. Maybe this is just an *ordinary* deadly volcano."

"No," Steven replied. "We know Kim is here, so this has to be one of Maxwell's bases. I just can't believe the big jarhead left it undefended."

"I *don't* believe it," Malik said.

Maxwell had kept a very low profile in the weeks since he'd stolen the Zodiac powers. He hadn't made any aggressive moves; his private army had pulled out of even its most routine military contracts. He seemed to have diverted his resources toward some secret objective, but every time Steven and Jasmine thought they were closing in on that secret, the trail went cold. The ex-Zodiac teams had explored a half dozen of Maxwell's former lairs, using information supplied by Nicky, Josie, and Malik. They'd come up empty every time.

"We've gotta keep searching," Steven said. "Find a way down to the next chamber. And remember: be ready to create a diversion, in case the second team needs one."

"Search covertly *and* create a diversion?" Malik shook his head. "Those are contradictory objectives. We can't risk this entire mission for one person."

Steven glared at him. Malik was a great fighter, even without Zodiac powers; the team was lucky to have him. But sometimes he could be *too much* of a soldier.

"Kim's a very special person," Steven said.

He turned away, thinking of Kim—the Zodiac's Rabbit. Steven had wanted to lead the other group, the one assigned to find her. But the mission required careful deployment of every team member, especially since none of them had their Zodiac powers anymore. Steven was the most likely person to locate the *jiānyù*, so he had to lead this group.

As team leader, he'd made that decision himself.

Josie was still staring at the ground. Steven crouched next to her, touched the uneven surface—and felt something. A rush of energy, warm and familiar, ran through him.

Zodiac energy.

CHAPTER ONE

A man's face appeared, filling Steven's field of view, wavering and shimmering as if it were made of fog—a very old man's face, with wrinkles all over and eyes sunken into the flesh below the brows.

Steven reached up for his HUDset, but it wasn't covering his eyes. This was a vision—one of the strange by-products of the Zodiac power. When the power had been stolen from him, the visions had gone with it. He hadn't had one for a long time.

He started to tumble forward. He felt Malik's and Nicky's arms steadying him, but their voices seemed very far away. The face filled his mind, focusing on him with an expression of alarm and concern.

Now Steven recognized that face. It belonged to an old man he'd met in Berlin, a man he'd seen die before his eyes—the man who'd been the Tiger before Steven, before Steven had even been born, in fact.

"Don't," the old man whispered.

Somehow Steven knew what he meant. "I must," he replied.

The old man shook his head. "Do not seek out the power."

"I have to," Steven said.

The man grimaced. His face melded and shifted into a full body, the trim, small man Steven had met briefly in Berlin. He nodded, seeming to understand Steven's words, and pointed a finger downward. Then, in a flash, he was gone.

Steven shrugged away from Nicky and Malik, shaking his head to clear it. He looked down at the floor, at the spot the old Tiger had indicated. He glanced quickly at Josie.

Almost imperceptibly, she nodded.

Together they scrabbled away at the dirt. Nicky and Malik stared at them as if they were mad.

Josie's hands were rough, calloused from a lifetime of military operations. Steven had no such experience; he winced as his fingers began to bleed. But he kept digging.

Seven or eight centimeters down, they uncovered a round manhole cover. Steven grabbed hold of its edge and tried to pry it loose. It didn't move.

Josie grabbed it with both hands and flung it into the air.

The passageway stretched almost straight down. It was dark, curved, and narrow, no more than half a meter in diameter. Steven shone his flashlight into it, but he couldn't see the other end.

Once again, he heard the old man's voice. *Don't,* it said. A chorus of voices joined it, warning Steven in unison. *Don't,* they said. *Don't. Don't. Don't.*

He knew who the voices were. The other Tigers. The men and women, young and old, who'd wielded Steven's particular Zodiac power in the years and centuries past.

Josie's voice jolted him out of his vision. "If we're gonna do this," she said, "let's do it."

She hoisted herself up and vaulted into the hole feet-first. In less than a second she was gone.

Steven looked up at the others. Nicky spread his arms and shrugged. "You said we should find a way down."

Steven nodded. But in his mind, he could still hear the Tigers, warning him:

Do not seek out the power.

The passageway led down through the rock, its walls jagged and sharp. Malik led the way, with Nicky following and Steven bringing up the rear. The end of the passage remained out of sight, beyond a seemingly endless series of twists and turns.

"Can't see Josie at all," Malik grumbled.

As they made their way down, Steven's sense of discovery grew stronger. *We're close,* he thought. *This is the place. The power is here, somewhere.*

The tunnel began to widen. "Finally!" Nicky said. "I was tired of smellin' you guys' armpits."

Malik gestured for Nicky to be quiet. The passageway veered sideways, almost leveling out. When it grew large enough, Steven climbed down next to Malik and Nicky. He could see light just ahead, where the tunnel ended.

They crept up to the lip, looked down—and froze. The chamber was smaller than the one above: barely three meters high, with fluorescent lights mounted on the ceiling. Luminescent blue stones lined the walls.

Josie stood below, her back to them, hands raised in defeat—facing a virtual wall of Maxwell's Vanguard agents, all in full body armor and protective helmets. Their glowing energy rifles were raised and pointed at the hole in the wall where Steven's team had appeared. Malik hissed in a breath.

"Come on down," the lead soldier said. "Slowly."

"Affirmative," he said. "Shielded."

Steven felt the soldiers' eyes on him, even through their opaque helmets. He looked around, frantic, at the chamber below. Door-sized entryways were arrayed along the walls, but there was no way Josie—or the rest of them—could reach one before the soldiers picked them off.

I'm the leader, he thought. *I have to figure out what to do—*

"I'm surrenderin'," Nicky said. "Unless you got a better plan."

Steven shook his head.

Nicky slipped down out of the passageway, followed by a reluctant Malik. As he watched them, Steven remembered the Tigers' warning: *Do not seek out the power.*

Looks like we don't need to worry about that anymore, he thought.

He raised his hands and dropped to the floor, the Vanguard energy rifles tracking his every move.

CHAPTER TWO

A BOLT OF ENERGY sizzled past, two centimeters above Roxanne's head. She flinched, assumed a defensive stance, and opened her mouth to cry out.

Nothing. No Zodiac power, no sonic assault—just a strangled noise, deep down in her throat.

A second bolt grazed her cheek. Jasmine grabbed Roxanne by the shoulder and pulled her down behind the rocky barrier.

"Use your brain," Jasmine said, "not your instincts!"

Roxanne felt sheepish. She rubbed at the warm spot on her cheek.

CHAPTER TWO

Her team was pinned down in a small corridor, deep inside the volcano. They'd just rounded a bend when a trio of energy cannons came jutting out of the wall, aimed straight at them. Fortunately, the floor in that area had been broken up into large chunks of debris, presumably by some previous earthquake or magma flow. They'd barely managed to dive behind a rocky shelf, low to the ground, before the firing began.

Now they were trapped. They couldn't move forward without being tagged by the energy guns. If they turned around and went back, the whole mission would be for nothing.

Roxanne risked a quick peek over the barrier. She couldn't see very far; the corridor curved ahead, just past the weapons mounted on the wall. She ducked back down as another beam flared out.

"Is there, uh, someone firing those guns?" she asked.

"Doubtful," Duane replied. "This area is controlled by the complex's computer system."

Roxanne turned back to look at him. Duane sat cross-legged on the uneven ground, his dreadlocks concealed beneath his mission cap. As he tapped furiously at a small tablet, a network of circuitry snaked and wove its way across the screen. Security/password windows flashed open and closed.

"So this is Maxwell's automatic intruder-defense mechanism," Roxanne said, watching the beams flash by overhead.

"Not Maxwell," Jasmine said. "Not anymore. He's just the Dragon now."

Roxanne turned to Duane. "Can you deactivate those guns?"

"That is my intention."

Jasmine looked around. She seemed confused, distracted. Her eyes locked on to a large backpack lying on the floor next to Duane. Staying low, she crawled along the floor to grab it, her long ponytail whipping back and forth.

Roxanne watched, frowning. Jasmine was the founder, first leader, and former most powerful member of the Zodiac team. But lately, ever since Maxwell had stolen the last of the shared Dragon power for himself, she'd seemed stressed. *Post-traumatic stress disorder,* Roxanne thought. *The Dragon is the most potent of the Zodiac powers—and Jasmine held it inside her for almost a year. What would that much power do to a person?*

"Jasmine?" Roxanne asked. "You okay?"

Jasmine peered inside the backpack, then hurriedly zipped it shut. She shook her head, dismissing Roxanne's question. "Our first priority is to protect Duane," she said. "He's the only one who can get us inside."

"Even without his powers?"

"Duane was a master hacker long before we got our powers."

Roxanne clenched her fists. Without her Rooster power, she felt helpless, useless. *I am definitely quitting,* she thought. *As soon as this is over. I've said it before, but this time I mean it.*

Another beam stabbed the air overhead. *Assuming we survive, of course.*

"Priority two," Jasmine continued, hefting the backpack. "Keep this safe."

"You gonna tell me what's in there?"

Jasmine gave her a strange look. "It's a weapon."

An energy beam burned straight into the front of their protective rock shelf. The barrier sizzled, melting slightly, but it held. The beam switched off just as another one seared by over their heads.

"Couple more shots like that," Roxanne said, "and we won't have a hiding place left."

"Duane?"

"Working on it. Maxwell's—the *Dragon's* firewalls are formidable." Duane's fingers were a blur over the tablet. "I am not sure if I can do this."

Whoa, Roxanne thought. *He never admits that.*

"Looks like this might be up to us," Jasmine said.

Roxanne stared at her, incredulous. "Without our powers?"

Before Jasmine could answer, the energy barrage abruptly halted. The cannons' hum faded to silence as the weapons retracted soundlessly into the corridor wall.

Duane moved to join them. "Booyah!" he exclaimed.

"Duane?" Roxanne asked.

"Yeah."

"Don't ever say 'booyah' again."

Jasmine rose to her feet, shrugging the pack onto her back, and stepped over the barrier. Cautiously, Roxanne followed her. They moved forward, keeping their eyes on the wall where the energy guns had emerged.

"Dead as disco," Roxanne said. "Good work, smart man."

Duane grinned. He leaned in close and whispered in Roxanne's ear: *"Booyah."*

"Come on, you two," Jasmine said. "We're not safe yet."

As the corridor wound downward, its walls turned smooth. Roxanne followed her friends across the jagged floor, squeezing through narrow passages. They stopped at a crossroads, where the corridor branched off in two directions.

Jasmine ran a hand along her brow. "It's getting hotter."

"There's magma—molten rock—a hundred meters below us," Duane said, studying his tablet. "Also some very strange electromagnetic readings."

"Is this volcano going to erupt?" Roxanne felt a stab of panic. "I was assured this mission would be eruption-free."

"There were no signs of subduction premission," Duane replied. "However, the erratic nature of the Zodiac powers, combined with the inherent uncertainty of plate tectonics, dictated that certain precautions be observed."

Roxanne gave Jasmine a helpless, questioning look.

"The area around the mountain is being evacuated,

just in case," Jasmine translated. "But we didn't detect any signs that the volcano was becoming active."

"I don't see any now, either," Duane said, frowning. "But I've also never seen this energy pattern before."

Roxanne looked from the left branch of the corridor to the right. "Too bad Steven's got the only fancy headset on the team." She pointed at Duane's tablet. "Does that thing tell you which way we should go?"

"This way," Jasmine said, before Duane could reply.

Roxanne and Duane exchanged puzzled glances. But Jasmine was already heading down the left passageway.

"Have you noticed," Roxanne whispered, "she's been doing that all along?"

"Choosing our route as if she knows where we're going?" Duane frowned. "Yes."

There was a crunching noise up ahead. Roxanne led the way around a bend, with Duane right behind. Jasmine was on her knees, clutching her head. They rushed over to her.

"Easy," Roxanne said, sitting Jasmine up against the wall. "What's going on with you, anyway?"

"It's like . . . there's this weird knowledge in my head," Jasmine said. "I've never been here before, and we don't exactly have a map of the volcano. But I know exactly which corridors to take."

Roxanne frowned. "Something left behind by the Dragon? When you held its power?"

"I don't think so. This wasn't a Dragon base back then." Jasmine shook her head. "I'm all right. Duane, have you managed to . . . Duane?"

Duane didn't answer. He was wiping his hand against the wall, which—Roxanne noticed—looked different in that branch of the corridor. It was white and almost featureless, a stark contrast to the unfinished rock they'd seen so far in the volcano.

"Duane?" Roxanne called.

He lowered his hand, revealing a shallow pattern in the surface of the wall. It bore a carved symbol, a stylized representation of a character from some ancient language: the brand of the Vanguard Company, Maxwell's paramilitary organization.

"Well, that's proof, I guess," Roxanne said. "This is definitely . . ." Duane was staring at her. "What?"

Without a word, Duane lifted his tablet and pulled up a video. He turned it to face Roxanne and Jasmine.

The screen came alive with the image of Kim, the former Rabbit—the youngest member of the Zodiac team. She looked scared and tired. She stared out at them with wide eyes.

"Guys," Kim said. "Help—"

The screen went black.

Roxanne nodded. That was the two-second message they'd received from Kim, who'd been missing for the past seven weeks. Duane had traced the signal to Indonesia, then narrowed the location to the mountain.

CHAPTER TWO

"We've seen that," Jasmine said. "It's why we're here—"

"Watch it again," Duane said.

He hit the replay icon. "Guys," Kim said again. "Help—"

Roxanne sighed impatiently. "Duane. *What?*"

"Look at the wall."

She leaned forward. As the clip played a third time, she noticed: the wall behind Kim was white, just like the walls in the corridor. Duane paused the video and pinched the screen, magnifying the image. He panned the image past Kim's frightened face. There, barely visible, was the same stylized Vanguard symbol embossed on the wall.

"Whoa," Roxanne said. "Jackpot—"

A sharp pain stabbed her neck. She cried out and staggered against the wall, then dropped to her knees. A fog, a dark haze, seemed to creep over her.

"Don't move, guys," said someone with a familiar voice. "For reals."

Roxanne tried to turn her head. It didn't want to move. Jasmine and Duane took up positions in front of her, shielding her from the attacker. She peered around their legs.

"Mince," Roxanne gasped.

The girl called Mince, Vanguard's teenage genius scientist, stood blocking the corridor. Her cruel face swirled before Roxanne's eyes.

With the last of her strength, Roxanne reached up to her neck and pulled out a tiny needle-thin dart. *Drugged,* she thought, tossing it away. *She drugged me!*

"He said you'd come," Mince said, "looking for your little Rabbit."

Roxanne struggled to stay conscious. Mince, she saw, wore multifinger rings on both hands. Metallic swirls linked her fingers together, and each knuckle was studded with a sharp metal dart—just like the one that had struck Roxanne.

Roxanne felt her consciousness fading. *Useless,* she thought again. *Without my powers, I'm just a target for every psycho that wants to kill us. I should have quit the team earlier. . . . That would have been better for everyone.*

Jasmine glared at Mince. "What have you done?" she asked, gesturing at Roxanne. "What's going to happen to her?"

Mince held up her hands. Her rings displayed a pair of words in block letters, linking the knuckle darts together. The left hand read LIVE and the right one DIE.

"Could be one," Mince said, smirking. "Could be the other."

Jasmine said something in reply, but the words seemed to fade into the air. Roxanne barely noticed Duane's hand on her forehead, warm and comforting. "Sorry," she said to him. "Sorry I . . . failed. . . ."

Then the drug caught up with her and she fell into darkness.

CHAPTER THREE

STEVEN COUNTED the soldiers: nine—no, ten. They stood in a perfect semicircle, their shoulders almost touching. Visored helmets concealed their eyes; their energy weapons all glowed the same shade of red in the blue-lit cavern.

They look like clones, he thought. *Or ants. Robots, maybe, each one identically programmed and tested.*

"Hey, guys," he said, moving forward to stand next to Josie. "You, uh, seen the new *Star Wars* yet?"

Malik and Nicky moved up to flank him. The soldiers said nothing.

"Effects were banging," Nicky offered.

The lead soldier raised a hand to his earpiece, as if he was receiving orders. Then the wall of soldiers parted and a pair of figures in civilian clothes stepped forward. The first was a small woman with sharp, hard features. The other, a man, was almost twice her size. They wore wraparound sunglasses and crisp matching black business suits.

Steven didn't recognize them, but Josie clearly did. Her eyes narrowed, and her mouth curled into a sneer—the blank expression on her face turning to one of anger.

The dark-suited woman took in each of the group members in turn. She shrugged at Nicky, dismissing him, and laughed silently in Steven's direction. Her gaze lingered on Malik for a moment.

Then she walked straight up to Josie and raised her sunglasses, revealing hard dark eyes.

"Josie," the woman said. "The powerful Horse."

The man laughed. "She don't look so powerful now."

Josie said nothing, but her hand closed into a fist.

"Beta," Malik said to the woman. "And Alpha. Been a while."

"Malik," the woman—Beta—replied. "You were the first to walk out on the Dragon."

"You mean Maxwell?" Steven looked around, mock casual. "He around?"

Alpha, the big Vanguard agent, laughed. "You ain't

asking the questions around here, shorty." He gestured at the soldiers, who hadn't moved a muscle.

Shorty, Steven thought. *I'll remember that, you big goon.*

Beta smiled. "Here's the thing," she said, pacing back and forth dramatically. "Some of us actually believe in loyalty. Some of us don't turn against our employer every time things get rough."

"Maybe you don't know how rough things can get," Malik rumbled.

She ignored him. "That loyalty . . . that reliability, that sense of honor . . . sometimes it's rewarded. And some of us manage it *without* magic powers."

"I remember you!" Nicky stepped forward, frowning at Beta. "You used to work in Maxwell's accounting department. You turned down my expense report a couple years ago."

Beta shot him a withering look. "Fifty-five showings of *Up* is not a valid business expense."

Nicky looked hurt. "I love that movie."

"Look," Steven said. "We're, uh, we're sorry we stumbled into your mountain. Honest mistake, could happen to anyone. If you just wanna lower those guns, we'll get out of your way and you can get on with, with, with whatever big-fun shooty party you've got going on here. Just give our apologies to Maxwell or the Dragon or whoever's in charge here—"

"You're not going anywhere," Beta said, pulling a small

energy weapon out of her suit pocket. "As for who's in charge, that would be me."

"You?" Josie asked.

She took a step forward. The soldiers all moved half a step closer, their weapons trained on her.

Beta motioned the soldiers back. She reached out to touch Josie's chin. Josie's eyes flared, but she didn't move.

"Like I said, Maxwell rewards loyalty. He's promoted me to director of this facility."

"He gave *me* this cool gun," Alpha said. He held up an energy rifle the size of a cannon.

Nicky nodded. "That is a big gun."

Beta smiled at Josie, taunting her. "So while *you've* squandered your almighty Zodiac power and made nice with your enemies, we've done pretty well for ourselves. What do you think of that?"

Again, Josie was silent. Her eyes panned across the line of soldiers.

"This facility wasn't in the old Vanguard files," Malik said. "What is it?"

"It's a holding center," Beta replied. "And . . . well, other things, too."

A holding center, Steven thought, his heart beating faster. *Kim . . .*

"What 'other things'?" Malik asked. "Do you know what Maxwell is up to here?"

"We don't ask a lotta questions," Alpha replied. He

pulled out a cloth and started polishing his gun's barrel.

"Here's a question," Steven said. "Have you noticed anything weird about Maxwell lately? Does he seem like himself?"

"He's been distant lately," Beta replied. "But he's Maxwell."

"He gives me a gun like this," Alpha said, "he can be as distant as he wants."

"Here's how this is going to go," Beta said. "You're all going to come with us to the holding cells. You, kid . . ."

"Steven."

"Steven. I'll have to check with Maxwell, but I doubt he cares much about a kid with no powers. He'll probably just let you go."

Steven wasn't sure whether to feel relieved or insulted.

"You two . . ." She gestured at Malik and Nicky. "You've violated your terms of employment with Maxwell. Again, it's up to him, but I'm planning to recommend you be tried for treason in a private military court. If you're lucky, you won't be sentenced to death."

"Very generous," Malik growled.

"As for this little witch . . ." Alpha walked up to Josie again. "You threw your weight around with me before, 'Horse.' Bad mistake."

Josie clenched her other fist.

"So there's no mercy for you." Alpha circled around her, studying Josie like a laboratory specimen. "I'm gonna make this personal. I'm gonna take it slow. I'm gonna find out all your weaknesses, make sure there's no way out. Maybe I'll even pay a little visit to your *dad* up in *AWWWK—*"

Steven hadn't even seen Josie move. But in a heartbeat, the former Horse had slammed Alpha up against the wall and locked an arm across the Vanguard agent's throat, cutting off Alpha's breath and pinning him firmly.

"Little *too* personal," Josie hissed, grabbing the energy rifle from her captive's hand.

Malik and Nicky tensed. Beta growled quietly and gestured at the soldiers. They moved toward Josie and Nicky, their energy rifles cocked and glowing.

"Go ahead," Josie said. "Shoot. Think you can hit me before I blast your boss?"

The soldiers exchanged unsure glances.

Josie cast a look at an opening in the wall, about a meter away from where she stood. She started edging toward it, dragging the protesting Alpha along with her. The soldiers tracked her every move, drawing closer.

She's trying to escape, Steven thought. *But she'll never make it.*

Almost too fast to see, Malik grabbed the nearest soldier's gun. The soldier, a woman, cried out. Malik twisted the gun around in a

practiced motion, thumbed the control to STUN, and fired. A bolt of energy stabbed out of the muzzle, dropping the soldier to the ground.

Two other agents scrambled toward Malik, firing their weapons. He leaped and dodged, squeezed off two shots, and took them both down.

Alpha squirmed and struggled in Josie's grip. Josie held on tight.

Malik backed up slowly toward Steven, firing his stolen energy gun at the advancing line of Vanguard agents. Beta whirled toward them, raising her weapon. She stalked toward Malik from behind, aiming at the former Ox's back.

"Guess we're doin' that diversion thing," Nicky said.

He ran forward and leaped onto Beta's back. The Vanguard agent yelped in surprise. Malik whirled, sized up the situation in an instant, and grabbed Beta's weapon out of her hand. Nicky started beating on Beta's head with his bare hands, and together they crashed to the ground.

As Steven watched, the room erupted into chaos. One group of Vanguard soldiers started firing wildly in Malik's general direction. The rest surrounded Josie, who still held Alpha pressed up against the wall. A distant fury burned in Josie's eyes.

I should help them, Steven thought. *But they're all trained combat veterans—on both sides. And without my powers . . .*

He saw it again: the face, the wrinkled visage of the

old man. It was sharper, more vivid than before. As Steven watched, a multitude of other faces joined it, all staring at him. A large man with tired eyes. A young woman, dark hair upswept in a regal fashion. Soldiers, revolutionaries, politicians, artists.

All long dead, passed away into history. And all part of Steven's heritage: the legacy of the Tiger.

"Don't," they said once again. This time the voices were so loud, they forced him to his knees.

"I must," he said.

"Don't," said the chorus of Tigers. "Do not seek out the power."

Steven forced the vision away. In the underground cavern, the soldiers had Josie cornered. Malik was backed up against a wall, still picking off soldiers but severely outnumbered. Beta had thrown off Nicky, who was staggering away, dazed.

"I must," Steven repeated. "I have to get my powers back." An energy bolt struck the rocky wall, centimeters from his head. "Otherwise we're *all* finished!"

Don't.

Gritting his teeth, he closed his eyes and concentrated. *Tell me,* he thought. *Tell me where to find the* jiānyù.

The chorus in his head fell quiet. His consciousness seemed to expand, taking in the chamber, then the entire mountain. He saw the other team for just a moment, trapped in another of the volcano's dozens of tunnels.

Roxanne lay on the ground, unconscious; Duane and Jasmine were facing off against someone, but he couldn't see who it was. *They need help,* he realized.

Tell me where the powers are!

The Tigers seemed to nod, acknowledging his need. Steven felt his mind sinking down, past the level that held Roxanne's team. Down through more levels of solid rock, past mazelike passages, through pools of superheated magma . . .

"I know," he whispered.

He opened his eyes and turned toward the wall. One of the openings, the passageways leading out of the chamber, was close enough to reach. He'd have to avoid drawing the soldiers' attention, but he knew he could make it.

Nicky and Malik stood together against the wall, facing off against five soldiers. Nicky had picked up one of the fallen soldiers' energy rifles; he held it up in front of him, squeezing off shots. Alpha twisted in Josie's grip; Josie kneed him in the stomach.

Steven felt a pang of doubt. He'd run out on Josie and Nicky once before, in the tunnels below Maxwell's Australian complex. That act, that guilt, had haunted him ever since. Could he leave them *again*?

"I know!" he cried. "I know where it is!"

Malik and Nicky didn't answer. Nicky waved his energy rifle in an arc and, with a single blast, dropped one of the guards. Four more stepped into his place, advancing and firing.

They're completely outnumbered, Steven realized. *They won't survive this battle—unless we get our powers back. And neither will . . .*

An image of Kim appeared in his head. Determined, but frightened. *She's here,* he thought. *She's somewhere inside this mountain!*

He turned to Josie. "I have to—"

"Kid," she yelled. *"GO!"*

He turned and darted into the passageway.

The sounds of battle, the blasts of energy fire and grunts of combat, receded into the distance. And as they faded, the Tigers' voices rose again in Steven's mind. *Don't,* they said. *Don't do this. Do not seek the Zodiac power.*

It will be your doom.

CHAPTER FOUR

JASMINE LOOKED around the narrow passageway. Mince loomed just ahead, grinning that unbalanced grin of hers, holding up both hands to reveal her deadly rings.

Mince was the immediate threat. There was no way forward until she was dealt with. But several other things cried out for Jasmine's attention. Duane stood against the wall, his eyes flitting from Mince to Jasmine and back again. Roxanne lay on the floor, making small weak noises.

And then there was the pack on Jasmine's back. The weapon.

CHAPTER FOUR

Roxanne whimpered once and went silent. Jasmine glanced at her, alarmed.

Mince gestured at Roxanne's unmoving form. "Go on," she said, her tone a mockery of kindness.

Jasmine knelt down, keeping an eye on Mince. The floor felt warm, almost alive. The molten rock of the volcano was supposed to be several kilometers below them, but she swore she could feel it flowing beneath her feet.

She lifted Roxanne's arm and touched her wrist. A strong, steady pulse beat against Jasmine's thumb. She rose to her feet, flashing Duane a relieved look.

Mince took a step forward and held up her left hand, the one with LIVE spelled out across the knuckles. "Lucked out," she said. "But next time . . ."

Mince's other fist shot forward. From one of the rings labeled DIE, a tiny dart flashed through the air. Jasmine ducked one way; Duane dodged the other. The dart *whooshed* between them and struck the rocky wall with a light *clink*, then fell to the floor.

"Never know," Mince said, her grin even wider now. "Ah-ah, brainiac. Touch that screen and I drop you."

Duane froze. He had been reaching down, surreptitiously, for his tablet computer, which lay discarded on a rock.

Jasmine looked around. *We need a diversion,* she thought. *But Mince is impossible to outwit. She doesn't act rationally.*

"What now?" she asked.

"I haven't decided." Mince held up both fists and cast

her eyes back and forth: DIE, LIVE, DIE. “I could stun you and leave you here for your friends to find. Or I could let you pass, try and find your friend.” She laughed, a high unpleasant sound. “Or I could just kill you.”

Take this slow, Jasmine thought. Duane stood against the wall, waiting for her to give him a signal.

“Is that what your boss wants?” she asked. “Maxwell?”

“Forget Maxwell.” A flash of anger crossed Mince’s face. “If you want to live, you’ll have to beg *me*.”

“He’s not really Maxwell anymore, you know. The Dragon has taken him over completely. There’s not a trace of humanity left in him.”

Mince shrugged. “Humanity’s overrated.”

“The Dragon doesn’t care about anyone. I know.” Jasmine paused, remembering. “For a year, I had that power all to myself. The Dragon is . . . it’s inconceivable, impossible to describe. Like all the fire in the world, burning behind your eyelids. Like a star.”

Mince rolled her eyes. “So what?”

“So now it’s gone. Wrenched out of me by your boss—the walking corpse we call Maxwell.”

Mince walked right up to her and reached out a hand. Jasmine struggled not to pull away as the girl’s fingers, studded with metal, caressed her cheek. DIE swooped in and out of her field of vision.

“Walking corpse,” Mince repeated. “I like you. You’ve got a dark side, Jaz.”

Jasmine flinched at the nickname.

CHAPTER FOUR

"Oh. Sorry." A look of mock regret crossed Mince's face. "Isn't that what *he* used to call you? Carlos?"

Jasmine felt as if a dagger had struck her in the heart. She struggled to keep the hurt from showing.

"I know why you're here. The other reason, I mean." Mince activated a device on her wrist, and a hologram rose into the air. It showed a bronze sphere, dented and tarnished with age.

"The *jiānyù*," she continued. "It's here, all right. But where? Where, oh where, oh where?"

Jasmine's pulse quickened. *If that thing really is in this complex somewhere,* she thought, *then the team has a shot at getting their powers back. I've gotta keep her talking!*

"What do I care?" she asked nonchalantly. "*My* powers aren't in it."

Mince smiled. "Nice try, *Jaz*. But I think we both know how important this is to you." She studied the *jiānyù*'s image, her smile turning to a sneer. "Crude little device. Carlos built this, too, didn't he?"

This time Jasmine's face betrayed her. Mince snapped off the hologram and moved in closer, raising an eyebrow. She looked like a cat that had spotted a mouse.

"*Carlos*," Mince repeated. "He was a lousy scientist. The Dragon's much better off with me." She twisted her face in front of Jasmine's, like a snake hypnotizing its prey. "How is old Carlos? Still crazy as a bedbug, locked up in some cell with mattresses all over the walls?"

"Shut up," Jasmine hissed.

"Oooh." Mince clapped her hands in delight. "I knew you two were close, but . . . are you kissy close? Do you LOOOOVE him?"

Jasmine clenched her fists, furious. She'd been trying not to think about Carlos the entire mission. It wasn't hard; she'd been avoiding thinking about things for most of her life. But now . . .

Don't, she thought. *Don't let her bait you. Don't let her win!*

"It must suck to be you," Mince continued. "Are you gonna get married? Word of advice: don't have any sharp knives at the ceremony."

That's it, you little psycho. You've crossed the line.

Jasmine turned away, assessing the situation coldly. Roxanne lay unmoving on the floor. Duane stood a meter away, watching.

"Poor Jasmine," Mince said. "The boy she wants to kiss is a drooling psycho. Poor, poor, poor little *Jaz*."

Jasmine put her head down and pretended to cry.

Mince laughed again. "I *should* kill you!" she said, holding up her DIE hand. "You'd be better off."

Jasmine shot a glance at Duane, showing him that her eyes were dry. With a small sharp motion, she cocked her head toward Mince.

Hope he gets the idea, she thought.

Duane nodded, an almost imperceptible movement. As he stepped past Jasmine, Mince held up both hands, aiming all her darts at him.

CHAPTER FOUR

"One more step, kid, and you'll look like a porcupine."

Duane held up both hands in a surrender pose, showing that he'd left his tablet behind. "I was just wondering," he said, "if you knew the story of Mount Merapi."

"Mount what?" Mince asked.

"Merapi. This volcano." Duane gestured around at the rocky walls. "The locals call it the Mountain of Fire."

Mince rolled her eyes. "Duh. It's a *volcano*."

"They believe this mountain was originally situated on the far side of the island," Duane continued. "But Batara Guru, leader of the gods, was displeased. He wanted the mountain in the *middle* of the island so the whole place would be balanced out." Duane flashed a grin. "I think he was a little OCD."

Mince just stared at him. She jabbed her hands through the air, one after the other, like a boxer: DIE, then LIVE. Then DIE again.

That's it, Jasmine thought, shrugging the backpack off her shoulders. *Keep your eyes on him.*

"But two men were already engaged in holy work in the center of the island," Duane said. "They refused to leave. So in his anger, Batara Guru dumped the mountain right on top of the men."

Mince stared at him, incredulous. "So. Freaking. What?"

Duane shrugged. "I just thought there might be a lesson there—about ordinary people like you ignoring the forces of nature, trying to use this volcano for something unnatural." He smiled sheepishly. "The gods could get angry."

Jasmine reached into the backpack.

Mince marched straight up to Duane. She had to look up to stare him in the eye, but her attitude was mocking, superior.

"There are no gods. No Zodiac powers anymore, either." She held up her dart-rings. "The only power here is me."

Duane quivered but held his ground. "They also believe there's a whole kingdom of ghosts inside the mounta—"

"I think I'll kill you now," Mince interrupted, "because of these boring stories. Did you really think they'd make me change my mind?"

"No," Duane said. "I merely hoped to distract you for a moment."

"From wha—"

Jasmine lunged toward Mince, grabbing her from behind. Mince whirled, but she was too late. Jasmine reached up and clamped a pair of metal electrodes on Mince's temples.

Mince swiped out, panicked, with both sets of rings. But Jasmine dodged away and, with one quick motion, fastened a second set of electrodes to her own forehead. A length of cable stretched from the electrodes to a small device in Jasmine's hand.

"What *is* this thing?" Mince screamed.

"Something else he created. Carlos." Jasmine twisted

a knob on the device, and it hummed to life. "And for the record: even half-mad, he's twice the scientist you'll ever be."

Mince howled and clawed at her temples. But the electrodes were stuck tight.

"I really don't *want* to know what's inside your head, psycho," Jasmine said. "But I've gotta find out where Kim is."

Two sharp tones sounded from the device, indicating that it was ready. Jasmine pressed a button—and the whole chamber vanished. Duane, the smooth walls, even Roxanne's unconscious form on the floor: all gone.

Jasmine stood in a small dingy room. Paint peeled off the walls; the bed was just a bare mattress, sagging in its frame. A TV with a cracked screen sat on a little table.

A scared feral-looking girl's face appeared, startling Jasmine. The girl couldn't have been more than five. She glared at Jasmine with wild eyes.

Mince, Jasmine thought. *This is her, when she was a little girl!*

"Go away!" the girl screamed. "Leave me alone!"

The face wavered and disappeared. Jasmine found herself back in the real world, in the corridor of the volcano. Duane stood by her side, touching her arm in concern.

Mince flailed at the end of the cables, still linked to the machine. She seemed dazed, blinded, waving her arms around.

"You cried out," Duane said. "Are you okay?"

LIVE
DIE

"I've got to keep her off balance," Jasmine said, shaking Duane off. "You just watch out for those rings of hers."

Jasmine concentrated, pouring mental energy into the machine. Her brain impulses traveled down the cables and into the device, which magnified their power and fed them out through the second set of cables.

Mince turned and blinked. She seemed to have realized what was happening, but it was too late. The mind energy struck her straight on; she grabbed her head and arched her back in pain—

—and Jasmine found herself inside Mince's mindscape again, in the dirty room. But this time two figures, gaunt and angry and tired-looking, stared down at her. A wiry man with cruel eyes and a cringing woman.

"Don't!" the man yelled at the woman. "Don't you argue with me!"

Jasmine looked around: *Where's the little girl?* And then she realized: I'm *the little girl. This is a memory from Mince's childhood.*

The man raised his hand. The woman cowered.

These were her parents.

As the man struck the woman, Jasmine felt a rush of painful emotion. Rage, terror, helplessness. The world exploding, a little girl's childhood shattered forever.

As the horror of Mince's past washed over her, Jasmine felt a pang of guilt. *I shouldn't be watching this,* she thought. *These are her secrets. This is wrong; it's private. How would* I *feel if someone exposed my . . .*

CHAPTER FOUR

Then she remembered: *We've got to find Kim. This is a horrible thing to do—but it's our only hope!*

The image shifted and wavered. But the corridor didn't return this time. Jasmine found herself staring at a computer screen covered top to bottom with tiny mathematical symbols. *Equations,* she realized. She recognized some of them from Carlos's notes.

Mince's emotional storm had calmed. As Jasmine's eyes ran across the lines of numbers and symbols, a feeling of pure bliss filled the mindscape. She felt the sense of order, the sheer mathematical beauty of the world within the computer.

This was her escape, Jasmine realized. *When her home life became too horrible, young Mince took refuge in numbers. In cold uncaring formulas, things that couldn't hurt her.*

No, Jasmine warned herself, *don't feel sorry for her! But . . . but no child should have to live through this. . . .*

A shadow fell over the computer. The air all around, the entire tenor of the mindscape, changed in an instant. Jasmine looked up and saw a fist, huge and hairy and masculine, poised to strike.

No, she thought. *No, no, no. Not now.*

Not the equations!

The fist slammed down, smashing the computer screen. Glass flew in all directions, tiny sharp fragments of a fragile life. Mince screamed.

Pain lanced through Jasmine—her face, her cheeks, her nose. All at once, she found herself back in the corridor.

Duane was staring at her, alarmed and concerned. *Why?* she wondered. *What's he looking at—*

Then an iron grip clamped down over her windpipe. She choked, almost gagged, and again felt a stabbing pain on her cheeks and nose.

"Don't," Mince said, and Duane looked down at her. "Don't move. I'll kill her."

Jasmine realized what had happened. Mince had swiped a whole set of poison dart-rings across her face. The cuts weren't deep—hardly any of the poison had actually entered her system—but they'd stung enough to shock her out of the mindscape.

Then Mince had grabbed her by the throat and twisted her around. Now Jasmine was backed up against Mince, who stood against the wall. Mince had her arm around Jasmine's throat in a wrestler's grip, holding her like a human shield.

The machine dangled in the air, its cables still fixed to both women's temples. With a swipe of her free hand, Mince sliced the cables free. The machine fell to the floor with a dull crack.

Which hand? Jasmine wondered. *Which hand did she hit me with?*

Mince raised one hand in a dramatic motion, holding it up in front of Jasmine's face. The rings read LIVE.

"Lucky for you I'm left-handed," Mince hissed in her ear. "Need my DIE arm to hold you."

CHAPTER FOUR

Jasmine wished she could see the girl's face, read her emotional state. But Mince's iron grip held her tight, turned away. Jasmine pictured the scared little five-year-old, watching her father explode into violence.

"I—I saw what happened to you," Jasmine croaked. "I'm sorry."

"Don't you *dare* pity me."

Duane fidgeted but didn't move. His eyes were fixed on Jasmine.

"I've signaled for reinforcements," Mince continued. "They'll be here in a few minutes. Which ought to give you time to think about the horrible thing you just did to me. Then the Vanguard soldiers will take you away, and nobody will ever remember the great, powerful pig man and dragon lady again."

Jasmine squirmed, but it was no use. Mince was a small woman, but her madness gave her strength. Without the Dragon power, Jasmine couldn't break her grip.

A slight rumble sounded beneath their feet. "Volcano's acting up," Mince said with a laugh. "Believe me, this is only the beginning."

The air seemed hotter now, the walls narrower. Roxanne still lay unconscious. Duane looked at Jasmine, his eyes pleading for guidance.

But Jasmine was out of plans, out of power, and out of ideas. There was nothing to do but struggle for breath, deep in the heart of the volcano, and wait for the end.

CHAPTER FIVE

STEVEN LEE RAN along the winding passage. The tunnel grew darker, narrower, steeper; he found himself skidding down a rocky incline. The air tasted thick and stale.

The voices in his head had become quieter. But their distant chant was like a drumbeat: *Don't. Don't. Don't.*

The passageway leveled out slightly. He flipped the HUDset down over his eyes, hoping to use it to guide his way. The schematic appeared, a scaffold of jagged green lines. The tunnel continued for at least half a kilometer, winding its way downhill.

CHAPTER FIVE

Then he noticed the battery level: 22 percent. At that rate, the HUDset would lose power within minutes; better to save it for an emergency. He switched it off and stashed the HUDset in his pack.

As his eyes struggled to adjust in the dark tunnel, the old Tiger appeared before him again. "Turn back," the man said. "There's still time."

"I can't," Steven replied.

The return of the visions meant something, he knew. In the past, they'd appeared only in connection with his Zodiac power—and usually when Steven was at a high altitude, in an airplane. There was a reason for that, something to do with the electromagnetic field of the earth. Duane had tried to explain it to him, but Steven couldn't follow the science.

This vision, however, seemed to be warning him *away* from the source of his power. And it had come to him in the farthest place possible from an airplane: in a volcanic cavern deep beneath the surface of the earth.

As he felt his way along the rocky walls, Steven remembered something else Duane had said—earlier that day in the premission briefing. The volcano, Mount Merapi, featured prominently in a variety of different regional mythologies. Some locals told a story about humans being destroyed carelessly by gods who had decided to move the mountain. But others believed something else: that the spirits of the people's ancestors actually lived in the mountain, guarding and protecting it.

Is that what's happening here? he wondered. *The Tigers . . . they're like my ancestors, in a way. Are they trying to protect me? Or are they guarding something* from *me?*

He cried out in pain as his head struck something. He shook off the vision and turned, squinting along the tunnel. He'd run straight into a stalactite hanging from the ceiling, which was less than half a meter above his head now. Angry, he punched the stalactite and howled again as pain stabbed through his hand.

Then he noticed the light.

He whirled around. A perfectly round metal plate filled the passageway dead ahead, blocking his way. It measured at least two meters in diameter, and it was glowing.

When Steven reached out for it, the voices surged again: *Don't. Don't.*

"Shut up," he said. He touched the cool metal.

The plate flashed bright, blinding him momentarily. When his vision cleared, a familiar face was glaring out at him—a cruel visage with short-cropped military-style hair and a square jaw.

Maxwell.

"Steven Lee," Maxwell said. "The one-time Tiger."

The voice sent chills through Steven. Maxwell had held him captive in the past, drained Steven's powers, even tortured his friends. *But I can't let him see me sweat. Got to stay cool!*

"Maxy," he said. "You look good. Been lifting?"

"Do not enter this chamber," Maxwell warned. "It will be your last act."

CHAPTER FIVE

Steven studied the edges of the metal plate. They were set right into the rock, sealed with some unseen fixative. "You on the other side of this, Maxy?"

"Do you think you can best me in battle?" Maxwell asked. "I am the Dragon, most powerful sign of the Zodiac. You have no power; you are just a boy. I will destroy you."

Steven paused, raising a hand to his chin. Something was wrong. Maxwell's answers were coming a little too fast, as if he wasn't even pausing to think. And his image looked a bit too perfect, a little younger than usual. Hadn't there been more wrinkles on his forehead before?

"I am the Dragon," Maxwell repeated.

Let's try something, Steven thought.

"I know who you are . . . mate," he said, deliberately putting on an Irish accent. "But you got me wrong. I'm not Steven Lee."

Maxwell blinked. "What?"

"The name's Liam," Steven continued. "I'm not the Tiger, uh, mate. You can call me Ram."

"Liam MacNeil," Maxwell said, with no pause at all. "The one-time Ram. I am the Dragon, most powerful sign of the Zodiac."

Steven rolled his eyes. Liam was the Zodiac's Ram, one of the key members of the team. A few weeks before, the Irish government had learned his secret: when he was younger, Liam had deserted from the army. He could have run away again, but he'd decided to turn himself in and pay for his youthful indiscretion. Now, as far as Steven knew, Liam was sitting in a jail in Dublin. He certainly wasn't talking to a plate inside an Indonesian volcano.

But Maxwell—or *whatever* Steven was talking to—didn't know that.

Steven turned away, thinking. In the light from the plate, the stalactite caught his eye.

"You have no power," the Maxwell image continued. "You are just a man. I will destroy you."

"Maxwell," Steven muttered, reaching out to grab the stalactite with both hands, "the great and powerful." He pulled and twisted, the rocky protrusion loosening in his grip.

"Do not attempt to enter this chamber. It will be your last act."

"You know something—uhhh—Maxwell?"

"Do not—"

"I'm tired of people telling me what *not* to do."

With a crack, the stalactite snapped free from the ceiling. Steven whipped it around and stabbed it into the plate. Electricity flashed out, knocking him away. The Maxwell image didn't even look surprised; it just blinked again, flared bright, and winked off.

Steven staggered back, stunned. When he looked again, the circular plate had swung slightly inward on a hinge, revealing a hidden room on the other side. He pushed the heavy, smoking door open farther. A damaged server computer hung on its back, whirring loudly.

"Nice try, Maxwell," Steven said, smirking at the

computer. "But this *boy* has been playing multiplayer games all his life. I know a bot when I'm talking to one."

His smirk faded quickly. In the end, the preprogrammed facsimile only reinforced the question that had been nagging at him all along: *Where is Maxwell, really? Where's the Dragon?*

And are they still the same person?

He edged his way inside, studying the room. It was about the size of a large den, dimly lit by recessed lamps, with a higher ceiling than the passage outside. No people, no furniture—just a gigantic pile of relics in the center of the room.

Steven knelt down to examine the objects. They were all artifacts, souvenirs of Maxwell's military exploits. An ancient Mesopotamian spear, a nineteenth-century Colt revolver. Steven recognized a Roman shield salvaged from the wreckage of Maxwell's former Australian headquarters.

That base had been filled with treasures stolen from around the world. Now they lay discarded, like a pile of trash that nobody had bothered to take out.

He studied a large wooden wheel—probably from some World War–era cannon. He picked up the revolver and tossed it aside.

Again, the Tigers rumbled in his mind: *Don't do it.*

"I have to." He dug deeper into the pile, uncovering the headpiece from an Egyptian sarcophagus.

It will be your doom.

He blocked out the voices. He kept digging, lifting

and then discarding one object after another. A teletype keyboard. A Chinese crossbow. A carved bust resembling the head sculptures on Easter Island, but much smaller.

Don't.

He felt compelled, gripped by some force greater than himself. As he dug farther down into the pile, the artifacts became almost exclusively Chinese in origin. A fighting staff. A thin *gong* with no arrows. A weapon with a fanned blade . . . a *yue*, his grandfather had called it.

"Ow," Steven said.

He shook his hand in pain. Near the bottom of the pile lay a thin *qiang*, or spear, another ancient Chinese weapon. He'd pricked his finger on it. A drop of blood glistened on its jagged blade.

On the floor in the exact center of the room, a small brown sphere caught his eye. As he reached down for it, the voices in his head grew louder: *Don't. DON'T.*

His hand closed over warm bronze. "The *jiānyù*," he whispered.

No, the Tigers said. *Do not seek out the power. It will be your doom.*

Ignoring them, he raised the sphere above his head. It pulsed and shimmered in the dim light. It seemed to speak directly to the Tiger, the immortal spirit still buried somewhere inside him.

The voices reached a crescendo: *SEE.*

The room seemed to dissolve into a haze of light. Steven shrank away, struggling to banish the vision. But it was the most powerful, most overwhelming vision he'd ever experienced.

A droplet of water appeared in the light. It hovered in the air, then fell to the floor. A second droplet followed, and then a third.

Drip. Drip. Drip.

The light softened, revealing a small group. Roxanne, her eyes wide with fear. Duane, tapping furiously on a small tablet. Liam, his uniform in shreds. Kim, the missing Rabbit, casting anxious glances behind her.

They stood in a circle, watching the droplets fall from the sky. Their eyes moved in unison, tracking the motion of the water as if it were a one-way vertical table tennis match. They seemed fearful, mesmerized, resigned to some terrible fate.

Drip. Drip. Drip.

As the last droplet fell, Jasmine appeared. She looked tired, guilty, as if she'd been carrying around some horrible secret. She lifted an arm and pointed upward.

The water had vanished. In its place, a gigantic Dragon claw descended from the sky, talons reaching down to menace the Zodiacs. They looked up, defiant but terrified. Powerless.

I'll save you, Steven thought, the pulsing *jiānyù* still clasped in his hand. *I'll get all our powers back. That's why I came here!*

No, the Tigers said. *Look.*

Steven whirled around—and saw *another* Dragon

claw reaching down from the sky. Its talons seemed even sharper, more severely hooked than the other's. Beneath it, two small figures cowered in fear, raising their arms to shield their vulnerable bodies.

"Mom," Steven whispered. "And Dad."

His father, dressed as always in a freshly pressed business suit, shouted up at the unseen Dragon. In response, its claw swiped through the air, grazing his mother's cheek. She didn't cry out, but she raised a hand to wipe away blood.

This, the Tigers said. *This is your doom.*

A cry of pain. Steven turned back to see Jasmine struggling, pinned beneath the first Dragon claw. Duane lay bloody on the ground, his tablet computer shattered beside him.

A scuffling noise. Steven whirled again. His mother batted her fists helplessly against the Dragon's claw. Mr. Lee hunched down beside her, clutching at a fresh wound in his stomach.

Steven wanted to help them—wanted to help *all* of them. But he was frozen, rooted to the spot. All he could do was watch.

The face of the old Tiger appeared again, filling Steven's view. When the old man spoke, the voices of the other Tigers vibrated behind him, echoing forward through the ages.

"If you reclaim your powers," the Tigers said, "you will be forced to make this choice: the Zodiac or a normal life.

Your friends, your teammates, your duty—or your family, the people who gave you life."

"I can't," Steven said. "I can't make that choice."

"You must. We did—all of us, every Tiger through history. We all lived through the cycle, were all tested. And all of us failed."

Steven felt cold inside. The warning was cryptic, its details shrouded in mystery. But behind it, he knew, was the truth. The end of the story, the dark secret behind the Zodiac powers.

"The result," the Tigers chanted, "is always the same."

The old man's face faded away. In its place, the Dragon filled the sky, coiled and menacing. Its fiery breath burst forth, a song of triumph over its enemies. The Zodiacs lay below: Roxanne, Duane, Kim—broken, slashed to bits. Only Liam still stood, defiant atop his friends' bodies. As he lowered his head for a final Ram charge, the Dragon swiped its claw at him, almost casually. He toppled and fell.

Steven's mother and father lay together, silent and unmoving, hands clasped in death.

Oblivion.

The white haze began to rise again. The Lees receded into the distance; the Zodiacs seemed to melt away. Even the Dragon became blurry, indistinct.

None among us may escape this destiny, the Tigers continued. *When our time was done, our enemies vanquished, we found that all trace of our powers was erased from the world. Even the memories . . . of ourselves, of the friends we cherished in love and in battle . . . all this was lost.*

The whole picture dissolved into light. Water began to trickle down again, just as before. *Drip. Drip. Drip.*

And just as it was for us, so it will be for you . . .

An inhuman roar rose. The crimson breath of the Dragon burned through the droplets, obliterating them.

. . . if you reclaim your powers.

All at once, the vision was gone. Steven sat on the floor of the cavern, surrounded by a thousand scattered relics. The room was cold.

The *jiānyù* pulsed in his hand. He could feel its power, the tremendous energies held captive within it. The fierce Horse, the unstoppable Ram. The Rooster with its piercing cry, the ever-searching Pig. Dog and Rabbit, Snake and Ox and Monkey and . . .

As he watched, mesmerized, the sphere's surface began to flow and melt in his grip. Its shape became elongated and cylindrical, like a sausage. One end morphed into a thick whipping tail; the other became a tufted head with sharp bronze fangs.

The Tiger.

The others, the ancient Tigers, had receded. But Steven could still hear their warning in his mind.

He remembered the day he'd first received the Zodiac power, in a subterranean chamber very different from this one. He hadn't asked for the power, hadn't wanted it. But since that time, it had helped him save a lot of people.

He thought of his teammates. He remembered the battles they'd fought in the wastes of Greenland, the caverns beneath China, the Australian desert. He thought of his alliance with Ox, Dog, and Horse, who had once been his enemies.

The vision persisted in his mind: the Zodiac team cut down, slaughtered by the Dragon's power. And his parents, too. They'd always been distant, obsessed with their work. He'd never been close to them, never enjoyed a normal father- or mother-son relationship.

But I don't want them to die!

Was that what would happen if he took back the power? Would he inevitably be forced to choose between his parents and his friends? Was the Tigers' prophecy unavoidable?

Oblivion, they'd said.

The *jiānyù* grew warmer. It shifted and morphed again, back to a sphere of tarnished bronze. Its surface pulsed, thrumming like a heartbeat.

"Tell me," Steven said aloud. "Tell me what to do."

One more image came to mind. Kim, tired and hungry, held captive in a near-airless room. Desperate, scared.

Powerless.

He picked up the *qiang* and wiped the blood off its tip. Then he threw the *jiānyù* down on the floor and thrust the spear straight through it.

The *jiānyù* seemed to shatter into fragments of light. Power, raw Zodiac energy, mushroomed, flaring in all

directions through the room. Steven dropped the spear and took a step back.

For a moment, time seemed suspended. Energy flashed and whirled in the air, filling the rocky chamber. Within its blinding radiance, images seemed to flicker and fade. Sharp teeth, quick and primal. Spectral animals: a charging horse, a screaming rooster. A spiral galaxy, mirroring the swirling pattern of the power itself.

Just like the Convergence, Steven thought. *That night in Hong Kong, when the Zodiac powers burst free into the modern world.*

He blinked and the spell was broken. The energy seemed to burn white-hot at its core in the center of the room. Then a dozen beams flashed outward, blazing through the walls and ceiling, leaving the rock untouched.

No, Steven realized, *not* quite *a dozen.* The Dragon power wasn't there. Neither was Rat—but that was a whole different problem, one the team would have to sort out another time.

One power seemed to hesitate, remaining within the room. A bright orange light hovered, pulsing and shimmering, at Steven's eye level. It seemed to be studying him, sizing him up.

Steven felt his pulse quicken. He faced the orange light head-on. In its center he could see the old Tiger, shaking his head in despair. The man mouthed the word soundlessly, one final time:

Don't.

CHAPTER FIVE

A wave of doubt washed over Steven. *Last chance,* he thought. *Just like at the Convergence. I could bolt. I could turn and run as fast as I can, find someplace where nobody's ever heard the word* Zodiac. *I'd be free of all this, of the power and the burden and the legacy. Maybe we'd all be free.*

But there hadn't been any real choice, that night long before. And there wasn't any now.

"Hit me," he said, spreading his arms wide.

He didn't even see it coming. The light was everywhere at once, filling his body, blazing through every pore of his skin. It felt like ice and fire, like running and flying and swimming with the muscles of a god. It was as old as the cave and as young as Steven himself.

It felt like coming home.

He glanced down at the *jiānyù*. It lay melted and shattered at his feet. Its light had faded; no trace of the Zodiac energy remained inside its shell.

Gone, he thought, looking around at the walls. *Returned to its hosts, wherever they might be.*

Good or bad, they're Zodiacs again.

He opened his mouth and roared. The blazing form of the Tiger appeared above his head, echoing his primal cry. He flexed his arms and legs, reveling in the pride, the strength, the agility—the sheer physical joy of the Tiger's gift.

Then he turned and dashed out into the corridor. The Tiger leaped and ran, screaming its glory to the world, racing to join its brothers and sisters.

CHAPTER SIX

THE CEILING IS *two point four meters high,* Duane thought. *Roxanne lies point three meters from my feet; her breathing is shallow but steady.*

"I see what you're doing," Mince said. "Figuring the angles."

Mince stands three point one meters away, holding Jasmine by the throat. She called for assistance sometime between three point five and four point five minutes ago. No sign of the Vanguard soldiers yet, but they'll be here imminently.

"Don't think it's gonna save you," she continued. "Being smart tells you what people are gonna do, but it doesn't mean you can stop 'em."

CHAPTER SIX

Her dart-rings are aimed directly at me. If I lunge at her, she'll fire them before I can cover point three meters of the distance. She'll probably kill Jasmine, too.

"You gotta have power, too." Mince smiled again, that horrible unnerving smile. "Then you can do whatever you want."

Conclusion: I am helpless.

"Mince," Jasmine croaked. "You don't have to do this. Don't let your father—*ARRGGKK!*"

The smile vanished from Mince's lips. She tensed her arm, pressing tighter against Jasmine's throat. Jasmine struggled, tried to pry Mince's arm away. But it was no use.

"I told you," Mince said. "Shut up."

I've got to do something! Duane thought. But the equations, the cold facts of the situation, left him no options.

He felt a tingle in his spine—and went instantly alert. The feeling was so faint, most people wouldn't have registered it on a conscious level. But Duane's memory was precise, perfect. He'd felt this way once before, and he instantly knew what it meant.

The Zodiac power.

The wall began to glow, a blinding light emanating from the other side. Mince whirled in alarm, then ducked. But she kept a tight grip on Jasmine, pulling her to the ground.

The power flashed forth, leaving the wall undamaged but filling the corridor with light. Duane spread his arms and counted down silently: *Point five seconds. Point four. Point three—*

Energy surged through him, filling him, electrifying every atom of his being. He barely had time to think, *Hmmm. Miscalculated slightly,* before the raging, snorting form of the Pig rose above him.

Mince stumbled to her feet, wrenching Jasmine around in front of her.

Duane's mind felt alert, alive, open to every piece of information in the universe. Unlike most of the Zodiac abilities, Duane's power wasn't primarily physical in nature. It enhanced his own innate abilities, allowing his already brilliant mind to operate at many times its normal capacity.

With uncharacteristic emotion, he remembered: *This is cool.*

"Okay," Mince said, "you got your power back. One of your little friends must have found the *jiānyù* after all."

Duane took a step forward. Above his head, the Pig roared silently.

"But I've got your *other* friend." Mince held Jasmine like a shield. "And she's still out of luck in the powers department."

Jasmine glared. "Duane. Take her ou*wggktt—*"

Mince sneered at Duane. "You're the weakest Zodiac." She held up her DIE hand. "What can your stupid information-processing power do, anyw—"

Duane's eyes flared. He shot a glance at Mince's arm

and the holo-projector on her wrist exploded in a shower of sparks. Mince cried out and shook her arm in pain.

"That's one thing it can do," he said.

Jasmine saw her chance. She jabbed Mince in the stomach and burst free. Jasmine stumbled, coughed, and slammed into Duane, knocking him off balance. They tumbled to the floor.

When Duane looked up, Mince was standing over them. Her left fist, adorned with the rings labeled LIVE, was aimed at him. Slowly, Mince turned to Jasmine and clenched her right hand into a fist.

"C-can you take out her dart shooters, too?" Jasmine gasped.

Duane shook his head. "They're simple mechanical devices. My power only affects electronics."

Jasmine tried to speak but burst out coughing again. The word DIE hovered less than a half meter from her face.

"You first," Mince hissed.

A low whine filled the air. Jasmine turned her head, looking around in puzzlement. Mince's fists didn't waver, but her eyes narrowed.

Duane just smiled.

The whining sound rose in volume, becoming a high-pitched shriek. Mince took a step back, raising her hands to cover her hears. "Stop it!"

"It's not me," Duane said. "It's her."

They all turned to follow his gaze. Roxanne stood in an action stance a short distance down the corridor, her mouth open in a feral scream. She looked fierce, furious, a righteous angel of vengeance. Above her head, the ghostly form of the Rooster cried out in unison with its human host.

Mince turned both hands toward Roxanne and fired. Roxanne cried out even louder, a scream of rage. The darts struck the sonic barrier and dropped harmlessly to the ground.

All at once, the sound stopped.

Mince looked down at her empty dart-rings, then back up at her attackers. Three angry forms moved toward her. Duane with the raging Pig, Roxanne and the now-silent Rooster, and angriest of all, Jasmine.

"Okay, girl," Jasmine said. "That's it."

Mince glared at her, petulant. "What?"

"I don't feel sorry for you anymore."

Jasmine punched her in the face. Mince pitched backward, falling to the ground. Duane reached for Jasmine, who shook him off.

"I'm all right. Just had to get that off my chest." Jasmine smiled at Roxanne, shaking her hand in pain. "Welcome back to the party."

"I still feel like crap." Roxanne stumbled. "But the Zodiac power . . . I think it's purging the drug from my system."

Duane gestured down at Mince, who lay dazed on the floor. "What do we do about her?"

CHAPTER SIX

"I'll tell you what to do," someone said. *"Don't move."*

Duane whirled around; Jasmine and Roxanne mirrored his movement. Three large Vanguard soldiers stood in the passageway, blocking the way back to the surface. Their energy rifles were cocked and aimed, the tips glowing dangerously red.

"Technically," Duane said, "that's what you want us *not* to do."

Jasmine and Roxanne stared at him.

"These little details bother me," he explained.

Jasmine turned to the soldiers, an amused look on her face. "Better back off, boys." She gestured at Duane to her left and Roxanne on her right. "In case you're late getting the news, my friends have their powers back."

"These weapons have been optimized to deal with Zodiac-enhanced individuals," the leader said. His eyes were hidden behind his helmet; his voice was magnified electronically. "The Dragon takes no chances."

"The Dragon," Roxanne said, "isn't here." She opened her mouth to scream.

The three guards swiveled their weapons toward her. The first one's finger twitched on his trigger—

But he flew backward, his body spinning in midair, his gun's energy beam sizzling harmlessly against the ceiling. Duane thought he saw a flash of gray pants, a dark boot. The second man cried out as something incredibly fast—a dark fist? A red sleeve?—chopped into his neck. He went

LIVE
DIE

down, his energy rifle twisting around to strike him in the stomach.

The last soldier stumbled back, trying to aim his gun. But before he could get off a shot, the newcomer leaped onto his back and wrenched off the soldier's helmet. The man flailed, twisting his head around in the bulky uniform, struggling to see his attacker.

When he caught sight of the raging Tiger, the man cried out.

"G'night," Steven Lee said.

He leaned forward, still clinging to the soldier's back, and slammed the man's exposed head against the wall. The soldier groaned, dropped his weapon, and passed out.

As his enemy crashed to the ground, Steven leaped into the air. He reached out with his arms and legs, soaring gracefully. As he touched down in a perfect four-point landing, the Tiger above him roared in triumph.

Roxanne ran over to hug him. "That was awesome!"

Even Jasmine seemed impressed. "I don't think I've ever seen you move that fast."

"Guess I was excited. It's been a while." Steven grinned. "What's the matter, Duane? Don't *you* want to tell me how great I was?"

But Duane was busy scanning the room. His instincts—and his perfect memory—had kicked in again, enhanced by his newly returned powers. He counted the people in the corridor: Jasmine, Steven, Roxanne. Three soldiers lay on the floor: two unconscious, one dazed. But . . .

"Mince is gone," he said.

Steven looked around, his Tiger eyes confirming Duane's observation. The three guards lay on the floor, but there was no sign of Mince. In the confusion, she'd managed to escape.

"Ah," Roxanne began, "what harm can she do? I don't *believe* I just said that."

"I can track her," Steven said, pulling out his HUDset. "Unless . . ."

"She's shielded." Duane gestured at the soldiers on the floor. "If we couldn't see them, we're definitely not going to find her."

Steven was overcome by a sudden wave of emotion. Seeing his friends in action again, their Zodiac avatars blazing above them—it was like coming home. Fighting alongside Duane and Roxanne . . .

I didn't realize how much I missed it.

Jasmine staggered and raised a hand to her head. As Steven reached for her arm, he noticed the tiny cuts across her face.

"Are you okay?" he asked.

"Some of Mince's poison . . . got into my system." Jasmine gestured at the wall. "Think I better sit down."

Duane took her other arm. Together he and Steven led her over to a corner where the corridor twisted. "Thanks." Jasmine chuckled. "Remember when I used to be the most powerful Zodiac?"

"You still are," Steven said. "Where it counts."

He saw the gratitude in her eyes. *She's still one of us,* he thought, *even without her powers. But she needed to hear me say it.*

He heard a crashing noise coming from just around the bend in the passageway. "Um," he said, pulling Jasmine away from the sound. "Maybe you better sit over *here.* . . ."

The noise grew louder. And something else, too . . .

Laughter.

Three Vanguard soldiers tumbled around the corner, grunting. A huge yellow-furred arm reached out from inside the human tangle, flinging one man aside. A second soldier tried to raise his energy rifle, but an even larger *foot* with sharp curved claws caught him straight in the stomach. He flew back, gasping for breath.

The Vanguards' attacker stood revealed. He wore the same uniform as earlier that day, and the scar still dominated his face. But every centimeter of that face, and his body, was now covered with blond fur. His laughing mouth gaped wide to reveal deadly fangs.

"Dog," Roxanne said.

Nicky—his Dog powers restored—turned to face the third Vanguard soldier, who cast a nervous glance backward at Steven and his team. He looked down at the floor, where five of his fellow soldiers had already fallen. Then he looked back up at Dog.

"RAAHR!" Dog growled, lunging forward.

The soldier stumbled back in fear, half tripping over one of his fallen comrades. Dog howled, then burst out laughing.

Steven turned sharply toward the side wall. He could still hear crashing noises, even though Dog and the soldiers had already arrived. The sound seemed to be coming from *inside* the—

"Get down!" he yelled.

He ducked, pulling Jasmine and Duane down with him. The wall burst apart from the other side, filling the air with bits of plaster and stone. A chunk of rock the size of a trash-can lid came flying toward them; Steven held up a hand to block it.

And then Roxanne was there, leaning over him. She opened her mouth and shrieked, forming a sonic barrier. The rock bounced off and crashed to the floor.

Steven looked up, waving away plaster dust. A man-sized hole gaped in the wall, revealing four more Vanguard soldiers. A huge figure, almost too big to be human, strode through them, jabbing and punching. He moved with heavy, measured steps, absorbing each of his enemies' attacks and blocking them with practiced ease. Above his head, a fierce Ox with long curved horns snorted and raged in the air.

"Man," Roxanne said. "I'd forgotten how tough Malik is."

"He makes a pretty good hero figure," Steven replied, "for a former villain."

He glanced over at Nicky. Dog held his last opponent in the air, stretched out at the end of a thick yellow-furred arm. Ox was holding his own, but the first two soldiers he'd thrown were starting to recover.

"Should we assist them?" Duane asked.

Roxanne turned to Steven, grinning. "You're the boss."

Steven eased Jasmine down to a sitting position. He glanced nervously at the dazed soldiers strewn across the floor. "You okay here?"

She grunted, reached over, and grabbed an energy rifle from one of the fallen soldiers. "Locked and loaded."

Steven smiled and rose to his feet. Roxanne and Duane jumped toward him, dodging as one of Ox's opponents struck the floor.

"Let's go," Steven said.

Roxanne led the charge, her sonic cry forming a protective shield. Duane followed, surrounded by a halo of Zodiac energy. Steven leaped and ran, skirting the edges of the corridor with catlike grace.

He reached out with his Tiger power and linked the three of them together, just as he'd done so many times before. He felt the fierce cry of the Rooster, the slow mastery of the Pig. The Tiger prowled among them, strengthening their abilities and drawing strength from them in turn. Steven's already-sharp senses grew sharper, his enhanced reflexes guiding him at superhuman speed.

Two soldiers turned at the sound of Roxanne's piercing cry. For a moment, Steven imagined what they saw. Three young people moving in perfect unison, like human weapons, and three spectral beasts raging and snarling above them: the screaming Rooster, the charging Pig, the savage Tiger.

Ox stepped back, allowing his teammates to crash into the soldiers. Roxanne reared her head back and shrieked again, even louder, directly into a soldier's face. The man grabbed his ears, screamed, and dropped to the ground.

The second soldier raised his gun, aiming shakily. Duane reached out in a casual motion, Zodiac energy sparkling from his hand. The gun exploded.

Steven glanced around. Three soldiers were still on their feet. Ox traded punches with one, backing the man slowly up against a wall. Dog seemed to be playing with another. The yellow-furred Zodiac slapped the gun out of his opponent's hand. When the man snatched the gun off the floor, Dog slapped it away again.

"So you're the Tiger," said someone with a deep voice.

Steven whipped his head around—and saw the man in the black suit, the Vanguard agent from the cavern above. *Alpha,* Malik had called him. He raised his enormous energy rifle and aimed it straight at Steven's chest.

Steven gestured at the gun. "Does that thing really work? It's hilariously large."

"See for yourself."

Without even thinking, Steven dodged the energy bolt. As the Tiger's instincts kicked in, he found himself leaping straight up. He twisted in midair, the Tiger avatar roaring with power, and kicked at Alpha.

But the Vanguard agent was surprisingly fast. He raised his weapon and fired off two more shots in rapid succession. Then a third. Steven reached out and bounced off the corridor wall, pausing to kick a guard—the one facing off against Dog—in the head. The man groaned and dropped, stunned.

"Zodiacs," Alpha muttered, squeezing his trigger again. "Can't stand 'em. That's why I volunteered to test this quantum particle rifle, even though they warned me it might overheat and expl—"

The energy rifle blew apart, setting fire to the arms of Alpha's suit. He cried out, dropped the smoking remains of the particle rifle, and staggered back. When he saw the flaming arms of his suit, he started batting at them and flailing.

Steven leaped up and landed behind Alpha. He paused, considering a final jab at the man's

competence and/or judgment. Maybe "Hey, there's no smoking in here" or "Good luck getting the deposit back on that suit" or "People don't kill people; ludicrously huge guns kill people."

"Never call me shorty," he said.

A thick fist smashed down on Alpha's head, dropping him to the ground just as the last of the flames died down. The fist belonged to Ox. The burly Zodiac stood over the bodies of two more soldiers, cocking his head wryly at Steven.

"Sorry, kitty," he said, indicating Alpha's unmoving form. "Looked like you were playing with your food."

The fighting had stopped. Steven counted the number of fallen Vanguard soldiers. Ten—no, eleven of them lay stunned on the floor.

"You were right, Malik," Dog said, moving toward them. "These kids fight pretty good!"

"Pretty well," Jasmine said.

They all turned to look at her. She sat propped up against the wall, waving the energy rifle. She looked weak but was still conscious.

"Well. The kids fought *well*," she repeated, slurring her words slightly.

Ox nodded slowly. "It shows you what the Zodiacs can do. When we're not trying to kill each other, I mean."

"Yeah." Dog grinned. "But that's kinda fun, too."

Jasmine staggered to her feet. Steven started toward

her, but Dog was closer. He held out a thick-furred hand, and Jasmine clasped it firmly.

Steven cast his eyes across the group. Roxanne and Duane seemed barely winded, energized by the return of their powers. Ox and Dog were powerful engines of battle, back in their element. Even Jasmine, weak and depowered, projected a confidence he hadn't seen from her in months.

The fight wasn't finished yet. They hadn't found the Dragon or rescued Kim. Steven's vision still haunted him, too. There was plenty to do, he knew, before they left the Mountain of Fire.

But for that moment, the Zodiacs stood triumphant. And Steven had to admit: it felt good.

CHAPTER SEVEN

"OH," DUANE SAID. "Oh, this is bad."

"What?" Steven asked.

Duane sat crouched against the corridor wall, holding a small analyzer device in one hand and his tablet in the other. As his eyes darted from one to the other, the Pig avatar flashed on and off above his head.

"I've been taking soil samples," he explained, "analyzing the level of gas contained in the rocks, the chemical composition, temperature, state of oxidation, and—"

"Duane! The point?"

CHAPTER SEVEN

Before Duane could answer, a massive rumbling shook the passageway. Steven dropped into a Tiger crouch, instantly alert. Malik and Nicky ran to different ends of the passageway, stepping nimbly over the unconscious Vanguard soldiers. Roxanne took up a position at the large gap in the tunnel wall.

"Nothing coming from this side," Malik said.

"Here either," Nicky said.

"Nothing inside the ginormous hole in the wall," Roxanne said. "Oh, wait. Yes there is."

Steven crept up next to Roxanne, tensing for action, and peered into the hole. The Tiger avatar rose above him, snarling. The tunnel revealed by the hole was dark, lacking the artificial light that suffused the corridors and filled with dust from the various impacts.

Duane moved up next to Steven. "I should tell you—"

Steven motioned him to silence.

Inside the hole, two figures lumbered into view: a large woman holding a much smaller woman by the collar of her suit jacket.

"At ease, boys," Josie said. "It's just me. And Betty here." She held up the smaller woman as if she were presenting identification.

"It's Beta," the woman said. Her black suit was torn and charred, and she wore a dazed expression. "My name is Beta."

Josie stepped into the main passageway, shaking the

woman roughly. A ghostly Horse appeared over Josie's head, pawing the air and snorting.

She's got her powers back, too, Steven thought. Strangely, the knowledge made him uneasy.

"Betty's been telling me some very interesting stuff," Josie said.

"It's *Beta*—ow!"

"This is fairly important," Duane said.

Josie ignored him. "Tell 'em, Betty."

"I—"

Duane cleared his throat. "If I could just—"

Horse shook Beta again. "Tell 'em what you told me!"

"Mince has triggered an eruption of the volcano!" Beta exclaimed.

"That's what I'm trying to tell you!" Duane yelled.

Steven sucked in a breath. He reached out with his Tiger senses, taking in the subtle sounds of the mountain, the temperature and humidity of his surroundings. At the very edge of his awareness, he could hear the rumbling of molten rock flowing far below.

It was growing louder—pressing upward, moving toward the surface.

"It's true," he said.

Duane tapped at his tablet. "There's no way for me to tell exactly how long the evacuation will take. The eruption could still kill hundreds of people."

The chamber shook again. Roxanne lost her footing,

tripped over a fallen Vanguard soldier, and almost slammed into the wall.

"Mince," she said. "She'd kill all those people out there just to make her escape."

"Yeah," Steven said. "And one person in *here*, too."

Duane's eyes opened wide. "Kim."

"Excuse me," Beta said. "Can you people put me down?"

Josie adopted an exaggerated expression: *I'm thinking about it.* Steven gestured to her. She shrugged and set Beta down on the floor.

"Why did you tell us about the eruption?" Steven asked.

Beta averted her eyes. "I didn't take this job to kill kids."

"That's admirable, I guess"—Roxanne rolled her eyes—"in a least-you-can-do-to-be-a-human-person sort of way."

"We've got to get outside," Malik said. "People are going to need help."

"Plus," Nicky added, "flowing lava. It's kinda bad for the fur."

"But we can't just leave Kim!" Duane exclaimed.

Then all eyes were on Steven. *Leadership,* he thought, not for the first time. *Sometimes it sucks.*

A moan came from the floor. One of the soldiers was starting to awaken.

Steven turned to Beta. "You want to get your people out of here?"

She nodded.

"Do it."

Beta crouched down and started jostling the soldiers. One by one, they sat up, shaking their heads.

"But leave the guns," Steven added. Beta hesitated—and then she saw the Tiger above Steven's head, roaring a silent warning. She nodded hastily.

The chamber shook again. Steven gestured to the assembled Zodiacs.

"Get out," he said. "All of you. Get to the evacuation zones, do what you can to help the local authorities."

Roxanne frowned. "But—"

"I'll get Kim."

She stared at him. "You'll be killed."

"I'm the Tiger," Steven said, trying to sound confident. "I'm the fastest one here."

"I dunno, kid," Nicky said. "We ain't had a race yet."

Beta gathered the Vanguard soldiers together. Their armor was dented and ripped, their expressions dazed and disoriented. One by one, they dropped their energy rifles in a heap on the floor.

"Duane," Steven said, "can you locate Kim?"

Duane stabbed at his tablet, almost punching it in frustration. He shook his head.

"She's on level echo," Beta said. "It's the bottom floor of this complex—holding cell three."

"Thank you," Steven replied.

Beta nodded grimly. Then she turned, gestured up the

corridor, and started toward the surface. The line of soldiers followed, boots clomping on the hard floor.

Steven whirled back to address his team. "What are you guys waiting for?"

"I'm staying, too," Malik said.

Steven started to argue, then nodded. He could use Malik's Ox strength.

A faint moan rose from the far end of the passageway. Jasmine lay forgotten, her head propped up against the wall. They all rushed over to her.

"She's barely conscious," Roxanne said.

Duane leaned in. "I think she's trying to say something."

Steven crouched, wincing at the small cuts all along Jasmine's face. *Another thing Mince has to answer for,* he thought.

"Don' worry." Jasmine's voice was faint, her words slurred. "I'll get us outta . . . volcano. All of us. Drag'n power can do . . . anything. . . ."

"She doesn't *have* the Dragon power anymore." Josie snorted, the Horse above her mimicking the motion. "She's delirious."

"She's been drugged." Steven thought furiously. "Sorry, Malik."

"What?"

"I coulda used your help. But you've got to get her out of here. You're the only one who's strong enough."

Malik hesitated.

"Otherwise," Steven continued, "another innocent person will die."

Malik swore, then nodded. He reached out and, in a single swift motion, hoisted Jasmine onto his shoulder.

"Hey," Jasmine protested, her voice even fainter now. "Unhand the mighty Dragggg'n."

"Get her out of here," Steven said, locking eyes with Malik. "Get them all out of here."

"You got it."

Malik turned without another word, still carrying Jasmine's helpless form. He marched up the corridor toward the surface. Josie and Nicky hesitated for just a moment, then turned to follow.

Duane and Roxanne hung back. "Steven," Roxanne said, "we can—"

"Sorry, guys. This is *my* job. Duane, compute the lava pattern the best you can on the way out. That way you'll be ready to help the rescue teams." He forced a smile. "I'll be right behind you."

Then he turned and bolted down the corridor, heading deeper into the mountain.

I have to do this, he thought. *And I have to do it fast. But the truth is, it's kind of crazy—and I'm really scared. So I can't afford to give anybody the chance to talk me out of it.*

He didn't look back.

CHAPTER SEVEN

Steven ran deeper and deeper into the mountain. The passageway grew darker, the downward slope steeper. He couldn't be sure, but the walls seemed closer together than before.

He came to a fork in the path. The two choices looked identical; each branch curved out of view a meter down the corridor. *Great. Which way now?*

He flipped the HUDset down over his eyes. The green schematic glowed faintly and was hard to make out. To the left, the passageway seemed to open into a large, detailed structure made of flickering lines. On the right: a dead end.

The schematic blinked off, then on. His eyes flashed to the readouts: BATTERY LEVEL 0%. Then the screen went black.

He tore off the HUDset and flung it away. It hit the wall, let out a sharp burst of static, and fell to the ground.

Steven looked around, panicked. What was he doing so far underground? The walls seemed to be closing in; he felt an overwhelming sense of doom. *I'm gonna die here,* he thought. *I'm gonna die alone!*

Then he realized, to his surprise: *That's not me. It's the Tiger.*

Usually, the Tiger gave Steven strength, lent him its spirit and ferocity. But not this time. *It senses the magma flowing below, the molten rock that could incinerate us. So it wants to run away. It doesn't understand why I'm running* toward *the danger, instead of fleeing.*

It's the one panicking, not me!

"I appreciate the self-preservation instinct," he said aloud. "But we've got a friend to rescue." He paused, suddenly self-conscious. "And now I'm talking to myse—"

Another tremor struck—the biggest one yet. Steven tottered, almost lost his footing, and then took off down the left-hand branch of the corridor.

At least the other voices have gone quiet, he thought. *Maybe the presence of the actual Tiger power somehow pushes them back. Or maybe they gave up after I ignored their warning.*

The vision returned to his thoughts: the prophecy, the warning that either his friends or his parents would fall, inevitably, to the Dragon's power. He forced it away, using techniques Jasmine had taught him to clear his mind. *Later. Worry about that later.*

The Tiger roared in protest.

The corridor grew even narrower, so tight that Steven had to slow down and squeeze his way along. Then the path widened and disappeared abruptly. He stopped short, barely managing not to fall off the edge.

The sight took his breath away.

The pathway ended at the edge of a short cliff. About three meters below, a strange floor stretched out for about a kilometer. It was composed of slate tiles, thousands of them, arranged in a mosaic pattern. It reminded Steven of a surface his grandfather had laid down in their backyard, meticulously, one flat stone at a time.

CHAPTER SEVEN

Then he noticed: the tiles were moving. They slid back and forth, side to side. They seemed programmed, interdependent; they moved in concert, one tile shifting sideways to allow the next one to take its place.

He looked up. A map of the world covered the ceiling, high above. Continents glowed, lit from behind as if the ceiling itself were some sort of parchment covering an unseen light source. He could make out Africa, Europe, North and South America—but something was wrong. The shapes seemed twisted, distorted somehow.

What is this place? he wondered. *Did the Dragon build it?*

He frowned, calculating quickly. He couldn't be sure, but at a guess, he'd descended about two levels since leaving the others. Based on the earlier scans, level echo had to be at least two stories farther down. And the only way down was . . .

He leaped off the cliff, reaching out with all four limbs like a cat. He landed with his legs on separate tiles and both hands on a third. The two back tiles slid sideways, forcing his legs apart. He almost fell but somersaulted forward and repositioned himself on another, slower-moving tile.

"Tiger style!" he said, smiling. Then: "Let's never say that again, right? Right."

He turned to look back at the rocky cliff face. His Tiger senses detected no doorway, no way out of the chamber other than the passageway above. But he could hear something: a very low humming, almost out of the range of human hearing. *The machinery,* he realized. *The hidden tech that runs this place.*

The tile beneath his feet lurched, almost knocking him down. He took off running, away from the cliff and the narrow corridor. His eyes darted back and forth, side to side. He took in the motion of each individual tile, calculating exactly where, and how fast, to move his feet.

There didn't seem to be a way to get below that level. The tiles stretched out in all directions, shifting and moving in their heavy ballet. The chamber's walls might have held an elevator or stairwell leading down, but they were barely visible, far off in the distance.

Up ahead half a kilometer or so, the floor turned darker. Maybe there . . .

Steven leaped and ran, sometimes vaulting up high, other times lunging forward to somersault onto the next tile. As the tiles slid in all directions under his feet, he started to laugh. The action distracted him, cleared his thoughts, banished the fear from his mind. But still he wondered: *What was this place built for? It's not much of a security measure. The Tiger can navigate it easily, but even an ordinary person could slip and roll his way through it eventually.*

He leaped off a fast-moving tile—and caught another glimpse of the ceiling. Russia loomed directly above him, with the rest of Asia just beneath it. Like the other continents, it looked wrong . . . distorted, somehow. . . .

CHAPTER SEVEN

They're backwards, he realized. The whole image was flopped, reversed, as if he were looking at it in a mirror.

Or from inside the earth.

He looked down, a bit distracted, and almost twisted his ankle on the landing. The Tiger growled inside, a warning. *Pay attention,* it seemed to say. *You have the power again, but you're not invincible. Stay alert.*

That's how the Tiger survives.

As he approached the dark section of tiles, a grinding noise filled the air. Steven slowed, eyeing the expanse ahead. He shifted his feet more slowly, traveling across the tiles almost by instinct—as if he were treading water against a slow-moving tide.

The tiles ahead were black, polished as dark as newly laid pavement. At first they seemed stationary, a static surface, unlike the moving field beneath Steven's feet. As he watched, the grinding grew louder and the black tiles began to move. But their pattern was completely different. Instead of slipping over and under each other, the tiles slid away from each other in pairs, revealing a hundred gaps leading to the level below.

The tiles halted, along with the grinding sound. Steven drew closer. The holes varied greatly in size. Some were barely big enough to drop a bucket through, while others were elevator-sized.

Grimacing, he leaned forward and stared down one of the larger holes. Hot air wafted up, accompanied by a thick sulfur smell. But all he could see was blackness.

The tiles began to grind again—and to move. The gaps began to close.

"Oh, well," he said, and jumped.

The air in the chamber was heavy, humid and warm. The fall was farther than he had expected. He twisted midair, reaching out again with all fours. The Tiger, he knew, always landed on its feet.

He caught sight of another group of tiles below. These ones were jagged, with rough pitted surfaces and broken rocks sticking up at odd angles. He leaned forward, reached out his hand, grabbed hold—and yelled in surprise.

The tile was *hot*.

He pushed off the rock, vaulted over a large boulder, and landed on his feet. The rock beneath him was warm, but his boots shielded him from the heat. He couldn't see far; the lighting was dim, the air suffused with smoke. He heard a distant noise like crunching rock. But the source was out of view, even to his Tiger eyes.

Another tile, even more uneven and jagged, was lurching toward the one he stood on. One couldn't really call them tiles, he realized. They were more like flattened boulders, rattling around on some unknown surface. And that surface was very warm. The magma, the molten rock of the volcano, couldn't be far beneath his feet. He didn't want to think about that.

Steven braced himself and waited for the tiles to slide

past each other. He looked around, considering options. A third tile approached from the side—

The three tiles collided with a massive crash, their surfaces splintering. Steven flew into the air, swatting away chunks of stone with both hands. He cried out as a rocky shard grazed his neck.

He executed a midair somersault and glanced down. Two more boulder tiles met, shattering the smaller one into three even smaller pieces. Those pieces began to move independently, sliding and lurching toward other rocks. One of them struck yet another, sending softball-sized chunks flying.

Okay, he thought. *Now* this *is a security measure.*

He landed on a large rock, then leaped up again just as it made impact with another one, like a ship hitting an iceberg. He leaped and danced, avoiding shrapnel, trying to get a better view of the entire chamber. *I'm running blind,* he thought. *No HUDset and I can't see twenty feet in front of me. This should be level echo . . . but how do I find Kim?*

Then, as he jumped up again, he saw it: a wall, just ahead. A narrow walkway with no railing curved around it, only half a meter or so above the level of the chaotic rock tiles. The wall was lined with doors labeled with large numbers: 1, 2, 3—

Three, he thought. *Beta said Kim was in holding cell three!*

Another collision knocked him off his feet. He swore,

stumbled, and regained his footing. Ahead, one of the tiles was moving toward the wall. He jumped for it, his legs pumping comically in the air. He touched down, leaped back up, and stumbled onto the landing. He staggered, grabbed for the floor, and barely managed to avoid falling back onto the moving rock path.

He leaned against the wall, catching his breath. Below, the rocks continued to churn and slam together, spitting slate and basalt into the hot-sulfur air.

How do they work? he wondered. *Do they just keep breaking down into smaller and smaller chunks? Or does the machinery, the unknown tech of the Dragon, replenish the surface with fresh boulders?*

He shook his head and thought: *Kim.* Two doors rose before him, both with solid opaque surfaces. The one to his left read 2, the right one 3. He whirled to the right and banged on the door.

"Kim!" he called. "Are you in there?"

No answer.

"Kim!"

He studied the door. It was made of wood, with a hinge that swung inward. Surprisingly, it didn't seem very thick. He lunged forward, striking it with his shoulder. The door buckled slightly but didn't open.

He started back across the moving boulders, grimacing. *Maybe with a running start . . .*

He ran and jumped along the boulders, then turned

back toward the door labeled 3. He glanced down and saw a small globule of molten rock bubble up between two tiles. As soon as he noticed it, it simmered back down and vanished.

That's not good, he thought.

He started running, building speed. He leaped up and shot forward, soaring over the walkway, and slammed his shoulder into the door again.

"Ow," he said.

He stumbled back, rubbing his arm. The door had a small vertical crack along the wood grain, but it was still sealed.

He gasped for breath. *Gotta try again,* he thought. *I can't quit now!*

The third time he crashed into the door, it felt as if his shoulder would break. The fourth time he almost passed out. Only one thing kept him going: the thought of Kim, youngest of the Zodiacs, held captive in that boiling magma trap far beneath the earth.

The fifth time, the hinges snapped and the door buckled inward. Steven rolled and tumbled. He rose catlike to his feet, all his senses on high alert.

His heart sank. The cell was small and neat, with white walls marked with the Vanguard symbol. A screened-off bathroom area in the back, a simple cot with bedclothes, a washbasin and soap. On a small conveyor belt near the wall, a tray of food sat half-eaten.

But no Kim. After all that effort, she wasn't even there.

Behind him, the rocks crashed and split apart. Below his feet, molten rock roiled and rumbled at the command of unseen machinery. And in the little cell beneath the earth, Steven Lee hung his head in despair.

CHAPTER EIGHT

STEVEN HAD NO IDEA what to do. He'd gone halfway around the world, led the mission, risked the lives of the whole expanded Zodiac team. He'd braved the tunnels of Mount Merapi, regained his powers, and fought his way across a bizarre rocky obstacle course. He'd bashed down a door, nearly breaking his shoulder in the process.

All to find Kim.

For Steven, it had always been about her. And she wasn't there. Wherever she might be, whatever the Dragon had done with her, she wasn't in that cell.

CHAPTER EIGHT

He stepped out onto the walkway and stared at the number 3, painted on the loose-hanging door. *The soldier, Beta—could she have lied about the cell?* he wondered. *Maybe she just wanted to lure me down here. . . .*

He clenched his fists and looked out over the sea of moving rocks. He felt frustrated, more helpless than ever before. *The Dragon,* he thought. *This is all part of his*—its—*plan. Where is he? What has he done with Kim? What are his plans for all of us?*

Two rocks collided. Steven's neck hairs pricked up—but not at the crashing noise. The Tiger had heard something else, a softer sound drowned out by the collision below. A soft *poof.*

"Hey," said someone with a familiar voice.

He whirled around, not daring to hope. Kim stood against the wall, smiling. Her blonde hair was in need of a trim; her head was cocked in that cute way she had.

She looked wonderful. For a moment he just stared at her.

"What?" she asked. She raised a hand to her cheek. "Is there something on my face?"

He wailed loudly, dropped to his knees, and started to cry.

"Hey." She stepped closer and laid a hand on his shoulder. "It's okay. It's okay!"

Steven struggled for breath. He wanted to hug her, to talk, to ask her a million questions. But he couldn't help it. He couldn't stop crying.

"I'm *fine*," she said, sinking to her knees in front of him. "I'm good! They treated me okay . . . even gave me pizza when I asked for it. Side note: Indonesian pizza kind of sucks."

He laughed and looked up at her. Kim's eyes were as big and kind as ever, but something was different about her. She looked older, more grown-up. *I haven't seen her for weeks,* he realized. *This ordeal . . . what has it done to her?*

"They took away my powers," she continued. "Maxwell and that creepy girl, Mince. Then they locked me up here. It got pretty lonely."

He smiled and sniffled. "I bet."

"But just, like, an hour ago, my powers came back. Just like that!" She snapped her fingers. "So I took a chance and teleported out here."

He nodded, still gasping for breath. The air seemed even hotter than before. Just beyond the walkway, magma simmered up from beneath the rocks, giving off little bubbling noises.

"I'm okay." She reached out and touched him on the cheek, staring at him with those earnest eyes. "Really."

He burst into tears again.

"Hey. *Hey!*" The sharpness in her tone made him look up. "We're gonna get out of here. Right? And when this is all over, when Maxwell's just a bad memory and the Dragon slinks its whipped tail back into some Peter Jackson movie, we're gonna go someplace. Just you and me."

"By ourselves?" He smiled. "We're just kids."

"We're *awesome* kids. With mad powers." She smiled back. "You told me about that safari park, right? Near where you grew up?"

He nodded. "Wild Adventure."

"We're gonna go to Wild Adventure. We're gonna watch the animals and go on rides and eat popcorn till we burst. And we're not gonna think about volcanoes or supervillains or parents or Zodiac powers or *anything*. We're just gonna be us."

"That sounds . . ." He trailed off.

She threw up her hands. "*What?* Do I have like a ginormous zit or something?"

"I just never thought I'd see you again."

She bit her lip. "You had to say that. . . ."

Then *she* was crying and he was comforting *her*. He leaned in close, reached out a hand to wipe away her tears. She grabbed his hand, held it tight, and stared into his eyes.

She tilted her head up. Her lips were parted, ready to meet his. He moved in closer for . . . for . . .

. . . for our first kiss.

A bubble of magma the size of a medicine ball burst up between two boulder tiles, less than half a meter from the walkway. Steven and Kim flinched, shrinking back against the wall. As the bubble died back down, they both laughed in embarrassment.

"So much for *that* moment," he said.

She nodded. "Another one we owe Maxwell."

"He, uh, he might not be Maxwell anymore. But later for that."

He looked over the edge of the walkway. The rocks seemed to be moving faster now, crashing and rebounding off each other like bumper cars. Magma seeped up between them like red-hot rain pooled in sidewalk cracks.

"We've gotta get out of here," he continued. "Did I mention the volcano is erupting?"

"I had a bad feeling. But I was trying to stay positive." She gestured down the walkway, which vanished into darkness thirty meters or so away. "I've been scouting around. . . . This platform just dead-ends into a wall on both sides. There're more cells, but they're all empty."

"There might be a way out on the other side of the cells."

"Yeah. But I can't teleport unless I know what's on the other side, remember?"

"And the other walls are too far away." He gazed out grimly over the crashing boulders, tossed on a rising sea of molten rock. "We'll have to go back the way I came. It's gonna be tricky. . . . That lava stuff wasn't so angry-melty when I came in."

"That's how a volcano works, right? Pressure building up until it explodes?"

Another magma bubble burst in the air. "I guess," he said.

CHAPTER EIGHT

"We can do it. Remember the drills we did? Using our powers together?"

He smiled at her. "I'm a little rusty."

"Some leader!" She punched his shoulder playfully. "Follow me."

She grabbed him around the waist. He leaned in and took hold of her the same way. She felt good, warm and tense under his arm.

"Okay," she said. "Jump."

Together they leaped over the walkway's edge. Kim's Zodiac avatar, the Rabbit, appeared over her head, bounding from side to side. Steven's Tiger rose to join her, clawing the thick air. He looked down at the rocky mass and grimaced.

As Kim squeezed her eyes shut, the world vanished with a soft *poof.* They reappeared in midair, higher than before. He looked back: the wall was now thirty meters or more away, barely visible in the dim light.

Kim squeezed him tight. "Your turn!" she said.

He looked down. A large rock was moving, grinding against a few others; two magma fountains splashed up on opposite sides of it. Steven reached out with both legs and his free hand, bringing them both down to a safe landing.

Less than two seconds had passed since Kim's teleport move.

He looked up and saw another large boulder headed toward them. He twisted to the side, lifting Kim, and

jumped. They landed on a third rock as the first two crashed into each other, sending rubble and magma flying.

Kim's hand touched the flat rock. "Ow," she said. "It's hot!"

He smiled at her, squeezed her waist. "You ready to 'port again?"

She nodded and leaped upward, just as Steven's Tiger sense stabbed an alarm through him. He turned and saw a tall column of magma—the biggest one so far—shooting up and arcing straight toward them. "Ki—"

Poof.

"—m!" he finished, looking around frantically in mid-air. The wall with the cells in it was gone, no longer visible in the gloom.

Again he sized up the grinding chaos below and landed safely. As he cast his Tiger sense around, seeking the next jumping point, Kim squeezed his hand.

"We still got it," she said.

Three *poofs* later, they stood on a flat rock, staring up at a familiar ceiling. Light from the brighter chamber above streamed down through several dozen holes.

Kim gestured up at the holes. They were closing, becoming smaller, sealing up. "I can't 'port us if they close. I don't know what's up there."

"Just wait," Steven said.

The holes slid shut, sealing off the chamber. He felt the burning-hot tile beneath their feet; molten rock bubbled and rose all around them. The rock tile tipped sideways, borne on the tide of the rising magma. He grabbed Kim and jumped, landing safely on an adjacent boulder.

Kim stumbled and looked down at the magma. "It's getting angrier down there." There was a slight tinge of panic in her voice. "Also meltier."

He gestured upward, indicating the holes in the ceiling. They began to open again. "We've gotta time this right."

She followed his gaze. Her big eyes scanned the sea of tiles, stopping on one of the larger openings. It stretched two meters wide, revealing a hint of the map-patterned ceiling of the chamber above.

"Now," she said. They leaped together.

Steven held on tight. He caught a quick glimpse of molten rock blasting up, flowing over the surface of the rocks beneath. Magma sizzled and spat, eating away at the rock, melting it and washing it into the larger flow.

Poof—and then they were in the upper chamber, directly above the large hole. The edge, he realized, was a couple of meters away. He stretched out with his whole body, reached forward, and roared. As they started to fall, he grabbed the edge of the hole and brought them to a wrenching stop.

Kim hung on to him, looking down at the bubbling sea below. "It's *all* angry-melty now!"

The hole is closing, too, he thought. But he didn't say it aloud; he didn't want to panic her any further. With a tremendous effort, he clawed his way forward and hoisted her up onto the surface.

Behind them, the hole slid shut with a clacking noise.

Kim leaned on him, breathing hard. "Those multiple jumps . . . take a lot out of me. Especially with somebody else along."

"We're halfway there." He started forward, towing her behind, onto the next expanse of moving tiles. "This floor is much calmer: no melty, no angry, no crashing rocks."

She grabbed on to his waist again. He led her across the floor, moving and dancing from one shifting tile to another. After the deadly boulders on level echo, it was a cinch.

"I don't really know what this level is for." He twisted sideways, moving expertly from one tile to another. "But the hard part is over. . . ."

He felt it before he heard it: a blast of heat on his back. Kim turned in alarm, then jumped forward with a *poof*.

They landed thirty meters ahead and tumbled awkwardly to the tile floor. Steven pulled Kim to her feet, and together they stared back the way they'd come.

"Whoa," Kim said.

A bright red river of molten rock bubbled up behind them—in the exact spot where they'd 'ported up to that level less than a minute before. The magma had erupted, forcing its way through the porous floor, eating away everything in its path. The sea of holes was *gone*.

Steven glanced down and shifted sideways to adjust to a new tile pattern. "Did I actually say, 'The hard part is over'?"

CHAPTER EIGHT

"You say a lot of dumb things," she replied.

The magma bubbled, rose higher. It began to flow outward, filling the chamber. One branching stream flowed toward them like the arm of an octopus. As it drew closer, sparks shot up from the space below the tiles. The humming in the background turned to a high whine; hidden circuits melted, dissolved, and exploded.

"Here's another dumb thing," Steven said. *"Run."*

They sprinted across the chamber, beneath the bizarre ceiling showing the reversed continents. China passed by overhead, then the Persian Gulf and northern Africa. Kim was puffing, breathing hard, but she kept up with him.

He stole a glance back. "The lava," he said, "it's gaining on us!"

She grabbed him and leaped up. "It's not—"

Poof.

"—lava. It's magma."

He glanced down and chose a landing spot. "What's the difference?"

"It's magma while it's in the volcano. It only becomes lava when it gets *outside*, into the air."

"But it's the same stuff!"

"I don't make the—"

Poof.

"—rules."

They both laughed. He clasped her hand, flashed her a quick smile, and started running again.

All at once, he knew: *We're going to make it. This will be okay.*

We're together again, and that's what matters.

Fiery magma flowed upward, destroying everything its path. Rocks melted, ash filled the air, hidden machinery sparked and died. And as the Dragon's lair dissolved into molten slag, the Tiger and the Rabbit ran hand in hand, sprinting and jumping through the Mountain of Fire to safety.

CHAPTER NINE

ONE LAST *poof* and they were outside. Kim tumbled free of Steven's grip as he landed roughly on the uneven ground.

He paused for a moment, catching his breath. The soil was a mix of red clay, dark rock, and gray ash left over from previous volcanic eruptions. Smoke filled the air, rising in a slow cloud from the volcano.

Steven scanned the area through the Tiger's sharp eyes. The mountainside angled sharply downward, a treacherous slope covered with more dry ash. After about a kilometer, the land flattened out and trees, whole forests, began to poke through gaps in the ash.

A few kilometers away, a small village was nestled in the trees, surrounded by green fields plowed in arcs and whorls. Low houses spread out at odd angles from a central hub. They looked like toys, like the building blocks Steven had played with as a little boy.

They're so exposed, he thought. *So vulnerable. What would it be like to live there? Under the constant shadow of death?*

"Hey," Kim said.

He turned to see her standing at the very peak of the mountain. He climbed up to join her, the Tiger guiding his steps. The volcano's opening gaped wide, leading into the chambers below. Kim waved away a plume of ash and pointed down into the volcano.

"Look," she said.

He peered over the edge. The jagged rock floor, the streams of water, the ropes his team had used to enter the mountain—all of it was gone. Molten rock filled the chamber, seething and rising, bubbling like a teakettle ready to overflow.

"Mince." Steven shook his head. "She destroyed the whole installation, just to get rid of us."

"She's crazy," Kim said.

He looked up. Ash blocked out the sun, but he guessed it was midafternoon. "We better get out of here."

She looked at him, and he saw how tired she was. "I can't 'port any more."

"We better radio for . . ."

He trailed off as he touched the spot on his temple where

the HUDset should have been. Then he remembered: *I threw it away.* He turned to explain to Kim—

—just as she stumbled backward, tripping on a rock. "No!" she cried, looking past him. "Stay away!"

Steven whirled in surprise. Nicky—Dog—approached around the curve of the volcano peak, stalking through the cloud of ash. Thick yellow fur still covered his body, including his scarred face. He wore a small Bluetooth earpiece.

Kim stared at him in terror.

Steven laughed. "It's okay," he said. "Nicky's with us now."

Kim took another step back. "He used to chase me. Like, a lot."

"Yeah," Nicky acknowledged, stepping over a rough patch of ground. "I used to have trouble with what you call impulse control."

Kim moved close to Steven, still eyeing Nicky. "Don't worry," Steven said. "He's learned some, uh . . ."

"New tricks?" she asked.

"Ha! Good one." Nicky clapped Steven hard on the back. "They sent me up to find you 'cause I'm the best climber. What happened to your headset, kid?"

Steven shrugged. "Batteries."

"Well, while you were breakin' blondie out of her cell—"

"I broke *myself* out," Kim protested. She seemed calmer now.

"—we evacuated the village." Nicky gestured down the mountain, toward the houses in the distance. "Now we're waitin' to hear from Duane about how bad the eruption's gonna be."

"What about the Vanguard soldiers?" Kim said. "There must have been at least a hundred of them in the base."

"Ah, don't worry about them," Nicky replied. "They're okay. A big Vanguard airship blasted out of a hidden entrance halfway down the mountain half an hour ago."

Steven stared out at the village. Trucks rolled away from the houses, tiny figures running alongside and clinging to the doors of the vehicles. Only the Tiger's eyes could have picked them out at that distance.

The mountain rumbled beneath their feet. "Blondie," Nicky said, "you feel like doin' that *poof* trick? Get us outta here?"

"I can't. I'm exhausted."

"A'ight," Nicky said. "We'll do it the hard way." He touched a furry claw to his earpiece and spoke in low tones.

Steven was barely listening. He stared at the village, at the houses surrounded by trees and ash. It all reminded him of something, but he couldn't remember what.

Kim touched his shoulder. "That lava's getting pretty high," she said, gesturing at the volcano's opening.

He smiled. "You mean magma?"

Before she could reply, the mountain shook. Steven leaped up, his Tiger reflexes kicking in. He whirled, growling, just in time to see Kim lose her balance. She cried out and fell backward down the mountain slope.

CHAPTER NINE

He leaped toward her, the Tiger rising above his head. But she was too far away.

"No worries, boss," Nicky said. "I got 'er!"

Before Kim could hit the ground, Nicky leaped ahead of her and landed on all fours. He dropped to his back and rolled, using his furry stomach to cushion her body as she fell. The impact flung them both down the slope; Nicky grabbed hold of Kim and pulled her tightly to him, shielding her as they rolled over a patch of rocks.

When they came to a stop, he opened his arms. Kim staggered to her feet, dazed.

"Thanks," she said, "You're pretty soft, when you're not trying to kill me."

"Don't tell nobody," he replied, winking his one good eye. "I got a whole tough-guy image goin'."

Steven ran to join them, keeping an eye on the volcano's mouth. A thick cloud of smoke filled the air. He coughed and waved it away, grimacing as a thin spout of magma burbled up.

Lava, he corrected himself, *not magma—*

"Let's bounce," Nicky said.

They ran, stumbling and coughing their way down the steep mountain face. Behind them, more smoke billowed out of the volcano. They could hear the lava now, the deep rumbling sound of superheated liquid rock rising to the surface.

Then, all at once, Nicky stopped. "Look!" he cried, pointing back toward the top of the mountain.

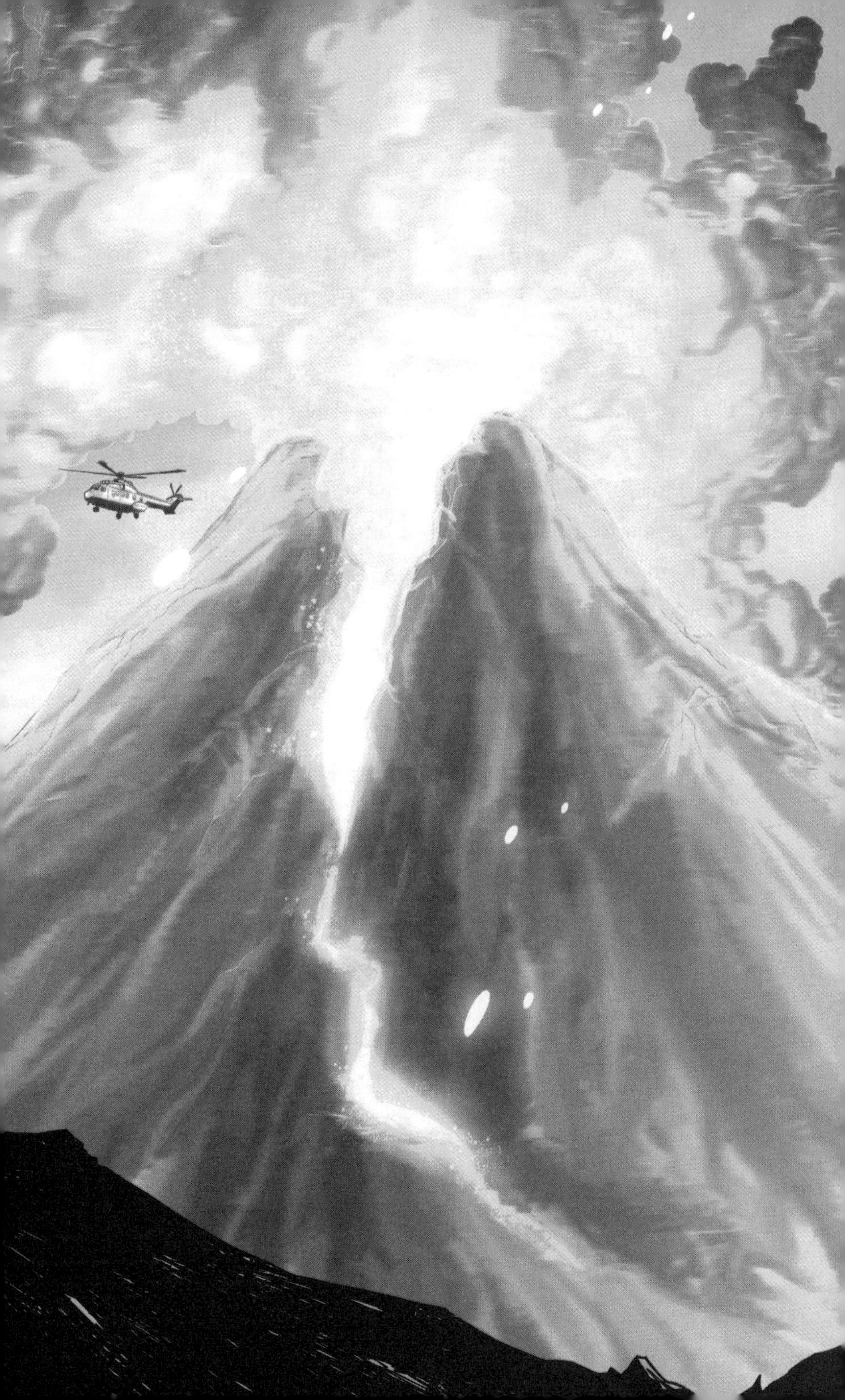

The smoke was thinning out. A single gout of lava burst out of the volcano's mouth, spreading to cover the near side of the summit. It flowed down a meter or so, then stopped short and dried, cooling rapidly.

Kim blinked. "Is that it?"

"Yup." Nicky touched his earpiece again. "According to Duane, that's all there's gonna be. Looks like Mince only triggered a *little* eruption."

"Huh," Steven replied. "So she didn't wipe out a whole village just to take a shot at us, after all."

Kim frowned. "Maybe Mince has got a tiny little conscience someplace inside that hot mess of a brain."

"Maybe." He gazed at the rock around the volcano's mouth, sizzling as the last of the lava cooled. "Or maybe the Dragon's volcano tech just isn't out of beta yet."

Suddenly, he felt tired. He looked down the mountain face, past red rock and long stretches of dried ash. The village seemed a long way away.

Kim gave him a weary smile. "Guess we better start walking."

"Walkin'?" Nicky laughed. "No way. Now that the dust cloud is clearing . . ." He pointed up.

Steven squinted into the sky. The sun was beginning to poke through, low on the horizon. And just above it, a thick tubular shape swooped through the air, moving closer.

"Malik, baby," Nicky said into his earpiece. "How 'bout a pickup?"

CHAPTER NINE

The vehicle resolved into the form of a large military helicopter. Malik—Ox—sat alone at the controls, steering steadily toward the volcano. He pulled up on the stick, tilting the copter's rotors to avoid the last sputtering plume of ash. Then he slowed and came to a hover.

Kim clapped her hands in joy, then leaned over to kiss Steven on the cheek. "See you on board!" she said.

With a *poof*, she was gone. Steven glanced up in time to see her reappear in the copilot's seat.

Two ropes dropped from the bottom of the copter. Nicky leaped up and grabbed one, swinging and barking theatrically.

"Malik hates it when I do this!" he said, laughing.

Steven reached out and clasped the second rope. With the crisis past, his adrenaline was fading. He'd been so pumped by the return of his Zodiac power, he'd forgotten it wasn't inexhaustible. Even the Tiger needed rest.

The copter rose, lifting him into the air. He looked down again, over the ashy mountain, the scattered forests. The copter drifted slowly away from the volcano, toward the populated area beyond.

In the distance, trucks circled back, returning to the village. Tiny figures leaped off the vehicles, landing on the ground and embracing their fellow villagers.

Under the shadow of death, he thought again.

The copter lurched slightly. Steven hung in the air, gripping the rope tight. Nicky swung himself up and grabbed hold of the copter's landing struts.

The volcano belched once more, rumbled, and went silent.

Suddenly, Steven realized what the village reminded him of. *My vision. The terrible choice: my parents or my team. My two families.*

The villagers faced a similar choice every day: between the home they loved and the safety of their loved ones who lived there. *They escaped death,* he thought, *today at least. And they decided it was worth it . . . to stay in their homes, with the people they care about most in the world.*

He hoped he could choose as wisely, when the time came.

PART TWO
MINDSCAPE

CHAPTER TEN

DESPITE ALL THEIR newly recovered power, the Zodiacs found themselves short on transportation options. Their stealth plane had recently crashed in Australia, and the military helicopter had to be returned to the Indonesian government. So the eight teammates crammed themselves into tiny seats on a commercial airliner and flew coach back to their headquarters in Greenland.

Kim held Steven's hand the whole time. That was nice. Halfway through the flight, his phone beeped a text alert.

"Hey," he said. "I've got some news."

Kim looked up, sleepy. "Mmm?"

"Your parents are waiting for us. At HQ."

"What?" She blinked. "Why?"

"You just escaped," he explained. "From Maxwell, the Dragon, whatever. We don't want him going after your folks, so Jasmine had 'em moved where we can protect them."

"Mom. Dad." Kim shook her head as if trying to clear it. "I was so worried about them. My dad . . . he had a stroke. . . ."

"I bet they want to see you."

She turned and touched his cheek tenderly. "Thank you," she said.

She leaned in closer. Steven barely hesitated a microsecond, but it was time enough for Roxanne to poke her head over the seat ahead and say, "Oh, just kiss her!"

He fell back in his seat, humiliated. But the sound of Kim's laughter almost made the whole thing worth it.

As soon as they arrived, the team scattered. Jasmine disappeared immediately into the bowels of the high-tech headquarters. Kim *poofed* away to see her parents. And Steven seemed distracted. When Roxanne suggested they grab some food, he mumbled a hasty apology and ran off.

Fine, Roxanne thought. *I'll just eat by myself.*

The small galley was crowded. Two women in lab coats, scientists on a short lunch break, grabbed sandwiches from a lighted shelf and brushed past Roxanne. A group of Chinese refugees sat huddled over a table, talking in low tones with a couple of the maintenance personnel. From the beginning, Jasmine had insisted the Zodiacs provide refuge for people whose communities had been devastated by Maxwell's private army. This group had recently arrived.

At another table, Duane sat talking with Dafari, a brilliant computer scientist. And in the corner, the three ex-Vanguard agents—Malik, Nicky, and Josie—sat together. They gestured wildly, clearly thrilled by the return of their Zodiac powers. Malik banged his fist on the table to make a point. Josie turned away, but Nicky leaned over the table, growling. In a matter of seconds, his formerly clean-shaven face sprouted thick yellow Dog fur. As he bared his teeth, sharp fangs jutted out.

Then he and Malik both laughed and clapped each other on the back. The refugees shot them brief nervous looks.

Roxanne grimaced. Josie and Nicky had just joined the Zodiacs for the latest mission; Malik had been there a bit longer, but only by a few months. They were all older than Roxanne's team, and they'd been trained in Maxwell's fierce, uncompromising military culture. They wanted to belong, but they hadn't managed to completely fit in yet.

And now, just like us, they've got their powers back. How's that *going to work out?*

Roxanne grabbed a sushi plate and slid into an empty seat next to Duane and Dafari. Almost instantly, she regretted it.

"The volcano," Duane said, "was equipped with some sort of tech that triggered a partial eruption." He shoveled a forkful of eggs into his mouth.

Dafari shot him a sharp look. "That would require a tremendous amount of pressure to be exerted on the magma from below."

Duane glared back at him. "Obviously."

"Did you actually observe this 'tech'?"

"Only hints of it. Defensive weapons, engines humming behind the walls." Duane paused. "But I remain convinced that the Dragon is performing experiments for some larger, as yet unknown reason."

"What basis do you have for this conviction?"

"I took extensive seismic and soil readings. They were highly irregular."

"I'll tell you what's irregular," Roxanne said, holding up her chopsticks. "This eel and avocado roll. Right?"

Dafari ignored her. "When you radioed in," he said to Duane, "I ordered a meticulous scan of volcanoes on all seven continents. We've detected no major seismic activity, no spike in island or continental eruptions. If the Dragon is indeed engaged in 'experiments,' he is performing them very quietly."

"Which does not mean he's not doing it."

"It doesn't mean he *is*, either."

"*Carlos* could figure this out in five minutes," Duane said. "I wish he were here."

"Technically, he *is* here. But he's in no condition to help."

"Well, boys," Roxanne said, rising to her feet. "I don't want to say this wasn't fun . . ."

They didn't even look up. "Perhaps when we've had time to debrief Steven and the others," Duane said, "and to analyze my findings . . . then we will have more to go on than your reflexive skepticism."

"I am merely pointing out the flaws in your rather *hurriedly* concocted . . ."

". . . but it wasn't," she murmured.

Sushi plate in hand, she crossed the galley, smiling briefly at the group of refugees. She felt uncomfortable, as if she didn't belong there anymore.

Without realizing it, she found herself standing before the ex-Vanguard table. Nicky and Malik were engaged in a heated discussion.

". . . not saying he can't do the job," Malik said, "but we've got a lot more experience."

"You just don't like takin' orders from a kid," Nicky said, laughing.

Josie just sat still, looking away. Her expression was grim.

"His mission parameters were sloppy," Malik said. "It

was a rescue *and* a snatch-and-grab. That's a dangerous split in priorities."

"We pulled it off."

"We were lucky. Lucky that psycho girl didn't blow the whole mountain to . . ."

They turned, noticing Roxanne for the first time. Malik stared at her for a moment, then gestured at the table's fourth, empty chair.

Roxanne drew in a deep breath, looked at the half-eaten sushi on her plate, and sat down. She felt like a rich kid who'd wandered into a bad neighborhood.

"Steven's a good leader," she said. "He saved my life more than once."

Nicky shrugged. "He a'ight."

"I've fought alongside him," Malik said. "He's a capable fighter and very energetic. I suppose I've just been wondering about the nature of the Zodiac powers . . . about the roles they force us into."

"Uh-oh." Nicky laughed. "Malik's been *thinkin'*."

Roxanne turned to look straight at Malik. Something about that phrase—"the roles they force us into"—echoed in her mind.

"Go on," she said.

"Steven is fast, agile, and powerful," Malik said. "But is he really a leader? Or do we just allow him that role because he happened to be born in the Year of the Tiger?"

"The powers," she said. "They sought out their hosts,

each of us, because we embody the principles of each Zodiac sign. I mean, if you believe all that stuff." She felt uncertain, as if she were venturing out of her depth. "Point is, it wasn't random. Steven isn't just a tiger . . . he's *the* Tiger."

"That's not true across the board." Malik gestured at the others around the table. "The powers may have sought you out—but not the three of us. *Maxwell* chose us."

I never thought of that before, Roxanne realized. *It's another way they're different from us.*

"I've heard you express doubts," Malik continued. "Can you tell me that you're absolutely comfortable with your own place on this team? With the part you've been chosen to play?"

A wave of anger washed over her. She liked Malik, but who was he to question her? To bring up these very real doubts that—yes—she'd been feeling lately, more strongly than ever?

"I'm just glad to have my powers back," Nicky said. He held up a hand, smiling as fur sprouted to cover it. "Maybe now we can start hirin' ourselves out for the big bucks. Right, Josie?"

Josie didn't answer. She sat turned away in her chair, staring at the wall.

"What's wrong with her?" Roxanne asked.

"Ah," Nicky said, "she's been like that for weeks now."

"Don't talk about me like I'm not here," Josie said.

"Why not?" Nicky snapped. "You never talk about yourself."

Watching Josie, Roxanne's anger grew stronger. She remembered a time, just over a year before, when the three people at that table—Malik, Josie, and Nicky—had mounted an assault on Zodiac headquarters, along with their then-teammate Vincent, who held the power of the Monkey. As soldiers in Maxwell's private army, they'd been following orders. And those orders had been to capture Steven's team at all costs.

At the time, Roxanne had only had her Rooster powers for a few days. Josie, already a trained soldier with the power of the Horse, had chased her down and taken her captive. Josie had bound and gagged Roxanne and dragged her, struggling and helpless, through the complex and outside.

Roxanne could barely reconcile that memory with the sullen, withdrawn woman who sat across from her now. She knew she should feel sympathy, should wonder what Josie had gone through. But all she felt was disgust.

"You don't look so tough now," she said.

Josie half turned, regarding Roxanne with a single eye.

"Back off," she said. Her voice was low, dangerous.

"Or what? You'll toss me out in the snow again?"

Nicky turned to Malik. "What is happening here?" Malik motioned him to silence.

"Maybe you'd like to throw down again," Roxanne continued. "I've been practicing."

CHAPTER TEN

The Rooster avatar rose, involuntarily, above her head. She knew she should stop, should walk away from the table. She was tired from the mission; they all were. But the memory of her humiliation at Josie's hands, combined with the blank look on Josie's face, made her blood boil.

I can't let this go, she thought. *The Rooster wants blood.*

"You're afraid," Roxanne said, still staring at Josie. "You're afraid to fight me."

"I'm afraid I'll kill you."

The Rooster avatar cried out a silent challenge.

Josie turned to face Roxanne for the first time. "Aren't you leaving this team?" she growled. "You seem to say that every ten minutes."

"Make me. Make me leave."

Josie's eyes locked on to Roxanne's. There was contempt in them, and weariness. Sadness, too, buried somewhere deep down. The raging Horse appeared above Josie, shaking its head in fury.

Then she stood and walked away.

"That was like old times," Malik said. "Little *too much* like 'em."

Roxanne reached for her chopsticks, then dropped them. Her hands were shaking.

"She's not herself," Malik continued. "Not here, and not on the mission. What happened to her?"

Nicky hesitated. He seemed concerned, more serious than Roxanne had ever seen him before.

"I dunno," he said finally. "After we escaped from

Australia, somethin' changed in her. She got real low, stopped working. Stopped goin' outside, even. I had to take care of her, bring her food."

Roxanne frowned. "But you both came, when Steven called?"

"I thought it'd be good for her. Practically had to drag 'er here." Nicky smiled sadly. "I hoped gettin' her powers back would snap her out of it. An' I really thought she was back to her old self when she whooped Beta. But as soon as we got back . . ." He gave a helpless shrug.

"Josie has her demons," Malik said. "We all do."

They were silent for a moment—lost in separate dark thoughts.

"I just wanted my powers back so I could make a livin'," Nicky said. His eyes were fixed on the exit, the door Josie had just walked through. "But I can't leave yet. I can't give up on her."

Roxanne nodded. Her rage had subsided; she felt slightly ashamed of herself. But a new purpose, a new path, seemed to tickle at the edges of her consciousness.

I can't give up on her.

"Maybe it's my turn," she said.

CHAPTER ELEVEN

STEVEN ROUNDED the corner, started down the hallway toward the living quarters—and froze. His Tiger senses rose to full alert; a rush of Zodiac power, almost like an electric shock, ran through him.

The door to the guest suite was ajar.

He crept up to it, listening for any noise from inside. Nothing. *This is where Kim's parents are staying,* he thought. *Why would they leave the door open? Has the Dragon found them already—here, in our own headquarters?*

He pushed the door wide and crept inside. The suite opened into a small kitchen. A thin archway led to a living area beyond, but he couldn't see much of it from that angle. Most of the living quarters were single and double rooms; this was one of the few larger suites. *That means more places to hide.*

He sneaked up to the arch. When he peered around the corner, his breath caught in his throat.

Kim's mother and father sat together on a small sofa. Her father looked older than Steven had remembered, his eyes slightly unfocused. He had one arm around his wife, whose friendly smile only partially hid the worry in her eyes.

His other hand was on his daughter's shoulder. Kim lay sprawled across her parents' laps, fast asleep. She looked very small, even younger than her fourteen years. She made a small noise and nuzzled her head into her mother's stomach.

Kim's father didn't seem to notice Steven's presence. But her mother looked up, nodded at Steven, and silently mouthed the words: *Thank you.*

Steven smiled back, embarrassed, and left. He pulled the door shut behind him.

The medical bay was just down the hall from the living quarters, easily accessible from the garage holding the trucks and land vehicles, and also from the plane hangar one level above. That day the bay stood nearly empty, rows of diagnostic beds attached to large blank monitor screens. The entire room held just one patient, strapped loosely to his bed: Carlos.

Jasmine stood in the middle of the large room, staring at Carlos. The small man lay unconscious, his eyes closed. Little hologram readouts rose from chips affixed to his bare chest, displaying heart rate, blood pressure, and other medical details that Steven couldn't understand. A compact diagnostic computer sat on the adjacent table.

He hesitated, not wanting to disturb Jasmine. But he had important things to discuss with her, and he wasn't sure they could wait.

A tall, severe-looking woman in a lab coat crossed in front of him, holding a tablet in one hand and a hypodermic needle in the other. She shot Jasmine a look, then jabbed the needle into Carlos's arm.

"A mild stimulant," the woman said. "If he does not respond to this . . ."

Steven moved to join them. The woman emptied the hypo into Carlos's arm and withdrew it, swabbing once to wipe away a teardrop of blood. It reminded Steven of lava bubbling from the lip of a volcano.

Carlos's eyes remained closed. He made no movement, no noise, gave no sign he was aware of the injection.

Jasmine turned to the woman. "Doctor Snejbjerg?"

"I'm very sorry, but I can do nothing." The doctor frowned. "We are at the bottom of my bag of tricks."

"We flew you in here." A hint of anger crept into Jasmine's eyes. "At great expense—"

"This is not a physical problem." The doctor waved a long-fingered hand at Carlos. "You said yourself this man is a victim of brainwashing."

"Brainwashing?" Jasmine snorted. "Calling what he experienced *brainwashing* is like calling a typhoon a little breeze."

"Be that as it may, the mind is not my province. And I believe it is his *mind*, not his body, that is keeping him in this state." The doctor turned toward Jasmine and reached for her face. "You should treat those cuts again. The poison may be—"

Jasmine pulled away angrily and slammed her fist on a nearby table. She glared briefly at Steven, then turned and stalked into a corner of the room.

Five months before, Maxwell had kidnapped Carlos and, using the power of the Dragon, altered his mind, turning him against his friends. That had almost destroyed Jasmine, who—Steven had come to realize—loved Carlos deeply. It had also given Maxwell access to Carlos's unparalleled scientific genius, allowing the Dragon to build weapons far more powerful than those he'd used in the past.

Steven, Jasmine, and the Zodiac team had risked

everything to rescue Carlos. In the end, they'd managed to pull him from the wreckage of Maxwell's Australian headquarters. But Carlos remained dangerously insane. They'd had to lock him up in a cell to prevent him from escaping or trying to sabotage the base—the same base that he and Jasmine had built from scratch, in happier times.

Every rant, every vow of revenge from Carlos's lips, struck like a dagger in Jasmine's heart. And over time his condition had deteriorated. A week before, he'd fallen into a coma; he hadn't moved or spoken since.

"I am sorry," the doctor said, adjusting Carlos's restraints. "I assure you I do not admit failure lightly."

Steven watched Jasmine, across the room. He felt bad about Carlos; he understood Jasmine's pain. But he really needed to talk to her about something else.

He turned to the doctor. "Could you, uh, leave us alone?"

The doctor raised an eyebrow. She checked a holo-readout above Carlos's shoulder and made a notation on her tablet. Then she left without a word.

Steven turned toward Jasmine. Before he could go to her, she walked over to him, carrying a small travel bag.

"I need to talk to you," she said.

"Yeah. I need to talk to you, too."

"I know, I know. She did everything she could." Jasmine waved in the doctor's direction. "I'll apologize later."

"That's, yeah, good. But it's not what I—"

"Steven, I don't have time for a debrief. You did good work at Mount Merapi, okay? I'm glad you found Kim, and got your powers back."

"Sorry we couldn't recover yours. Maybe when we catch up with Maxw—I mean, the Dragon."

"Yeah. That's me." She stared down at Carlos. "Powerless."

They stood silently for a moment, both staring at the body between them. Little readouts winked on and off in the air.

"Jasmine," Steven said, feeling the words start to pour out of him, "are you gonna forget me?"

She looked up sharply. "What?"

"In the volcano. I had a vision." He looked away, struggling to remember. "It was the old man, the old Tiger—the one who died in Berlin. He told me I'd have to choose between my family and my friends."

Jasmine grimaced.

"He also told me that when this was all over . . . when the choice was made, the enemy defeated . . ."

"What?" she prompted.

"I know you've done research on the past Zodiacs. You and . . ." He gestured at Carlos.

"Some. We've tried, but the records aren't clear." She frowned at him. "What did the old man say?"

"He said, he said that everything—all memory of the

Zodiac powers—would vanish from the world. And us, me and the others, we'd all vanish with it." He looked up at her. "Is that gonna happen?"

She turned away.

"Is that why you couldn't find the information?" he continued. "Because it was erased from the world?"

"Steven, I wouldn't obsess over the words of one dead man. Even your predecessor."

"It wasn't just him." He shivered, remembering. "I could feel them. All the Tigers, down through the ages. They all had their time, wielded the power, tried to make the world a better place. And in the end . . ."

Jasmine glanced down at Carlos again. She hefted her bag and circled around the bed, almost tripping over electrical wires. When she reached Steven, she looked into his eyes. He could see the tiny cuts that Mince's rings had made all along her cheeks.

"I won't forget you," she said. "You will not vanish from the world."

His reply caught in his throat. "Promise?"

"Promise."

He nodded and turned away, wiping a tear from his eye.

"Now," she said, "I need something from you."

"Of course," he replied. "Anything."

"Doctor Snejbjerg says Carlos's problem is mental, not physical." She rummaged in her travel pack. "So there's only one, desperate way to save him."

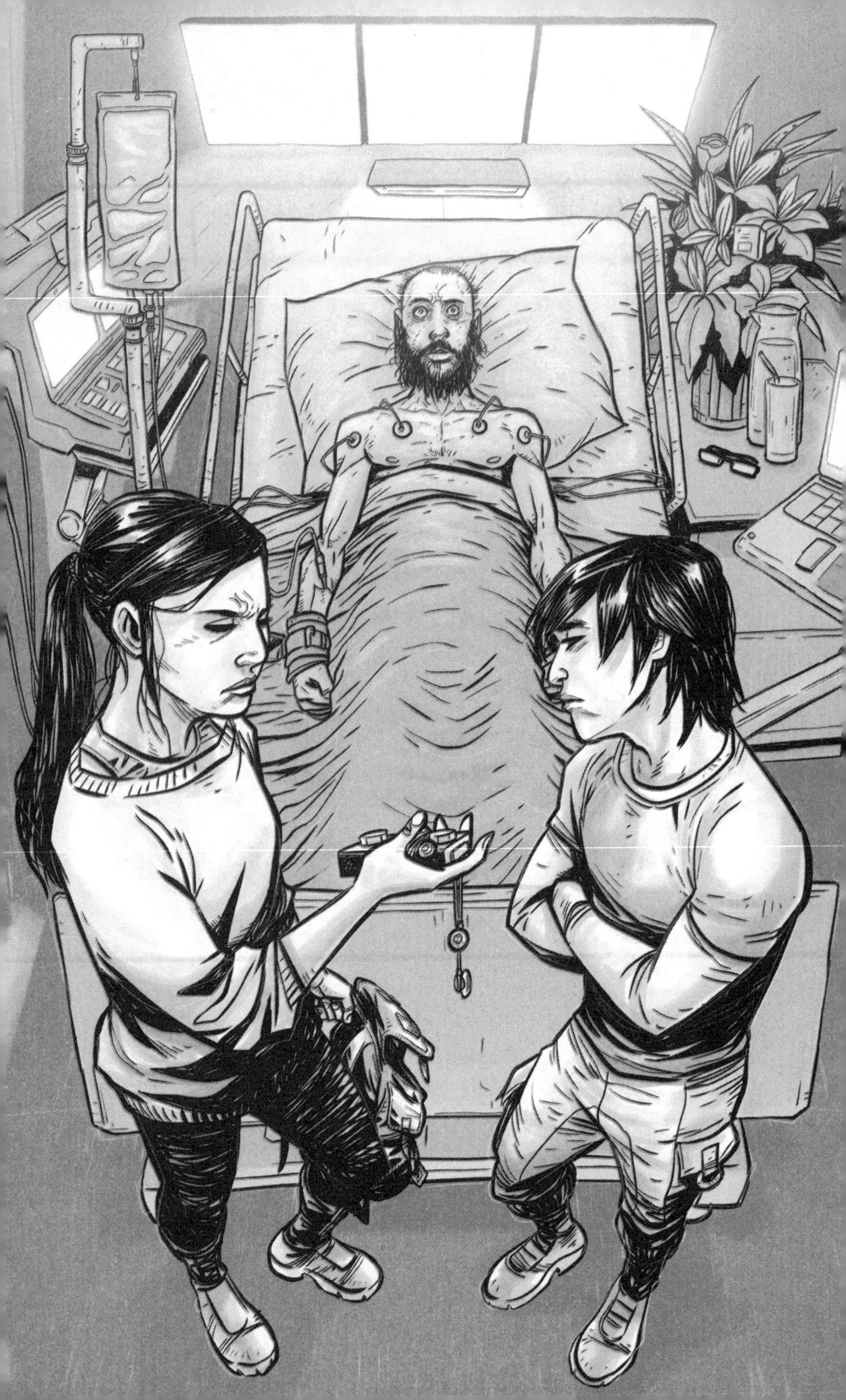

He turned to see her holding up a small metal box. Cables dangled from it, ending in two sets of electrodes fixed to flat patches. *The weapon,* he realized. *The one she used on Mince, inside the volcano.*

Jasmine stared at Carlos's unmoving form.

"We have to enter his mind," she said.

CHAPTER TWELVE

ROXANNE SLIPPED the kneepads over her boots. She picked up a smaller pad and started strapping it on to her elbow.

Josie watched her. "What are you doing?"

"Getting ready to kick your butt."

Roxanne tightened the second elbow pad and turned to face her opponent. Josie stood on the other side of the large training room. The floor was marked like a gymnasium, with a few punching bags and basketballs piled up in the corner. But the walls concealed an assortment of high-tech training devices.

CHAPTER TWELVE

"Ha!" Josie exclaimed. "As if you could."

"Guess we'll find out."

"I'm not going to fight you."

"Then why are you here?"

Josie didn't answer.

Roxanne tossed a tangle of knee and elbow pads across the room. "Put 'em on."

Josie just watched as the pads sailed past her. "Already got mine," she said, indicating the padded joints on her uniform.

"Suit yourself."

Roxanne stalked into the center of the room, hands raised boxing style before her face. Adrenaline surged through her, making her heart beat faster.

Hope I know what I'm doing!

Josie stood her ground. "What's this about? Do you still want revenge for the whooping I gave you?"

"You don't know anything about me."

"I know you're a lousy fighter. And a quitter."

Anger blazed through Roxanne. The Rooster avatar appeared, shrieking and cawing. She lunged the last meter and jabbed a fist at Josie's face.

Josie ducked, almost effortlessly. She dropped low and danced back about a meter. The Horse flashed above her, visible for just a second. Then it vanished again.

She's not even winded, Roxanne thought.

Josie stared at her. "You're determined to do this."

"*Oui.* That means yes."

"I know what it means."

Josie began to dance sideways in a circle, hands loose at her sides. Her eyes bored into Roxanne's. Roxanne mirrored the motion, keeping distance between them.

Josie gestured to the equipment at the side of the room. "Don't you want some mats on the floor? This is gonna hurt."

"I'll take my chances."

Josie's face went dark, intense. As she lifted her fists, the Horse rose above her, its mouth open in a silent scream.

Roxanne swallowed. *She's bigger than you,* she told herself, *and stronger, too. But the Rooster power is—*

Almost before Roxanne registered the motion, Josie grabbed both her arms and swung her around. Keeping one hand clamped on Roxanne's wrists, Josie locked the other one across her opponent's chest, just below the throat.

"This is . . . a basic combat move." Josie's voice dripped with condescension. "Designed to disarm the—"

Roxanne whipped her head around and screamed. The Rooster flared bright; a burst of sonic energy struck Josie in the face, breaking her grip and knocking her away. The two fighters fell to the floor on opposite sides.

When Roxanne looked up, Josie was laughing.

"That all you got?" Josie said, climbing to her feet.

Roxanne rose to join her. "Knocked you off your feet."

They moved closer together, glaring, and resumed dancing in a circle. "You're a child," Josie taunted. "A pampered girl with one trick, a power that fell out of the sky."

"Yeah? And what are you?"

"A soldier." They were so close, their noses almost touched. "Do you have any idea what you have to do to join Maxwell's army?"

"Give up all trace of original thought? I'm just guessing."

Josie grabbed Roxanne and threw her down. Once again, the action was so fast, so casual, that Roxanne was on the floor before she knew it. She shook her head, dazed.

Josie glared down at her. The Horse rose higher above her head, seeming to fill the room.

"You have to survive in the jungle for five days," she said. "Alone."

Roxanne struggled to rise. She scrunched her eyes shut and marshaled her energy. *One chance,* she thought. *I've gotta use every ounce of power I've got.*

"Stay down," Josie continued. "Like I said, this could hur—"

Roxanne opened her eyes and cried out. A look of surprise came over Josie's face as she flew across the room.

Roxanne rose to her feet, still screaming. *Got to maintain the assault. I'm rusty with the Zodiac power, but so is she!*

Josie struck a punching bag and rebounded, landing on the hard floor. Roxanne paused to take a breath—and in a second, Josie was on her feet again. Roxanne whipped her head back and screamed, the Rooster avatar crowing in time with her powerful cry.

Josie recoiled, but she held her ground. With great

effort, she moved one foot forward. Then the other. Slowly, she began to advance on Roxanne.

Impossible, Roxanne thought. *Nobody's ever resisted my sonic cry before. How is she doing that?*

"Determination," Josie gasped, as if she'd heard the question. "You might want to learn about it, girl. If you want to be a hero."

Roxanne opened her mouth wider. She called on the Rooster power, all she could marshal—every bit of will and determination inside her. The scream rose in pitch, shattering lightbulbs on the high ceiling.

Josie didn't stop. She pushed her way forward, step by step, through the searing wall of sound. The Horse reared, front hooves clawing at the air.

She's almost here, Roxanne realized. *And she's right; she's stronger, better trained, and physically larger than me. I can't beat her.*

But I didn't come here to beat her, did I?

Josie reached through the sonic wall and punched Roxanne in the stomach. Roxanne gasped as the breath was forced out of her. The noise stopped, the Rooster faded, and Roxanne fell to the floor.

She managed to roll onto her knees. But Josie was right there. She grabbed Roxanne and clamped a hand over her mouth. Then she slammed Roxanne down on the floor and laid her other arm tight across Roxanne's windpipe.

"Like I said," Josie hissed, "you've got one trick. And you can't use it if you can't catch your breath."

Roxanne twisted and struggled. The Rooster flickered

and flashed on and off above her. But Josie's grip was like iron. Roxanne couldn't move, couldn't breathe.

"Give up," Josie said. *"Now."*

Roxanne nodded quickly, frantically.

Josie released her. Roxanne tumbled away, coughing and gasping.

Josie dropped to all fours, breathing hard. "That trick of yours," she said. "It's not a bad one." She collapsed to the floor.

Roxanne lay down beside her. "You've got some moves yourself."

For a moment, the only sound in the room was the two women's labored breathing.

"You"—Josie gasped—"you didn't ask me here so you could kick my butt."

Roxanne said nothing.

"You knew I wasn't myself," Josie continued. "You thought you could snap me out of it."

"Busted," Roxanne admitted.

"Did Nicky put you up to this?"

"Not exactly. I just . . . I knew you weren't the woman I fought last year."

"My dad died."

Roxanne propped herself on one elbow. Josie lay on her back, eyes closed.

"I didn't like him much. He wasn't nice to my mom, back when she was alive." Josie sighed and opened her eyes. "But he was the only family I had left."

"I'm sorry," Roxanne said.

"And I wasn't there for him. I was wasting my time in a jail underneath Maxwell's Aussie complex." She shook her head. "Alpha, the Vanguard agent, he didn't know. When he mentioned my dad, down in the volcano, I almost killed him."

"I get it. When I first got my Zodiac powers, my *maman*—my mother—she threw me out of the house. I was devastated."

Josie just stared at the ceiling.

"I've been playing again," Roxanne blurted.

Josie turned to look at her. "Music?"

"Yeah. Privately, in my quarters. Just started a couple weeks ago, after Maxwell stole our powers." She closed her eyes. "I haven't told anyone."

"Electric guitar?"

"Just acoustic. Noodling around, really. But I wrote the beginning of two songs."

"Your usual save-the-whales crap?"

Roxanne looked over sharply. But Josie was smiling. "I checked out your stuff online."

"Music used to be my whole life," Roxanne said. "The Zodiac power ruined all that. . . . It was too dangerous for me to perform in public. I missed that, more than anything."

"So with your power gone, you thought you might be able to get back to playing music. But now your power's back." Josie frowned. "Why didn't you tell anybody?"

"I'm not sure. I guess maybe I thought the music

would go away on its own. That circumstances, or my own lack of inspiration, would take away this precious gift." She laughed. "That sounds *tres* pretentious."

"You *are* pretentious, little Rooster. But you're pretty inspired, too."

They lay side by side. On the ceiling, a broken bulb crackled and went dark.

"Do you have any happy memories of him?" Roxanne asked. "Your dad?"

"He taught me to rotate the tires on a Jeep."

Josie's jaw clenched reflexively and her eyes lost focus for a second. She shook her head, stood, and brushed off her uniform.

"If I can't quit," she said, "neither can you. Not now, anyway."

She reached out a hand. Roxanne took it and allowed the larger woman to pull her to her feet.

"Deal." Roxanne frowned. "Five days in the jungle? Really?"

"I cheated a little. Smuggled in some Cajun fries."

Roxanne laughed.

Josie clapped an arm around her shoulders. Roxanne winced under her grip.

"That Nicky," Josie said. "He's got a big mouth. Let's go find him and kick his doggie butt."

Josie nodded. "Then Maxwell."

"Yeah. Then Maxwell."

They walked out of the training room, arm in arm.

CHAPTER THIRTEEN

WHEN STEVEN LEE WAS SIX, he liked to pretend he was sick. Even at that age, he knew it wasn't a nice thing to do. But it got him a lot of attention from his grandfather, and it was practically the only way to get his parents to notice him at all. So he heated up thermometers to make it look like he had a fever, and practiced fake-coughing until it almost became real.

One day little Steven doubled over in pain, clutching his stomach. Grandfather glared at him, convinced that the boy was faking again. But when the spasms continued, Grandfather rushed him to the hospital. The doctor said they'd arrived just in time: Steven's appendix was about to burst.

CHAPTER THIRTEEN

The pain was almost unbearable. The doctor fit an anesthetic mask over Steven's face. The last thing he remembered was his grandfather's calm eyes gazing at him. Then the world dissolved into a dreamlike haze.

Jasmine's machine reminded him of that. He was sitting in the cold medical bay, fitting the electrodes onto his temples. He glanced over at Jasmine, who'd pulled up another chair on the opposite side of Carlos's bed. She wore the second set of electrodes, and she'd attached a third set to Carlos.

Jasmine grimaced, nodded, and activated the machine.

At first, Steven couldn't tell if anything had happened. There was no flash of light, no blurring of vision, no clear barrier between the outer and inner worlds. Just like in the hospital years before, one moment he was in the medical bay; then he was somewhere else.

Loose soil crunched beneath his feet: brown, rocky, devoid of vegetation. The sun burned blood red, low in the sky. The air smelled of sweat, smoke, and spices.

Steven felt a touch on his arm and whirled in surprise.

He knew instantly that the four figures facing him were Zodiacs. But if he'd had any doubt that he was in another world, now he knew for sure. They possessed the same powers as the Zodiacs, he knew, but they were different people entirely.

A withered man with a scarred neck staggered toward Steven. Above his head, an emaciated Snake crawled low, eyeing Steven with suspicion.

A large woman with tired eyes followed Snake. She sported a Ram avatar with a cracked horn.

A tall lanky man stared at Steven with concern. A blind Rat rose above him, its eye sockets bare.

And then there was Dog. But this Dog had dark fur, matted and patchy. The avatar above him was missing several teeth. Its tail was a stump.

With a shock, Steven realized: *This isn't a vision—not exactly. It's a memory. One of the other Tigers, centuries ago, lived through this. This was* his *team.*

"Boss?" Dog growled. "This don't look good."

That wasn't English, Steven thought. *It wasn't Chinese, either—at least not the kind Grandfather used to speak. But I understood it.*

Dog pointed off into the distance. Steven turned to look—and saw a low village made of timber and mud-brick huts, a few kilometers away across the rocky plain. Several of the huts were on fire, flames rising in the fading light.

Then he saw the riders—three of them, horses galloping away from the village.

Heading straight toward us.

"Tiger?" Rat touched his shoulder, an oddly gentle gesture. "What's the plan?"

Steven turned to look again at the unfamiliar Zodiacs. They seemed ragged, injured, exhausted. Something terrible had happened to them.

"Rabbit's gone," Ram said, her voice filled with despair. "Monkey, too."

"Pig?" Snake asked.

"She was in the village."

The hoofbeats grew louder. The riders wore gold armor, and even at that distance, Steven could make out the quiver of arrows on each one's back. Again he remembered the words of the ancient Tigers: *"Even the memories . . . of ourselves, of the friends we cherished in love and in battle . . . all this was lost."*

The lead rider drew up, pulling on the reins of his horse. The animal's forehead was covered with a close-fitting, intricately patterned plate of armor. The warrior's helmet matched his steed's and was fastened to tight chain mail covering his torso. His shield bore the crest of some long-forgotten kingdom.

The rider signaled with one hand. His two companions moved forward in formation, flanking their leader. They stared down at the Zodiacs.

They're going to kill us, Steven realized. *This is for real. It all actually happened, long ago. I can't stop it.*

A cruel smirk stole over the lead rider's face. He raised

a thick weapon, a high block of wood crisscrossed with metal and cords. A bow and arrow?

Somewhere inside Steven, an ancient voice explained: *A crossbow. Semiautomatic. It fires projectiles called bolts.*

Before the Zodiacs could react, the rider notched three bolts and fired them in quick succession. The first shot struck Dog in the heart; he howled and collapsed. The second and third shots took down Snake and Ram.

For the rest of his life, Steven would remember the noises they made as they died.

Rat's touch brought him out of his shock. The tall man moved up to whisper in his ear, eyeing the riders fearfully.

"We're the last two left," Rat said.

Steven looked up at the warrior. Their gazes met, and Steven shivered at the raw cruelty in his enemy's eyes. The man spat on the ground and hissed: "By the Emperor's command: no more Zodiacs. *No more.*"

The other riders fanned out, moving to surround the two survivors. Rat looked at Steven with fear in his eyes—and something else, too. Something Steven couldn't quite read.

"What do we do?" Rat asked.

"Run for it," Steven said.

He broke and ran, the Tiger rising above his head. He zigzagged around the three riders, pausing only to leap over Ram's body. Rat grabbed on to his hand and followed.

The village was three kilometers away, maybe four.

But Steven knew they wouldn't make it. The riders were already on their heels, laughing as they gained on the two running figures.

I could lose them on foot, Steven thought. *The Tiger is fast. But I can't leave Rat alone. They'll slaughter him!*

Then he realized: *That's what happened, centuries ago. He—the other Tiger—he couldn't leave his teammate to die.*

Clouds swept in to cover the sun. The world seemed locked in twilight, darkening fast. Even the fires raging across the village seemed dimmer than before.

"My Tiger," Rat gasped, puffing and falling behind. "It's over."

Steven skidded to a stop and turned to face the approaching riders. They were hanging back, taking their time. They knew there was no escape.

To Steven's surprise, Rat stumbled into his arms. There were tears in the tall man's eyes.

"If this is the end," Rat said, "then know that I have always loved you."

Steven heard the snap of the crossbow. Rat arched, gasped, and spasmed in his arms. The point of the bolt appeared, thrusting out of Rat's chest.

Steven closed his eyes in horror, waiting for the end—for the bolt that would take his own life. The Tiger roared, a howl of pain that seemed to shatter the world.

When he opened his eyes, that world was gone. No plain, no horses, no warriors calling for his death. No dead and dying teammates. Just utter blackness, thick and warm, stretching all around.

Steven paused, struggling for breath. He shook his head, trying to process what he'd just seen. *The death of the Zodiacs. The end of a cycle. The fate that awaits my team, too?*

Plus, I guess that Tiger was a girl. Or maybe he was gay?

It was all very confusing.

Darkness surrounded him like a shroud. *I'm lost,* he thought. *All alone in this limbo.* After the ordeal he'd just been through, it was oddly comforting.

Then a wheel appeared. It glowed in the air, many times Steven's size, pure white against the blackness. He took a step toward it.

He'd seen the wheel before. It was a graphic depiction of the Chinese Zodiac, with stylized images of the twelve animal signs arrayed along its rim. Long before Steven's time as the Tiger, his grandfather had taught the boy about his heritage.

Or tried to, anyway. I didn't listen to him much when he was alive. For the second time that day, Steven grimaced at a memory. He loved his grandfather; he wished he could express that to the old man one more time.

As he stared at the wheel, he noticed something odd. The animals along the rim looked strangely mechanical. The Rooster's legs were stiffly jointed; the Dog had a hinged metal jaw. The Tiger's tail looked like a computer cable, and its fangs sparked like open circuits.

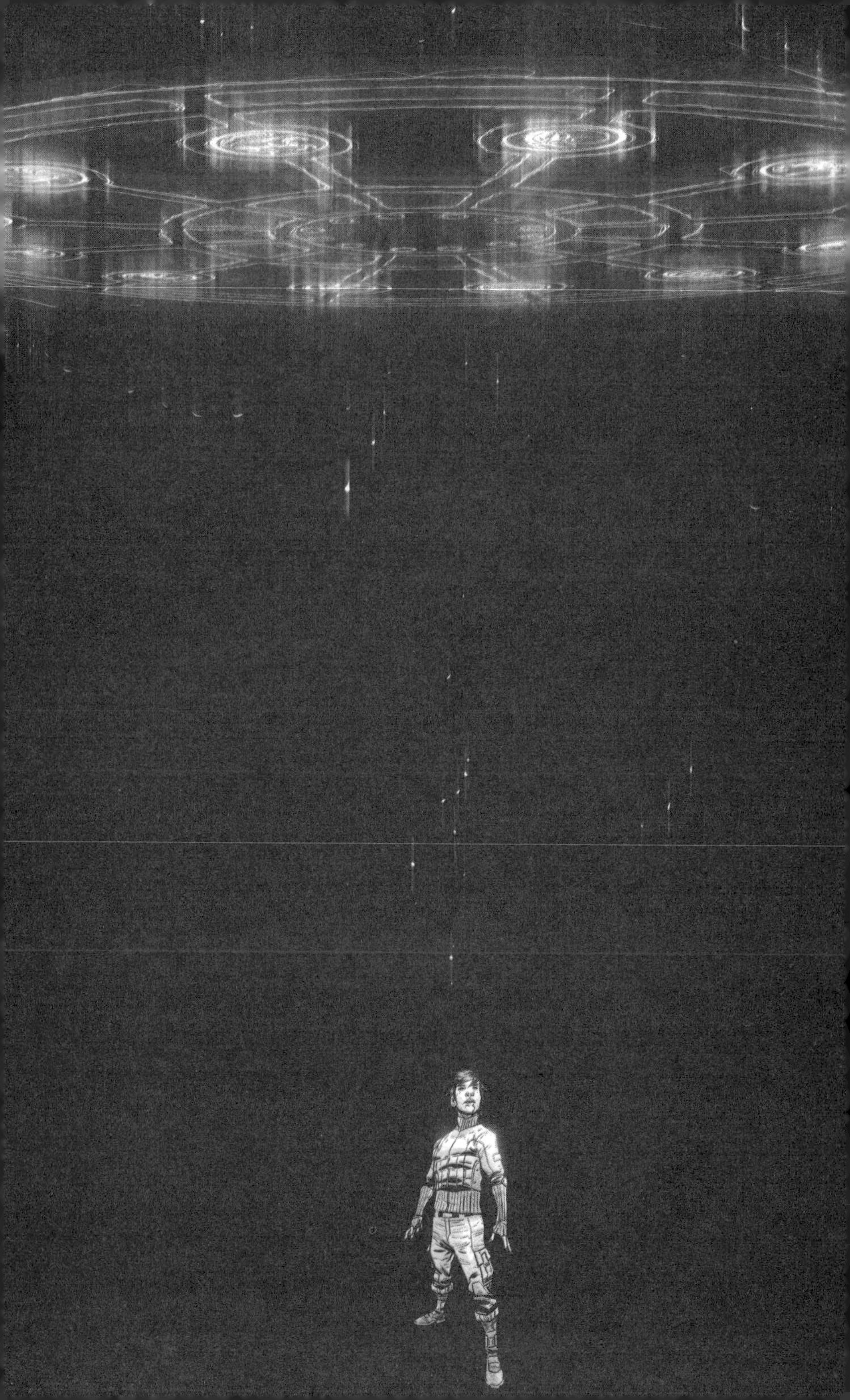

CHAPTER THIRTEEN

Carlos, he remembered. *We're inside his mind. And this is how* he *sees the Zodiac powers. To me, to the rest of us, they're almost mystical—creatures from ancient mythology. But Carlos is a scientist. He sees them as patterns of energy or marvels of engineering. As natural, as rational, as gravity or electricity.*

He reached out and spun the wheel a quarter of the way around. The Dragon locked into place in the top position: a fierce robotic construct with sharp metal talons and electric breath.

"Carlos?" he called.

The wheel began to turn again. Animals flashed before his eyes, each swooping to the top of the arc and then spinning down again. Snake, Horse, Ram. Monkey, Rooster, Dog. Pig, Rat, Ox, Tiger, Rabbit.

Faster and faster they whirled. As the images began to blur together, a voice filled the void. It was loud and insistent, as if desperate to communicate something.

The Dragon
The Dragon is order

"Carlos? Is that you?"

I thought I understood
Thought I knew him
Thought I knew the Dragon

"Jasmine, can you hear me?" He stared out at the blackness. "Are you in here?"

No answer.

"I think I found him," he continued. "I found Carlos!"

So I helped him
Helped Maxwell

At the word *Maxwell*, the world seemed to ripple and shake.

"Carlos," Steven said, turning back to the spinning wheel. "We're here for you. We came to find you."

I helped him
Because only Maxwell could do this
Only he could tame the Dragon

The wheel spun even faster. The signs formed a long continuous image, like all the Zodiac animals blended together: RatOxTigerRabbitDragonSnake . . .

Steven felt a rising panic. Again he recalled the words of the ancient Tigers: *We all lived through the cycle—*

But he failed
Maxwell failed

"Jasmine?" Steven looked around, frantic. "I need help. I don't think I can do this alone!"

The wheel lurched and wobbled, threatening to spin out of control. He reached for it with both hands. The edges whirled past, cutting his fingers. He cried out and shrank back. "Jasmine!"

Then she was there, grabbing his hand. She wore civilian clothes, just as she had in the medical bay. Her grip on his hand was *almost* solid.

"Where have you been?" she asked.

"You don't want to know." He shook his head, trying to banish images of Mongol warriors on horseback, of bolts plunging through helpless Zodiacs.

Now the Dragon is free
The Dragon is unleashed

"Is that really him?" Steven looked up and around, at the void beyond the wheel. "Carlos?"

"I think so."

"What do we do? How can we talk to him?"

"I've been trying. But I can't reach him." She tapped her temples, the spots where—out in the real world—the mind weapon was attached to her head. "Carlos invented this gadget. He's the only one who really knows how to use it."

Only Maxwell can leash the Dragon
But the Dragon cannot be leashed

Steven frowned. "I think he's trying to tell us something—"

That is the error
That is the fallacy

"That's it!" Jasmine exclaimed. "That's what's wrong with him—what he was trying to explain, back in Australia. Maxwell invaded his brain, convinced him that only he, Maxwell, could control the Dragon. But Maxwell failed. The Dragon took *him* over, instead of the other way around."

"And Carlos is a rational person. His whole life is logic, order." Steven nodded. "Now he's got two completely contradictory ideas in his head—"

" 'Only Maxwell can leash the Dragon. But the Dragon cannot be leashed.' " Jasmine stared at the wheel. "It's tearing him apart."

The Dragon flies free
The Dragon burns

"There's only one way to cure him." Jasmine stared at the wheel. "We've got to undo Maxwell's conditioning. We have to break the cycle."

"Carlos, buddy!" Steven cried. "We can help you. We can get you out of this." He turned to Jasmine and whispered: "Can we get him out of this?"

"We have to." Her voice was low, intense. "I love him."

"Look!"

Steven pointed at the wheel. Behind the blurry images,

barely visible, were the familiar contours of Carlos's face. They looked like pencil etchings, like crude sketches on a giant tablet.

The Dragon burns
The Dragon rages

Carlos's features grew sharper: his dark eyes, thin lips, the narrow mustache and goatee framing his mouth. The thin glasses he always wore when he worked.

Steven frowned. "He has glasses? In here?"

"It's his image of himself." Jasmine waved Steven's question away. "Just like Mince. She was a little girl inside *her* mindscape."

"I bet that was cheery."

Jasmine gave him a weird look. "She wasn't always bad."

Its breath boils the seas
Its touch scars the land

"Carlos, listen to me," Jasmine pleaded. She moved closer, staring into Carlos's eyes. "This isn't your fault—you're not to blame. Maxwell did this to you."

Carlos's eyes flickered. The wheel had almost completely transformed into a huge version of his face. He blinked down at Jasmine, struggling to focus.

The Dragon roars
The Dragon rages

"We can cure you," she continued. "Let us take you out of here."

Carlos blinked again, his eyes huge behind the narrow eyeglasses. He looked around, a hint of panic in those eyes—and all at once, Steven felt it, too, like bile rising in his throat.

Where's that coming from? he wondered. *Is Carlos's mental state infecting me? We're inside his mind, after all. Am I panicking because* he's *panicking?*

No, he realized, *it's the Tiger. Its instincts are crying out—prodding me, urging me to act. But what does it want me to do?*

The Dragon slays friends
It murders kinsmen
It kills the meek and the bold

Carlos's face twisted in pain. He opened his mouth in a silent scream of agony.

The cycle, Steven thought, the words of the Tigers echoing in his brain. *The cycle—*

It slays all
Loved and hated
Good and wicked alike

CHAPTER THIRTEEN

"Jasmine," Steven warned. He took a step back, driven by some unconscious instinct.

Carlos's eyes stared wide now, in mad terror. He opened his mouth.

The Dragon flies free
Where it passes no life remains
It burns it sears it slays
It scars kills boils murders rages

"Jasmine!"

Steven reached out to pull her away. She shook him off, staring straight ahead. Carlos's lips moved desperately, frantically. . . .

AND IT'S MY FAULT

Carlos screamed. His face exploded; the darkness shattered. As Steven flew backward, he reached out for Jasmine. He felt her hand clasp his, gripping him tight in the raging wind of the mindscape. They tumbled through time, through space, for a time beyond time, a distance that was no distance at all.

They landed on sand, hot and flat. The impact jarred Steven's back; he grunted in pain. When he looked up, the rays of the sun blinded him. He shielded his eyes and waited for his vision to return.

By the time he stood up, Jasmine was already staring at the hole in the ground.

The desert stretched all the way to the horizon. No clouds offered shade, no mountains or cities broke up the simplicity of the landscape. Just sand, sky, and the impossibly bright sun above.

And the hole. Four, maybe four and a half kilometers wide, like a crater in the sand. Char marks pocked its uneven edges, as if it had been burned into the landscape by some giant torch.

Jasmine walked up to the edge and peered down. "Careful," Steven called, running to join her.

"Look," she said, pointing down.

He stopped at the edge, fighting off a sense of vertigo as he stared down into the hole. At the bottom, in a pile of dark ash, lay fragments of buildings—stones and stairs and broken columns. A minaret that might have belonged to an ancient mosque.

Bones, too. Stripped of flesh, bleached by the sun. They no longer seemed to belong to any living thing.

"What—" Steven began. "What is this?"

"I know," Jasmine whispered, staring into the abyss.

"It's not from my mind." He looked sharply at her. "Is it a memory of yours?"

"No."

"Then it must belong to Carlos."

A strange movement caught his eye. Down in the hole, something shifted. A small rustling among the bones and wreckage.

"What is it?" he asked again. "What is this place?"

"It's Lystria."

He started to reply, then stopped. *Lystria,* he thought. *The murdered city. The place Maxwell destroyed during his rise to power. The town he leveled without mercy, just to tell the world never to mess with him. To cement his reputation.*

Steven had never been to Lystria. Neither had Jasmine. Carlos had, but he'd refused to speak of it to Steven or the other Zodiacs.

"If . . . if this is Lystria . . ." Steven paused, trying to gather his thoughts. "Then it isn't an accident. Carlos is trying to tell us something."

Far below, a small figure emerged from the pile of bones. He had dark hair, dark clothes, and ash-coated boots. He tossed aside some rubble and started to climb up the side of the pit.

"Someone is," Jasmine said.

A distant stench rose from the crater, carried on the low wind. The figure clawed his way up, drawing closer. When Steven caught sight of his face, he gasped and stepped back.

CHAPTER THIRTEEN

Jasmine stood her ground. When the newcomer clawed his way out of the hole, she was waiting for him.

"Human ashes," the man said, dusting off his pants. "They cling to a man."

"Maxwell," Steven said.

Maxwell stared at Steven for a moment, then looked over at Jasmine. A strange expression entered his eyes: part hatred, part confusion.

Then it passed. Maxwell's familiar, arrogant smile spread across his features.

"This guy better be inside Carlos's head," Steven said, rolling his eyes. "I sure didn't bring Maxwell in here, and I hope you didn't, either."

Jasmine didn't answer. She seemed to be studying Maxwell, as if unsure who he was.

Maxwell raised an eyebrow at Steven. "Your banter," he said, "is poorly timed."

"It usually is, yeah."

Maxwell strode past Jasmine, approaching Steven head-on. Steven struggled not to flinch. Maxwell's figure seemed very solid, more real than the searing sun above or the bleached bones below. More real, even, than the dying Zodiacs on the ancient Chinese plain.

"Carlos is correct," Maxwell continued. "The Dragon cannot be leashed. Not by you."

"Jasmine was the Dragon before," Steven said.

"For a time." Maxwell jerked his head back at Jasmine. "Ask her if she thinks she could control it forever."

Steven glanced over at Jasmine. She looked down sadly and shook her head.

"Jasmine!" Maxwell exclaimed. "You're growing wiser. No longer the headstrong young girl who worked for me, years ago."

A Tiger alarm went off inside Steven's head. *Something's wrong,* he thought. *The words coming out of Maxwell's mouth—it doesn't sound like Carlos's mind talking. But it's not Jasmine, either. . . .*

"Only I can tame the Dragon," Maxwell said. "Only I can stop the devastation to come."

Jasmine crossed over to join them, motioning Steven back. "What devastation?" she asked. "What have you done?"

Again, Maxwell smiled. He opened his mouth to reply. But Steven never heard the answer.

CHAPTER FOURTEEN

ONE MOMENT STEVEN stood in the desert with Jasmine and Maxwell. The next, without any transition, he was sprawled awkwardly in a folding chair, facing Carlos's hospital bed. Electrodes trailed from his temples to Carlos's unmoving body, then across the bed to Jasmine, who sat equally still.

He shook his head and pulled himself upright in the chair. He felt stiff, groggy; his vision was blurry. Across the medical bay, a cluster of people stood talking, but he couldn't make out who they were.

"Steven, mate!" someone with a familiar voice called out. "Yer alive!"

The group started toward him, led by a short, roundish figure. Steven blinked. *It can't be,* he thought. *It can't be him.*

"Liam?"

The Irishman leaned down, smiling warmly. It was him, all right: wide cheeks, thick glasses, a mop of unruly hair. Duane and Roxanne followed him.

"Liam," Steven repeated. "Are you real?"

How can he be here? Last I knew, Liam was in an Irish jail. Unless . . . A jolt of panic ran through him. *Am I still in the mindscape? Still hallucinating people . . . like Maxwell?*

Liam clapped Steven on the back, hard enough to make even the Tiger wince. "That answer yer question?"

Steven nodded. "How? What are you doing here?"

Before Liam could answer, Dr. Snejbjerg strode up and took Steven's head in both hands. With one quick motion, she ripped both electrodes off his temples. She snapped on a pocket flashlight and shone it in one of his eyes, then the other.

"Um," Steven said. "Ow?"

"You are indeed alive," the doctor said. "And you're lucky to be that way. What were you thinking? Entering the *mind* of a comatose man?"

Steven looked over at Carlos's body. He seemed deep in the coma, his condition unchanged. Past him, Jasmine sat rigid and unmoving in her chair. The control box lay in her lap.

Wait, Steven thought, his heart skipping a beat. *Jasmine! Is she . . . ?*

CHAPTER FOURTEEN

Dr. Snejbjerg circled around Carlos's bed and snatched up the control box. "She's alive, too," she said, gesturing at Jasmine. "But whatever's happened to her, wherever she's gone, we can't seem to bring her back."

"You brought *me* back," Steven said.

"Yes. Like so."

The doctor manipulated a few touch controls on the box. Jasmine stiffened briefly and murmured something, too quietly to make out. Then she went silent again.

"The best we can surmise," Duane said, "is that Jasmine doesn't *want* to come out of Carlos's mind. Or wherever she is."

"Duane, you're the smartest guy I know," Steven said. "Can't you get her out?"

"Carlos built the mind machine," Duane said. "I can't even find his notes."

Roxanne frowned at Steven. "Dude, where were you? What did you see in there?"

Steven stood up, suddenly restless. He remembered ancient warriors; assassins on horseback; a wheel in the sky; an enormous hole, blasted into the ground. And Maxwell, as imperious and smug as ever.

Out of all of it, only Maxwell seemed solid. The rest was like smoke, like a dream vanishing in the daylight.

"It's hard to explain," he said.

"Ah, we'll figure it out," Liam said, "now that we've got our powers back. Cheers for that, by the way."

Steven didn't answer. He paced away, trying to keep

hold of the fading mindscape images. Something about a mechanical Dragon . . . ?

"Hey, mate," Liam called. "Think fast!"

Steven whirled just in time to see Liam sprinting across the room, his head aimed straight at Steven's gut. The Ram avatar rose above Liam, its horns coiled into deadly spirals. Steven's Tiger senses kicked into gear; at the last minute, he dodged sideways. Liam slammed, laughing, into a diagnostic bed, shattering the screen on a large monitor above it.

Duane, Roxanne, and Steven rushed to him. But as always, Liam was completely unhurt. "Bloody hell," he said, still laughing. "I missed you guys!"

"Literally," Duane said.

They helped Liam to his feet. Steven found himself smiling, too. But when they all turned to face Dr. Snejbjerg, his smile died.

She jabbed a finger at Liam's face. "Get. Out. Of this medical bay."

Liam blinked. Something behind his eyes made Steven tense up. Liam was an old pub brawler. It wouldn't do for him to take the doctor's admonition as a challenge.

"It's okay," Steven said, stepping between them. "He's sorry. He won't do it again."

Dr. Snejbjerg glared. Roxanne started neatening the broken bed while Duane picked up pieces of the monitor screen.

Steven ushered Liam into a corner of the room, to a

large computer station. The Irishman shot the doctor a nasty look but allowed himself to be led away.

"This place used t'be more fun," he grumbled.

They pulled a couple of folding chairs together. Across the room, Dr. Snejbjerg glared at Roxanne and Duane as they swept up the mess.

"Is that how you got out of jail?" Steven asked. "Just smashed through a wall and kept running?"

"Nah." Liam turned away. "I had some help."

Something in his tone sent a warning tingle up Steven's spine. "Who?"

"People with clout." Liam grimaced. "Yer not gonna like it."

A detail from the mindscape rose to the surface of Steven's mind: the ancient Chinese Zodiacs. He saw, again, three rapid-fire bolts piercing the hearts of the one-time Dog, Snake, and . . . and Ram.

"I don't think anything can surprise me today," Steven said.

The Irishman's gaze darted to the middle of the room. Steven looked over and saw a pair of figures walking around the broken bed, giving the cleanup efforts a wide berth.

Wrong again, Steven thought.

The newcomers marched up to Steven and Liam. The woman wore a business suit with a long skirt and low heels. The man's suit was trim, dark, and fit every centimeter of his body to absolute perfection.

Reluctantly, Steven looked up. The man's face was rigid, his mouth turned down in a permanent frown.

"Hello, Son," he said.

"Dad. Long time." Steven swallowed. "*Very* long time."

Mrs. Lee met Steven's eyes for a moment, then took a step back. *She always defers to him,* Steven thought.

"Why are you here, Dad?" Steven felt an old anger building inside him. "Want to throw a ball around the yard? Oh, wait, no yard. Also, you never did that in your entire life."

Mr. Lee's lips curled even farther down. *His disappointed look,* Steven thought. *I sure remember that.*

"I am here—" Mr. Lee stopped, corrected himself. "*We* are here because of the Dragon."

Roxanne and Duane approached, watching the confrontation nervously. Liam shot Steven a concerned look.

"Well?" Steven asked.

"Not here," Mrs. Lee said. "Outside."

"Sometimes," Liam said, "I forget this place is in bloody Greenland."

Steven stood huddled with Liam, Roxanne, and Duane, a hundred meters from the ice wall that concealed the exterior of Zodiac headquarters. He pulled his coat tighter, shivering. Half a meter of snow lay on the ground, stretching all the way to the mountains in the distance. The temperature was well below freezing; even the glaring sun didn't seem to warm the air very much.

A few meters away, Steven's parents were assembling a strange machine on the snow. "You were kidding about going out in the yard," Roxanne said, gesturing at Mr. Lee. "He understood that, right?"

Steven shrugged. "He's never been much for sarcasm."

"That looks like a satellite dish." Duane peered across the snow. "They seem to be preparing to receive some sort of signal."

All at once, Steven had had enough. He'd survived a volcano, watched Zodiacs die, and lost Jasmine inside a hostile mindscape. Now he stood outside in the freezing cold, waiting for his parents to tell him what was going on. *Just like I've been waiting for them all my life.*

He strode over to them. Mr. Lee ignored him; the older man just kept screwing a roundish lens unit onto the base of the machine. But his mother turned immediately.

"Steven," she said. "I'm afraid we don't have time for pleasantries."

"Forget pleasantries. What is that thing? And why are we *out here* instead of inside where it's *warm*?" He winced when he heard his own voice; he sounded like a whiny little boy. But he couldn't help it. Somehow, his parents always brought out that side of him.

"Your mother has explained this," Mr. Lee said, not looking up. "It is a custom-built satellite unit, keyed to our private communications network."

"Are you using AES-256 encryption?" Duane asked.

Steven turned in surprise; he hadn't heard Duane follow him.

"Five twelve, actually," Mrs. Lee replied, a hint of pride in her voice. "Stronger than the U.S. government."

She stepped back, allowing Duane to see the device. It stood almost two meters high, bristling with lenses and projections. As Duane leaned in to look, the Pig flashed briefly above his head.

"Mom, Dad—we know you're important," Steven said. "Now can we tune in to your top-secret YouTube channel and get this over with?"

"We must wait for our private satellite to assume position overhead," Mrs. Lee said, consulting a smart watch on her wrist. "This footage is extremely sensitive. We cannot take any chance of its being intercepted."

A gust of wind blew up. Steven's teeth chattered; he turned his back on his parents. As he walked away, he heard Duane ask them, "Is the unit a secure server, as well?"

Roxanne greeted Steven, shivering. "So?"

Steven shrugged. "It'll be ready when it's ready."

"And we have to be outside to receive the signal?" Liam asked.

"Maybe. Maybe not." Steven struggled to keep his anger in check. "They're probably just making me suffer some more. All my life, they've been trying to toughen me up. I'm sick of it."

He turned away. *I'm worried,* he realized. *Not just about*

Mom and Dad, and not just about the Dragon. What is Jasmine going through, inside Carlos's mind? Will she ever get out again?

"Mate," Liam said.

Steven turned to see Liam glowing, the Ram power projected above him. Roxanne joined them, and Steven felt the Tiger reach out. He sensed Roxanne's fire, Liam's resilience. In the snow, against the wind, the three Zodiac avatars joined together, flickering like tiny flames in the cold.

"Keeps us a little warmer." Roxanne shrugged. "All this power . . . it's gotta be good for something."

Steven smiled, grateful.

The sound of Mr. Lee clearing his throat cut through the icy air. Steven turned to see him watching them, an impatient expression on his face.

"It's time," Mrs. Lee said.

A moment later they all stood gathered around the satellite receptor. A large round lens protruded from one side, glowing bright. *Great,* Steven thought, *home projection studio. Where's the screen?*

The lens flashed once. A cubed hologram appeared, over two meters long on each side, glowing above the snow.

Oh. No screen.

A three-dimensional cloud of static hovered in the air. It resolved into a peaceful vista: a narrow city, no more than four or five blocks wide, bordered by clear blue water. A highway ran through the middle of town, cutting the rows of one- and two-story buildings in half. The high spire of a church rose in the background, framed against distant, snow-topped mountains.

A location stamp appeared over the image:

AKUTAN ISLAND
ALASKA, U.S.

"Alaska," Liam said. "Another notorious cold spot. Did ye bring us outside to make us feel like we were there?"

The image panned down. The camera shook, tipping sideways more than once. It swooped past the highway, over the few cars headed through the city. The sea loomed ahead, choppy and seemingly endless.

"This was shot from a helicopter," Mrs. Lee explained.

"What was?" Steven asked. "A tourist video for Bleakville, USA?"

Then he saw it. A white spot in the water about a kilometer offshore. Churning, whirling, bubbling.

Liam frowned. "Is that a whirlpool?"

The bubbles grew larger, more agitated. The water seemed to rise, forming a spout that shot into the air. A hiss of steam accompanied it, darkening and thickening into a column of smoke.

People in heavy coats gathered on the beach, pointing and whispering.

With a flash of wings, the Dragon shot into view.

Water exploded all around, rising in the creature's wake and flying from its wings, like bathwater from a shaking dog's ears. The people shrank back, shouting in fear.

The Dragon's first breath of fire left the beach a charred, blackened ruin.

"Mon dieu," Roxanne said softly.

The beast reared back and roared in triumph. Its body snaked around, its bat-like wings flapping wide. It seemed to fill the sky, blotting out the sun.

"Aye," Liam said, "That's the Dragon, all right."

"Maxwell's Dragon," Steven added.

"Watch," Mrs. Lee said.

In the hologram, the Dragon seemed to pause in the air. It turned one way, then the other. Then it looked down at the city and its eyes flared red.

The view lurched abruptly, veering to point down at the land. On the central highway, a group of men and women in army fatigues had gathered quickly in the middle of the road. They aimed weapons up at the Dragon: handguns, grenades, even a semiautomatic machine gun.

They never fired a shot. The Dragon just leaned down, opened its mouth, and swept fire across them. The people fell, screaming, and died. A small explosion marked the machine gun's destruction.

"It's a slaughter," Roxanne said grimly.

"Look," Duane said. "Look what's happening."

The Dragon wheeled in the air—and as it did, it

seemed to morph and change. Its wings shrank and shriveled, becoming sharp claws. Its many teeth came together, sharpening into a few longer, deadlier fangs.

"That's a different Dragon," Roxanne said. "It looks more like the one that used to appear when Jasmine used her power."

"They are all the same Dragon," Mrs. Lee said. "Now that the creature has assumed full control of Maxwell's physical form, it exists in all its manifestations at once."

The Dragon swung low, its wings flapping over the church. It exhaled again, almost casually, and the church spire lit up like a candle. People fled from the building, running in terror.

"I don't want to watch this," Duane said.

Bit by bit, roaring and raging, the Dragon laid the town to waste. It swooped down, set a clutch of buildings on fire, then wafted sunward to survey its handiwork. It rose above the mountains, whirled, and flew low, like a World War II gun plane, spitting fire along the length of the highway.

The Dragon changed again. Its skin became steel, its joints and contours angular, machine-like. Its fangs sparked like open circuits. As a bolt of electricity issued from its mouth, Steven realized where he'd seen that Dragon before.

On the wheel inside the mindscape. This is yet another version of the Dragon—the one Carlos knows.

CHAPTER FOURTEEN

The slaughter continued. Liam and Roxanne winced repeatedly. Duane turned his back on the hologram.

But Mr. and Mrs. Lee kept their eyes on the image, resolute and firm. Steven forced himself to do the same. *If they can take it, so can I.*

The city lay in ruins, a burning scar along the coastline. Shards of highway lay at odd angles; the church's severed cross jutted up from the blackened beach. A plume of smoke rose from the mountains, as if nature were echoing the cataclysm in the town.

The image swung down to reveal a figure standing on the beach. An Aleut fisherman, dressed in a hoodie, cap, overalls, and yellow gloves. He stood in the ruins, staring up at the death image in the sky.

The only person left alive.

The Dragon paused above him. As the man stared at it, the creature began to shift and morph again. Its fangs grew even longer, its body stout and dark. Red eyes narrowed to dots of white; thick fur spread across its body. Its snakelike tail widened into a fin, like the tail of a walrus.

The Dragon rained down fire, engulfing the man. Then, incredibly fast, it swung its head up to look straight into the camera. For just a moment, Steven could make out a human figure at the heart of the beast: a familiar, muscular form.

Maxwell. Or his body, at least.

The Dragon opened its mouth again. The image shook and started to swing away. The creature's breath flared red and yellow, and the hologram turned to static.

Mrs. Lee reached out and snapped off the machine.

For a moment everyone just stood, completely silent. Steven felt numb. He couldn't even feel the cold anymore.

"The cameraman," Mr. Lee said, "did not survive."

"That footage was taken two days ago," Mrs. Lee said. "It has been successfully withheld from the general public. But if the Dragon strikes again, in a more populated area, such censorship will not be practical."

"When," Mr. Lee corrected. "Not if."

"There'll be panic," Liam rumbled. "Mass panic."

"Also death," Roxanne said.

"Yes," Mr. Lee said. "Much death."

"Cheery," Steven observed. "So what do we do?"

"We can provide expertise and specialized equipment," Mrs. Lee replied. "But we cannot predict where the Dragon will strike next. We had hoped that your group, with its experience in detection of the Zodiac powers, might be able to track the creature."

The stakes were high—possibly as high as the survival of the human race. But as Steven watched his parents, he couldn't help thinking: *They only visit me when they want something.*

They all turned at a rattling noise. The hidden garage door to the base was opening, forming a hole in the ice wall. Dafari, the African computer scientist, appeared in the doorway and ran toward them.

"Mister Pig," he said, holding out a tablet to Duane. "I have collated the data from the Indonesian volcano. I am forced to admit: you may have been right."

Mr. Lee frowned. "Indonesian volcano?"

"Dad," Steven began, "we've been trying to find the Dragon for weeks now. But we're a little shorthanded—"

"Steven. I do not wish to offend you." Mr. Lee held up a hand. "But this is a matter of large-scale strategic planning. Certainly there are older people here, better suited to these matters? The founders of this base . . . the people who recruited you?"

Dad, Steven thought, clenching his fists in anger. *If Jasmine and Carlos were available, I wouldn't be standing here having this stupid conversation with—*

Poof. "RAMMY!"

They all whirled around. Kim had appeared outside the complex door, running and jumping through the air. She *poofed* away again, reappearing several meters closer to them, then repeated the action two more times.

Liam held up his hands. "Whoa, little bunny," he said. "Not so—"

With a final *poof,* Kim appeared in the air right before Liam's face. She reached out and grabbed him in a bear hug, laughing. Together they tumbled to the snow.

"Easy, girl!" Liam cried. "Good thing I can't be hurt!"

"You big goof!" Kim wiped snow out of her face, still laughing. "I missed you like *crazy*!"

"Steven?" Mr. Lee said. "Time is not on our side. I suggest we take this up with—"

"Actually, Dad, the person to take it up with is me."

Mr. Lee looked at him sharply.

"Very well." Mr. Lee straightened his tie. "How do you suggest we proceed?"

Steven cast his eyes across the group. Duane and Dafari were conferring in low tones, pointing at the tablet in Duane's hand. Roxanne helped Kim and Liam to their feet, brushing snow off their uniforms.

"I'll let you know," Steven said.

Mr. Lee cast a look at his wife. Together they stepped forward. "Steven," Mrs. Lee said, "I suggest—"

"I'll let you know," Steven repeated, "*after* I consult with my team."

As he turned away and strode toward the open door, Steven was sure of two things. First: his parents were eyeing him with astonishment. He'd never spoken to them like that in his life. He wasn't sure he'd ever have the nerve to do it again, either.

The second thing he knew was that his team was right behind him. With Jasmine out of the picture, they would follow him anywhere.

Now all I have to do is be worthy of that trust.

"Classroom. Five minutes," he said in his most commanding voice. "Core team only."

CHAPTER FIFTEEN

"I TELL YOU, *mon frère*, we were *inside a live volcano.* Venting gas, hot magma, all of it. Very frightening."

"Ha! For real, Rox: I'd rather have been there than cooling me heels in a Dublin lockup."

Steven paused outside the door to the classroom, listening to the voices. It was good to have Liam back. His friendly manner had already lightened Roxanne's and Kim's moods.

"How *did* you get out of jail, anyway?"

"Ah, it ain't much of a story, Kimmy. One minute I'm eatin' beans out of a can, the next there's a flash of light and *bang!* My powers are back."

"So you just . . . rammed your way out?"

"Nah. At first I'm like, 'Look out, brick wall, here I come!' And then I remember, no no, Liam, yer in here because yer tryin' to make up for yer past. Right? Tryin' to do the right thing?"

"Also because the Irish authorities tracked you down, dude."

"Aye, there was that."

Steven took a deep breath. There were things he needed to tell his team, and advice he wanted to get from them. But there were also things he wasn't ready to tell them yet.

Some burdens are mine and only mine.

"Anyway," Liam continued, "I figured I'd just sit it out till my military trial. But it *was* a bit of a relief, I'll tell ye, when this mysterious couple showed up with my release papers."

Steven rounded the corner into the room. "That's my folks," he said. "Always where you need 'em."

His three teammates had pulled up chairs in a circle in the center of the room. Desks lined the walls, equipped with computer screens.

"Yer sarcasm is not lost on me," Liam said, a half smile on his face. "But I do owe the elder Lees a debt. I admit, though, when I first saw 'em, I thought I was bein' enlisted in some sort of international spy organization."

Steven dragged over another chair. "Where's Duane?"

CHAPTER FIFTEEN

"Busy with Dafari," Roxanne said. "They're trying to see if any of his readings from the volcano match up with your parents' data."

"He said he'd join us soon," Kim added.

"Right." Steven rubbed his eyes; he suddenly felt tired. "Liam, you've missed a lot the last few weeks."

"He missed a lot the last *twenty-four hours*," Kim said, smiling.

"I think I need some catching up, too," Roxanne said. "Steven, you haven't told us what you saw inside the mind machine."

Steven hesitated. He looked over at Roxanne, who gave him an encouraging nod. Straight across from him, Liam smiled his familiar easy smile. Kim touched Steven's arm and scooted her chair forward a little.

"Let's start from the beginning," he said.

So he told them. He described the descent into the volcano, the decision to break the group into two teams. He talked about working with Malik, Josie, and Nicky, the trouble he'd had commanding them and the enormous help they'd been against their former Vanguard coworkers. He explained how he'd found the *jiānyù* behind a door guarded by an AI with Maxwell's face.

"Maxwell-themed video doorbells?" Roxanne shook her head. "That's not gonna catch on."

He told them about the chase through the volcano, the HUDset, the bubbling pools of magma, and the weird,

crashing slate boulders. But he skipped the part about his vision, the deadly choice the Tigers insisted he would face.

When he mentioned finding Kim, his voice broke a little.

"I escaped from my cell before he got there," Kim explained, a playful look on her face. "But I let him *think* he rescued me."

"Sorry I wasn't there, kid," Liam said. "Every day I thought about bustin' my way out so I could help find you. It must have been awful."

"It's okay," Kim said, touching Liam's arm. "It was mostly lonely."

"The squirt managed to get a brief video message out," Roxanne said, smiling at Kim. "Led us right to her."

"That was a *total* fluke. Mince left a comm unit in my cell by mistake. She came back and ripped it out of my hand before I got three words out."

"Yer parents must be glad to see you," Liam said. "How are they?"

"Okay, I think." Kim frowned. "Dad seems better. But since the stroke, he has trouble finding words. When I arrived today, he couldn't remember my name. That was hard."

"They staying long?"

"Till we find Maxwell, I guess."

Steven felt something, a vague idea, tickling at the edge of his consciousness. "In the volcano," he said to Kim, "Mince used to visit you?"

"Only a couple times. Thank goodness." Kim shivered. "That girl is creepy with a capital *cree*."

"What about Maxwell? Did you see him at all?"

"Just once, early on." She looked troubled. "He was glowing, like he couldn't turn the Zodiac power off anymore. He only said a few words, to Mince. . . . I'm not even sure he knew I was there."

"What did he say?"

Kim furrowed her brow. "It was something about . . . they talked about a secret project. Project Firebird? And they mentioned a name. . . . It sounded like Huey Louie. His voice was all echoey. It was hard to understand."

"Huey Louie," Steven repeated. "Wait a minute . . . Hui Lu? Could that have been it?"

Kim shrugged. "Maybe."

"Steven?" Liam asked. "What's it mean?"

"I'm not sure. My grandfather . . . he used to try to teach me about Chinese mythology. I just wanted to watch superhero movies." He paused, trying to remember. "But I remember a fable about Hui Lu. . . . He was some kind of fire god. He kept all these birds, firebirds, a hundred or more of 'em. And when he set them loose, they rained down fire all across the land."

"That might be a clue to the Dragon's plans," Roxanne said. "Let's come back to it. Tell us about the mind trip?"

Steven nodded. He described the journey into Carlos's mindscape, skipping over the deaths of the past Zodiacs.

CHAPTER FIFTEEN

He described the wheel in the darkness and meeting up with Jasmine. That led to the giant hole in the desert and the arrival of . . .

"Maxwell," Liam said. "For a guy who's missing in action, he seems to pop up a lot."

"What about Jasmine?" Roxanne asked.

Steven shrugged. "She either wants to stay in Carlos's mind or she's trapped there." He noticed Roxanne staring intensely at him. "Why? What is it?"

"I don't know. But back in the volcano, she said something about 'weird knowledge in my head.' I think she's carrying around something . . . some secret."

Steven looked away, thinking of his own secret. He only hesitated for a fraction of a second—but in that time, all their eyes turned to him. *They know,* he thought. *They know me so well, they can sense I'm not telling them everything.*

"Remember," he said, changing the subject in a hurry. "We're not really up against Maxwell anymore. Whatever the Dragon's doing, it's completely taken him over."

"Jasmine's been saying that for weeks," Roxanne replied. "That the Dragon's all-powerful now, that Maxwell's not there anymore. I'm not sure I understand how that could happen."

"Aye," Liam agreed. "My power never feels like it's gonna *take me over.* It just lets me crash through walls without crackin' open my skull."

"Your power isn't the Dragon," Steven said. "I've

touched the Dragon, felt its power. It feels like . . . like we're all flickering matches and it's the whole blazing sun."

"If the Dragon took over Maxwell, then where did Maxwell *go*?" Kim asked. "His, whatever, consciousness?"

"I don't know. Maybe nowhere." Steven paused. "Maxwell was a maniac and a murderer, but at least he was human. The Dragon doesn't care about human life at all."

"Seems to me the important thing is the Dragon's *plan*." Liam stood up and started pacing. "Why attack a fishing town in Alaska? And what was all that crazy rock machinery it had set up inside yer Indonesian volcano? Is it just crazy, or does it have some big endgame?"

"The first attack was way up north." Steven pictured a world map. "Maybe it's starting up there and planning to work its way down? Something to do with the earth's magnetic poles?"

"Or the what? Ley lines? I don't know what I'm bloody talking about." Liam laughed. "We really need Duane."

"The Dragon kept changing," Steven said, "in the video my folks brought. I recognized the first three versions—but what was that last one? It looked like a walrus. Or a manatee, maybe—"

"It's called the Az-I-Wu-Gum-Ki-Mukh-'Ti."

They all turned to stare at Roxanne.

"Azziewhatnow?" Steven asked.

"Az-I-Wu-Gum-Ki-Mukh-'Ti," she repeated. "An Inuit myth. Their very own version of a dragon."

CHAPTER FIFTEEN

Liam blinked. "You part Inuit or something, Rox?"

She smirked and held up her phone. An artist's rendition of the Inuit dragon snarled out at them: long fangs and a walrus head, with a dog's body and a large fin at the back.

"Google, dude," Roxanne said. "It's your friend."

"The Dragon was menacing a local man," Steven said, "when it changed."

"Your mom said it—what was it?—exists in all manifestations now. Guess it adapts to fit the mythology, the fears, of whoever it's facing."

Steven nodded. He remembered his vision, back in the volcano: the terrible image of the Dragon filling the sky, menacing everyone and everything he loved.

"Steven?" Kim seemed hesitant. "I know you don't like to talk about your parents. But they did work with Maxwell for a while."

"Yeah," Roxanne said. "What did they do? Build Zodiac equipment for him?"

"You're saying they might know something they're not telling us." He grimaced. "Yeah, maybe. Dad's always got schemes inside his schemes."

"Sure, but they came to *us*," Liam said. "And yer mom helped us against Maxwell before, didn't she?"

"So did Rat. You trust *him*?" Steven shook his head. "You don't know them."

They all turned to him again, staring in concern. This time they didn't look away.

"Mate," Liam said softly. "What's wrong?"

Steven drew in a deep breath.

"Okay," he said.

He told them about the visions. The army of ancient Tigers whose voices rose to a deafening scream in that chamber beneath the mountain. He described the giant claws reaching down to slice his team to ribbons. He described the horrific sight of his parents, hands clasped as the Dragon swooped down to crush them with its deadly talons.

He talked about the Chinese plain, the team of past-era Zodiacs. His voice quavered as he described the ancient warrior whose unerring crossbow bolts had ended the Zodiacs' lives. He told them about patchy-furred Dog, the big female Ram, the old injured Snake. He told them about Rat, the tall weathered man who had loved a Tiger long gone from the earth.

And last, he told them about the choice. The inescapable fate, the doom foretold by the Tigers who had lived before him:

" 'The Zodiac,' they said, 'or a normal life. Your friends, your teammates, your duty—or your family, the people who gave you life.' "

His three teammates took in every word. Listening, seeking, struggling to help.

"They said they'd all faced the choice," Steven continued, "and every one of 'em had failed. And when they were done, nothing remained of the Zodiacs."

CHAPTER FIFTEEN

"So . . ." Roxanne began, "are you worried about failing? As a leader, I mean?"

"No. Well, yeah, but it's more than that." He frowned, struggling to sort his thoughts. "I just have a bad feeling that some sort of . . . *sacrifice* is coming."

Kim touched his arm. Roxanne squinted, thinking. Liam frowned.

"Sounds a little vague," Liam said.

"You didn't see the vision," Steven replied.

"No, I didn't. And until I do, I don't believe it. All we've got is the word of a bunch of ghosts in yer head."

"Nothing's set in stone, Steven," Roxanne said. "If there's a choice, you'll face it when you get there."

"We can take care of ourselves," Kim said quietly.

Steven nodded and reached for them. They scooted their chairs forward, stretching out for an awkward group hug at arm's length.

"Thank you," Steven said. He felt tears forming in his eyes. "*Man*, I've missed you g—"

"THE RING OF FIRE!"

Duane burst through the door, waving a tablet around. Steven and the others pulled apart slightly. They stared up at Duane, baffled, their arms still around each other's shoulders.

Duane paced around the chairs, holding up the tablet. "You know," he said impatiently, "volcanoes!"

"Mate," Liam said, "yer gonna have to dumb it down for us."

"Oh." Duane looked at the tablet. "Well. It was a matter of comparing seismic readings to soil samples. Then we plotted the results against—" He stopped in his tracks.

"Duane?" Steven asked. "What is it?"

Duane approached the group, the tablet hanging loose in his fingers. A sad expression came over his face.

"Did I miss the hugging?" he asked.

CHAPTER SIXTEEN

"THE PROBLEM we couldn't solve," Duane said, "was what had happened to the Dragon energy. Only the faintest traces were showing up on our scanners."

Steven frowned. "I thought Maxwell knew how to block our scans."

He leaned forward over a strategy table in the middle of the war room. Duane and Dafari stood at the front of the room before the large wall screen, which showed an image of the Dragon superimposed over Maxwell's face.

The war room had been refitted and expanded in recent months, with new computers and additional planning tables installed. Roxanne, Liam, and Kim were clustered with Steven. From another table, the ex-Vanguard Zodiacs watched the presentation warily. An assortment of nonpowered staff members stood farther back, around the computer stations.

Dafari nodded a bit impatiently. "That is correct. But the Dragon radiates much more energy than any of the other Zodiac signs—orders of magnitude more. Even Maxwell should not have been able to shield it from us completely."

Mr. and Mrs. Lee entered through the side door and stood stiffly against the wall. Mr. Lee shot a glance at Steven, then turned his attention to the big screen.

"So we broadened our search," Duane said. "Dafari contacted several Arctic research stations, hoping they might be of help. They provided wave readings that confirmed the Dragon's presence during the attack on Akutan Island. But as soon as that was over, the energy signature vanished."

"Then Duane had what you call a brainstorm," Dafari said. "Quite a brilliant one, actually."

"Why, thank you."

"Oh, it was well deserved."

"Knock it off, you two," Roxanne said, rolling her eyes. "Can we get to the point?"

Duane turned to the screen and pressed a button on

a remote control. The Dragon image faded, replaced by a video of a raging erupting volcano.

"I kept thinking of our experience inside Mount Merapi," Duane said. "Several of the readings didn't add up: timing of seismic waves, pattern of surface deformation, the levels of magmatic gas in the soil. The eruption was clearly unnatural."

"We know that," Steven said. "Beta told us. Mince triggered an artificial eruption."

"But how?" Dafari asked. "And why?"

"I needed more data," Duane said. "So I reached out to volcano observatories in Hawaii and Catania. It took us a frustratingly long time to collate the information. . . ."

Steven's eyebrows rose. Duane's "frustratingly long time" had been less than an hour.

"But eventually we found this."

Duane clicked the remote. The screen image changed to a simple map of the world, with Europe and Asia on the left and the Americas on the right. A thick line curved up and around the Pacific Ocean, starting to the right of Australia and swinging northwest toward China and the Philippines, reaching briefly over the islands of Malaysia and Indonesia. The line veered up the coast of Russia, swooping east to the Aleutian Islands and then turning to drop south down the North American west coast. It continued past the Panama Canal, all the way down past Peru and Chile to the tip of South America.

"The Ring," Duane said, "of Fire."

CHAPTER SIXTEEN

Mags, the group's caretaker/mechanic, spoke up from the computer area. "I know what that is. It's the area in the Pacific Ocean that contains most of the active volcanoes in the world."

"Yes," Duane said. "And it turns out that an alarming number of these volcanoes have recently shown signs of activity. The volcanology institutes have been keeping that information quiet—"

"In order to avoid panic," Mr. Lee said.

Malik—Ox—stood up and pushed his chair noisily under the table. Everyone turned toward him.

"Are you saying that Maxwell is triggering a massive chain of volcanic eruptions?" he asked.

"Exactly," Duane replied.

That must be hundreds of volcanoes, Steven thought, *all over the world. If they all erupt at once . . . what would happen?*

"This could lead to massive ecological disruptions, not to mention the actual fire damage from lava flows," Duane explained. "Billions would die or fall sick from the toxic gases. The sheer quantity of ash in the atmosphere would render air travel nearly impossible. Worst-case scenario: the end of the human race."

"I don't buy it," Josie said, rising to her feet. "I've worked for Maxwell. He doesn't want to kill everyone in the world. What would he gain from that?"

"Not Maxwell," Duane said, "the Dragon."

"This again?" Nicky—Dog—snorted. "Maxwell *is* the Dragon. What's the difference?"

"It's a big difference." Steven moved forward, turning to face the group. "Jasmine says the Dragon has completely taken over Maxwell's body. And the Dragon isn't human."

"It doesn't think the way we do," Duane added. "We believe it wants to wipe out all life on Earth and start over."

"Project Firebird," Kim said.

Steven nodded. "Raining fire across the land."

Billy, the team's quartermaster, gestured at the world map. "This, uh, sounds incredible," he said. "How could any entity do this? Even the Dragon? The technology required . . ."

"That's where Mount Merapi comes in." Duane turned to Steven. "Kim told me about your rescue. You had to pass through three different areas in order to reach her, correct?"

"Yeah," Steven replied. "But they weren't very dangerous, except maybe the last one. I couldn't figure it out."

"Those were not protective measures," Duane said. "At least not primarily. They were simulations."

CHAPTER SIXTEEN

"Simulations?" Steven echoed. "Of what?"

"Tectonic plates. The enormous moving rock shelves beneath the surface of the earth."

Roxanne nodded. "I thought that was a whole lot of tech just to booby-trap an underground jail."

Duane clicked again. On the big screen, a geological cutaway diagram appeared. It showed two flat layers of rock beneath the earth's surface, sliding toward each other. When they came together, one sheet of rock slipped easily past the other.

"This is called a conservative boundary," Duane explained. "Two tectonic plates passing each other without damage to either one. I assume it looks familiar."

"The first area," Steven said, "inside the volcano. The floor was made up of rocky tiles that moved like that."

"Conservative boundaries are not especially harmful. They can cause earthquakes, but that's about all. But there is another kind of tectonic plate activity . . . when the plates move *away* from each other."

Steven nodded, remembering. "The holes."

"And the third type: destructive boundaries. In this case, the plates collide and crash together. This can lead to deep trenches, subducted basins . . . and volcanic eruptions."

Steven thought of the third area, the expanse leading to Kim's cell. The grinding rock layers, magma bubbling up in the cracks between them.

"The Dragon," he whispered. "It built a little model of

the earth to work out the kinks. It was running tests . . . figuring out exactly how to manipulate the tectonic plates and trigger volcanoes."

"And Mince was its tester in chief," Kim said.

Steven's head was whirling. It all made sense. Even the inside-out map of the earth above the first chamber . . . as if a person interacting with the "tectonic plates" were looking *up* at the surface.

"Another clue," Dafari said, taking the remote from Duane, "in this video that the very gracious Mr. and Mrs. Lee provided . . ."

The screen lit up with a short clip from the Dragon's assault on Akutan Island. The Dragon swooped down out of frame, fire raging from its mouth. But Dafari froze the image, zooming in to show a column of smoke rising from the mountains behind.

"That is from Akutan Peak," he said, "one of the many newly active volcanoes along the Ring of Fire."

The screen returned to the world map. The thick line of volcanic activity seemed to press up against the continents, like a threat to their very existence.

"Kid," Malik said, staring at Duane. "Assuming this is all true . . . and I'm not convinced yet . . ."

"It's true," Duane said, a bit defensive.

". . . it still doesn't answer your first question. Why weren't you able to detect the Dragon energy?"

"That is child's play."

All eyes turned to Mr. Lee. He strode to the front of

the room as if he were conducting a board meeting, then whipped out a laser pointer and aimed it at the screen.

Steven rolled his eyes. *Does he carry that everywhere?*

The laser dot struck the map in the vicinity of New Zealand. Almost casually, Mr. Lee traced the path of the ring as it wound through the Pacific Ocean.

"Water," he said.

"That's, uh, correct." Duane looked a bit embarrassed. "Most of the volcanoes are deep underwater, often kilometers below the surface. The sheer bulk of seawater was obstructing our scans."

"I bet the Dragon planned on that, too," Liam said.

"Once we knew what we were looking for, we attacked the data from the observatories again. We compared our Dragon energy scans against lithosphere readings, subduction, oceanic-oceanic and oceanic-continental convergence studies . . ."

Steven tuned out Duane for a moment. *He'll get to the point eventually.*

". . . until we located the center of the volcanic activity."

The map zoomed up and in to an area near Japan. In the middle of the ocean, a red dot pulsed and burned.

"Tamu Massif," Duane said. "The largest volcano ever discovered."

"Actually," Dafari said, "there are larger."

"On *Mars*." Duane glared at him. "This is the cornerstone of the Dragon's plan. The large eruption that will trigger smaller ones around the world."

Kim stared at the screen, grimacing. "It looks a little harder to get to than Mount Merapi."

"It is approximately sixteen hundred kilometers off the coast of Japan and nearly two kilometers beneath the surface. The pressure at that depth is . . ."

"We get the idea," Roxanne said. "It's nasty."

"We're goin' there, aren't we?" Liam asked.

"An expedition seems inevitable," Duane agreed. "But I don't believe it will be sufficient. As Billy said, even the power of the Dragon isn't enough to pull off this level of tectonic change. Our enemy must have a huge complex of machinery somewhere, reaching deep inside the earth. All the way down to the asthenosphere."

"Well, it's not at Mount Merapi," Kim said. "That's just a pile of slag now."

"Awright," Liam said. "So where is it?"

"We have not been able to locate this complex," Dafari admitted. "Not as yet."

"It's at Lystria," Steven said.

Everyone turned to him.

"Lystria," Roxanne repeated. "The city in the desert, that Maxwell destroyed. How in the name of Jean Girard could you know that?"

"Carlos showed me," Steven said, remembering, "when I was inside his mind."

"It's possible," Duane said. "Carlos probably helped develop the Dragon's volcano technology, when he worked for Maxwell."

CHAPTER SIXTEEN

Steven nodded. It all added up . . . and yet something seemed wrong. His instincts told him something, some piece of the puzzle, was missing. Something about the Dragon . . . and Maxwell . . .

"Okay." Billy rubbed his hands together. "So we need to equip one team for an underwater mission and another for the desert. That'll strain our resources to the max."

"My husband and I can help," Mrs. Lee said. "Where is this Lystria?"

The room went silent.

"Malik," Liam said, turning to face the ex-Vanguards, "you ever been there?"

"Nope," Malik said.

"Before my time, too," Nicky said.

"Maxwell held on to that info pretty tight," Josie added.

"Carlos knows," Steven said. "He's been there. But unless Jasmine can wake him up, I don't think he'll be much help."

A murmur rose in the room. The various groups turned and began talking among themselves.

"Son," Mr. Lee said, his voice cutting through the noise. "When you were inside this gentleman's . . . *mind* . . . did you see anything specific? Features of the land, writing on buildings or documents?"

"I, I don't think so."

"Spoken languages? Star patterns in the sky?"

"Sorry, Dad. Just a lot of sand."

Mr. Lee shook his head. *Great,* Steven thought, turning away. *Everyone's looking at us. Which means everyone sees how disappointed he is with me—again.*

"We will review all the data," Duane said. "There may be something in the observatory feeds."

"I am not optimistic," Dafari said.

At the front of the room, Malik cleared his throat. As he pulled himself up to his full height, the raging Ox rose above his imposing figure. All eyes turned to him.

"Let's begin mission prep," he said, turning to Mrs. Lee. "Ma'am, you have specialized equipment that might help?"

"That's correct," she replied.

"Let's take a look. Quartermaster, please join us. Mags, can you do a full check of all air and ground vehicles?"

"Will do." Mags hesitated. "I'm not sure we have anything seaworthy."

"Let me worry about that. Let's go, people. There's plenty to . . ."

He paused, noticing Steven staring at him.

"Steven," Malik said, "this okay with you?"

Nicky and Josie joined Malik. They studied Steven, as though wondering what he'd do—whether he'd challenge their friend.

I was afraid of this, Steven thought. *These Vanguard guys . . . they're soldiers. Like Malik said, they're not used to taking orders from kids.*

"How are we going to carry out a mission," he asked, "when we don't know where we're going?"

Malik stood his ground, eyes steady. "I've got an idea about that, too."

"Steven? I must speak with you."

Steven whirled around. "Dad, I'm kind of busy here."

"This is important." Again, the look of disappointment. "You can avoid your filial obligations no longer."

"Avoi—I haven't *avoided* anything! You're the one who—Mom, tell him. . . ."

But his mother was already walking off with Malik, speaking in low tones. The others started breaking into small groups, making plans and beginning mission preparations.

Kim approached, but Steven waved her away. He wanted to scream; he wanted to smash something. But there was no time for that now.

Up on the big screen, the red dot burned like a scar in the middle of the ocean.

Dad's treating me like an infant, he thought, *and Malik's trying to take over my job.*

"Steven?"

Mr. Lee turned his back and headed toward the door. Furious, Steven clenched his fists and followed.

CHAPTER SEVENTEEN

"DAD," STEVEN BEGAN, steeling himself, "we don't have to have this conversation."

He held up his card, unlocked the door, and walked inside his room. His father followed one step behind. The older man made a quick circuit of the small room, pausing to raise an eyebrow at a shirt discarded on the floor.

"I mean it, Dad." Steven planted himself on the bed, grimacing. "I'd really rather not do the whole awkward father-son-bonding thing right now."

Mr. Lee ran a finger along a dusty mirror. "Surprisingly modest quarters," he said.

CHAPTER SEVENTEEN

"I'm trying to tell you, I understand. You had priorities growing up, important stuff. I just wasn't one of them."

Mr. Lee stopped midstride and shot his son a look. "We gave you many gifts."

Again, Steven felt the rage growing inside him. *Don't,* he told himself. *Don't lose your temper. That'll just show him he's right about you—that you're just a dumb kid!*

"Case in point," Mr. Lee added, gesturing upward.

Steven looked up. In his anger, he'd unintentionally manifested the Tiger avatar. It stared at his father, growling silently.

"If you mean the Zodiac powers," Steven said, "I'll remind you that you tricked me into receiving *that* gift."

"Do you regret it?"

"No. But it would have been nice to have a choice."

"You had a choice, not twenty-four hours ago. You risked your life to regain the power."

He's always got an answer, Steven thought. *Always a reason, a justification for whatever he wants to do.*

Mr. Lee sat down next to him on the bed—not too close, Steven noticed. The old man fidgeted.

"I understand you acquitted yourself well on that mission."

Steven looked up sharply. *Is he actually proud of me?*

No. No, don't fall into that trap. Remember: he always lets you down.

"At times, you remind me of your mother," Mr. Lee

continued. "She, too, is always dissatisfied. I expended much time and money bringing her father—your grandfather—over to the States from China. She took those efforts for granted."

"Poor Dad. Nobody appreciates you." Steven looked at his hands. "Of course, if you *hadn't* brought Grandfather over, you might have had to raise me yourself."

"He coddled you. Made you soft." Mr. Lee looked over sharply, anger in his eyes. "He indulged your fascination with American things. I recall an obsession you had with an old penny, the kind with an engraving of wheat stalks on the back. You carried it around for weeks."

"A penny? Expensive toy, Dad."

But he remembered the penny. What had the year been on it—1956? To a five-year-old immigrant boy, the wheat stalks had been a symbol of America, of the New World—a world that belonged to him, not to his parents.

"We spared no expense for you," Mr. Lee said. "And this is the result: a spoiled child. What have you accomplished with the gifts we gave you? What have you done in your life that is truly worthwhile?"

Steven stood up and stalked into a corner of the room. His father always knew how to hurt him—to reach right down and pull his son's worst fears, his greatest doubts, into the light of day.

What have *I done, really? Is all this power actually good for something?*

Or will I just be 'erased from the world'?

CHAPTER SEVENTEEN

"You wanted to show me something," he said quietly.

"Yes," Mr. Lee said. "Without your mother present."

Steven turned, his curiosity aroused. Normally his parents were inseparable.

"She is compromised in this area," Mr. Lee explained.

He touched a button on his watch. Light stabbed out from it, into the center of the room. A holographic image appeared—like the one they'd watched outside in the snow but much cruder, in lower resolution. It showed a scene from the end of the Dragon's attack on Alaska. The city lay smoking, the highway wrecked. The shadow of the Dragon's wings fell over the charred beach.

"Reruns?" Steven asked.

"Watch," his father said.

As before, the viewpoint zoomed down to pick out the local fisherman standing alone on the shore. The Dragon swooped low, facing the man directly. As it opened its mouth, fire dancing on its tongue, Mr. Lee froze the image.

"Do you see anything new?"

Steven scanned the image, walked around it. He shook his head.

"Perhaps with enhancement."

Mr. Lee manipulated the watch. The viewpoint zoomed in and panned away from the Dragon, to the back of the beach. A pile of rocks marked the land boundary—and among those rocks, a figure crouched, watching the drama. The picture was blurry, highly pixelated; Steven couldn't make out the figure.

His father tapped the watch three times in succession. The figure grew steadily sharper, resolving into a familiar shape with a sharp nose and a dark cloak.

"Rat," Steven said.

Mr. Lee nodded. "He was there."

Steven thought furiously. Next to the Dragon, Rat was the most dangerous of the Zodiacs. To him, the others were just pawns in an endless maze of schemes and double crosses. Steven had no idea where, if anywhere, Rat's true allegiances lay.

But he'd seen Rat just a few months before. With . . .

"Mom," he said. "He was working with Mom."

Mr. Lee nodded.

"Now . . ." Steven gestured at the blurry image. "Is he in league with the Dragon?"

"Possibly. Or perhaps he was spying on it. For himself or for some unknown master."

Steven nodded, his eyes wide. *The Dragon's about to destroy the world,* he thought. *Jasmine and Carlos are off the board, Malik is challenging my authority, and Dad's messing with my head as usual. Rat—he's a problem I could do without.*

"I must insist on discretion in this matter." Mr. Lee clicked off the hologram. "But I trust you to deal with the Rat if he should reappear."

Once again, the expression on Mr. Lee's face was unreadable. But for the second time, Steven allowed himself to hope his father might actually be proud of him.

CHAPTER SEVENTEEN

"There is something else," Mr. Lee said, touching the controls on his watch again.

Another image appeared in the air: a young man with a wide face, dark eyes, and close-cropped hair. He sat in an office of some kind, surrounded by computer screens. The screen images were blurry, but Steven could make out a smoking volcano and a series of wavelength patterns.

"Hello, Steven."

"Malosi." Steven swallowed. "This is, uh, a surprise."

That was an understatement. Malosi had been a soldier under Maxwell's command; in fact, Maxwell had chosen him to host the Tiger power. He'd deeply resented Steven, almost killing the boy in an attempt to grab the Tiger power for himself. Steven had convinced Malosi to turn against Maxwell—but then Malosi had gone off with his former master, vowing to do what he could to guide the Dragon onto a better path.

"Yes," Malosi said, as serious as ever. "I left Maxwell's employ weeks ago."

"Somebody make you a better offer?" Steven glanced at his father.

"Malosi," Mr. Lee said, "is able to admit his mistakes."

"You were right about Maxwell, Steven." Malosi frowned. "There's nothing left of him. It's all just this primal force, the Dragon, now."

"Okay, well, that's cool of you to say," Steven said. "And you know I love a good Tiger reunion. But are we through? 'Cause I'm really, really, *really* kind of busy right now."

Steven turned away, clenching his fists. He liked Malosi, but something about the situation was making him irrationally angry.

"Malosi has been working with our people on qi enhancement," Mr. Lee explained. "You will recall that qi was the basis for the company your mother and I founded. It allows ordinary people to enhance their gifts, granting them a much more modest version of your own Zodiac powers."

"Sure, I remember. You made a good living selling crystals to gullible rich people."

His father glared. "That is a gross mischaracterization."

"I also remember who funded most of your research: Maxwell."

"That part, sadly, is true. But we broke off all ties with Maxwell, long before the Zodiac Convergence and the assumption of your powers."

"Steven," Malosi said, "I know time is short. Your father wanted me to tell you about a weakness in the Dragon's armor."

"Sure. Awesome." Steven threw up his hands. "Fire away."

"It's Mince. The girl scientist?"

"I know who Mince is, Malosi."

"She's crucial to the tech the Dragon's using. And she's tough, vicious as a scorpion. But inside, she's just a kid."

"That's your great contribution to the fight? Mince is 'just a kid'?" Steven stared at the hologram. "How about something useful? Like where the Dragon's tech is centered?"

"I'm working on that. I'm analyzing qi levels and the volcano data, but I'm coming up empty." Malosi grimaced. "Sorry, man."

Steven turned away. When he and Malosi had met before, they'd fought like . . . well, like two Tigers. Malosi seemed much calmer now, more grown-up. That should have been a good thing; it meant Malosi was at peace with himself, and the Zodiacs had a new ally in their fight against the Dragon.

Somehow Steven found it infuriating.

"Steven." Malosi stared out of the hologram. "I know this is tough on you. I can only imagine what it's like, having to wrangle all those powered people. I'm impressed. I couldn't do it."

Steven paused, startled.

"I mean it," Malosi continued. "Nicky alone . . ."

Despite himself, Steven laughed.

"I'm glad you have the power now. I'm happier without it." Malosi paused. "I wouldn't want to have to make the choices you're facing."

"Thanks," Steven replied. "I guess."

CHAPTER SEVENTEEN

"Good luck." Something twinkled in Malosi's stoic eyes. "Tiger."

The hologram winked off. Then it was just Steven and his father again.

"Malosi had none of your advantages," Mr. Lee said. "He had no father at all. And yet look what he's accomplished."

Steven turned away. *Don't take the bait,* he thought. *Don't let him get to you.* But—

"I'm glad you found another son you like better," he said.

Mr. Lee let that hang in the air for a moment. Finally, he said, "Your own qi seems out of balance."

"Yeah, I'm a little gassy, too. I'll manage."

"Your team recently regained its powers." A strange tone entered Mr. Lee's voice. "Have you stopped to wonder why the Dragon allowed that?"

"Nobody *allowed* it." Steven turned, frowning. "We broke into the Dragon's lair and took our powers back."

"The Dragon is the most powerful entity on Earth. Do you think it couldn't have kept a bronze trinket secure if it wanted to?"

"We had the whole team." But the words sounded false, even to him.

"The Dragon doesn't care about you," Mr. Lee said. "It's so powerful—its plans are so far advanced—it doesn't believe it can be stopped. The rest of the powers, all eleven signs of the Zodiac, mean nothing to it."

Steven paused, blinking. *He's right,* he realized. *Dad,*

you've done it again. Cut through the crap and *tore me down to size, all at the same time.*

"Is the Dragon right?" he asked. "Is all this, everything we're doing—is it all for nothing?"

Mr. Lee's expression softened. "I don't know."

"You don't know." Steven stepped closer, facing his father. "All your fancy suits, your attitude, your big company. Your new-age pseudoscience, your zillion-dollar tech—you've got everything in the world and you still don't know anything."

Mr. Lee looked him in the eye. But for the first time, Steven saw him blink.

"You don't know whether we can beat the Dragon," Steven continued. "You don't know where Lystria is. Even your adopted son doesn't know—"

"Nope. But *I* do."

They both whirled around. A tall woman stood in the doorway, dressed in a skintight gray battle suit. Straight dark hair cascaded over one eye; her mouth was upturned in a smirk.

"Hey, Tiger," she said, peering inside. "Nice crib."

"Steven," Mr. Lee said, "who is this?"

Steven struggled to breathe. *If the situation was out of control before, this ought to drive it right over the cliff.*

"Dad," he said, "meet Snake."

CHAPTER EIGHTEEN

WHEN STEVEN ENTERED the two-story hangar bay, a rush of noise assaulted him. Hammers clanged, drills whirred, welding torches hissed. On the far side of the room, Malik stood with his back to Steven, supervising work on a vehicle of some kind, concealed behind a large screen.

Whatever that vehicle was, it had been crowded into a corner by the vast bulk of the Vanguard stealth jet. Snake patted the jet's door, smiling her slinky smile, clearly proud of herself.

"Thought you might want your toy back," she said.

Steven stared at the sleek gray plane. His team had stolen it from Vanguard a year before, then abandoned it after the assault on Maxwell's Australian base.

"How did you get it out of Australia?" Steven asked. "That thing was a wreck."

"You don't want to know." She rolled her eyes. "Tell you one thing, Monkey was no help."

"He's still working for Maxwell?"

"Until he dies."

"But you're not."

He tried not to make it sound like a question. But Snake raised an eyebrow. She stepped a little too close to him and looked into his eyes.

"I'm here because Malik called me," she said, "and because I agree that Maxwell has gone too far."

"We're not even, uh, sure he's Maxwell anymore."

"Whatever he is, he's got to be stopped."

Steven shifted from one foot to the other. Snake—Celine, that was her name—liked to flirt with him while reminding him constantly that he was just a kid. The combination made him nervous, a reaction that seemed to amuse her.

"I know you don't trust me. But consider this." She swept the hair from her eyes, which started to glow. The hissing Snake appeared above her head. "If I wanted to trick you—to *make* you believe me—you know I could do it."

"That's, uh, true." He looked away quickly, before her hypnotic ability could seize hold of him. Snake was only making a point, but she was one of the most powerful Zodiacs. He couldn't let himself be drawn into her games right now.

"Malik says the Dragon's tech is in Lystria," she said. "Or the hole that used to be Lystria."

"Yeah, well. *Malik* would know."

He shot a glare at Ox, on the other side of the bay.

"Can't say I'm surprised," Snake said. "From the day we carried out the Lystria op, I knew Maxwell would return there. He never wastes material."

She was there, Steven thought, *in Lystria. She participated in the slaughter, the murder of all those people. Maybe actively, maybe just by standing by. But she's the only Vanguard agent we know who worked with Maxwell back then.*

Which means she's the only one who knows where Lystria is.

"Where is it?" he asked.

"I don't think I'll tell you." She smiled. "But I'll be happy to guide an expedition there."

He stood, fuming. *This is all out of control. We're about to embark on the biggest mission of our careers, and nobody will listen to me. How can I trust these guys when—*

"Celine," Malik said, "stop playing with the boy."

He strode up and stared her right in the face. Celine touched his muscular chest playfully. "You want to make me?"

They both burst out laughing.

"I'm just messing with you, kid," Celine said. "Lystria is in Africa, just south of Egypt. I'll text you the exact coordinates."

"Stop calling me kid," he said.

"Sorry," Celine replied.

Steven turned away. *They don't respect me,* he thought. *It's just like dealing with Dad.*

"I wanted to show you something." Malik gestured toward the screen surrounding the unknown vehicle. He seemed all business again, his expression serious. Reluctantly, Steven followed him away from the stealth jet, toward the far side of the bay.

"Don't be a stranger, *kid*," Celine called. "I still owe you a drink."

Malik led the way around the wide jet. "Ignore her," he said, his voice barely audible over the sound of power tools. He pulled aside a flap in the screen and ushered Steven inside.

A group of five or six people in protective clothing swarmed around a familiar cone-shaped vehicle. They carried Plexiglas shielding and oxygen tanks, industrial piping, and searchlights. They crawled over the vehicle, welding attachments to the outside, hauling supplies and equipment inside through the small hatch.

"The drill-ship," Steven said. "That's the thing we escaped from Australia in."

"I had to pull all available staff to help. But I think we can equip it to function underwater."

Steven nodded, eyeing the oxygen tanks. "Two Vanguard vehicles to fight Vanguard," Steven said. "Good thinking."

A pair of technicians was installing a large rudder on the back of the ship. Billy entered the area with a hand truck, transporting a strange gadget. It was basically a long hose with a series of high-tech filters and an oxygen mask attached.

"That's the device Duane worked up," Steven said. "For Roxanne."

"We'll get it installed," Malik said. "Your parents have provided some useful equipment, too."

"That's them. Useful."

Malik looked over sharply at the tone in Steven's voice. When he spoke again, he seemed to choose his words carefully.

"Steven, I'd like to lead the other team. To Lystria."

Steven frowned.

"If you don't trust me," Malik continued, "I'll bring Liam along. I could use him. . . . He's good in a fight."

"Sure," Steven said. "That makes sense."

"I'd also like Duane. His power disrupts machinery. . . . He might be able to help knock out the Dragon's seismic equipment."

"No." Steven shook his head. "Duane has to stay here.

We need him to monitor the worldwide volcano situation and coordinate between the two teams."

Malik's expression grew dark. As he stared down at Steven, the faintest image of an Ox appeared above his head. "I really think—"

"Are you telling me that a squadron of ex-Vanguard agents can't manage to smash a couple machines? With the toughest member of *my* team along to help?"

A piercing whine cut through the air. Steven looked over to see a large drill boring into the side of the ship. Two technicians stood by with a missile launcher, preparing to mount it on the outer hull.

"We can smash the machines," Malik said.

"Good," Steven replied. "Just get this ship ready."

He turned and strode away, not wanting to see Malik's expression.

"It's worse than I thought," Duane said. "The seismic activity is increasing. Japan just experienced an enormous earthquake . . . and there's an even bigger one happening right now, in central Chile."

Duane gestured at the big wall screen in the war room. Steven looked up just as a news headline flashed onto the screen: CRISIS IN SANTIAGO, SURROUNDING AREAS. The screen was muted, but a grim-faced anchorwoman stood before a grainy film clip of buildings collapsing and people running for their lives.

CHAPTER EIGHTEEN

Duane sat at the main computer console, taking in information from a dozen screens: seismic levels, casualties, tomographic images, reports of volcanic activity, fluid analyses from the volcano observatories. Steven leaned in close to him and spoke in a quiet voice, too low for the technicians around them to hear.

"Have you reviewed my plan?"

A look of panic crossed Duane's face. "Yes," he said quietly.

"Well?"

"It's very risky. I—I cannot endorse it."

"You don't have to endorse it. Just don't tell anyone else." He stood up straight and spoke in a normal voice. "Break it down for me? The Dragon situation, I mean."

Duane grimaced and turned back to his screens. As his head swiveled back and forth, the glowing Pig appeared above him.

"It all comes down to Tamu Massif," he said, pointing at a blurry image of an underwater volcano. "Once that blows, the chain reaction will be irreversible."

"And when is that going to happen?"

"Four hours." A nervous edge crept into Duane's voice. "Maybe five."

Four hours, Steven thought. *That's not a lot of time.*

They looked up at a clanking sound. Roxanne and Josie clomped toward them in heavy diving equipment, holding round helmets. Roxanne jostled a technician at his station and hurriedly apologized.

Duane tensed at the sight of them. Steven leaned in and whispered in his ear: "Remember. Don't tell *anyone.*"

Roxanne elbowed Josie playfully. "The Horse here has been teaching me the basics of deep-sea diving."

"Best I could do on dry land, anyway," Josie said. "I hope we won't have to use these suits much."

Steven nodded. Whatever had happened between Roxanne and Josie, they seemed to have patched up their differences. He hoped Josie could keep it together in the field.

"So it's just the three of us on the deep-sea team?" Roxanne asked.

"I hope Kim can come, too," Steven said. "But it's up to her . . . depends on her parents. And we're running out of time."

"I should go along," Duane protested.

"No," Steven replied. "We need you here, coordinating from the Infosphere. You're the center of this whole operation."

Suddenly, Steven realized: *I do know this team. I know who I need in the field, and who works better behind the scenes. I know who to risk and who to keep safe.*

No matter what Malik, or Dad, or anyone else thinks: I know what I'm doing.

"Any change in Carlos's condition?" Roxanne asked. "Or Jasmine's?"

Steven shook his head.

CHAPTER EIGHTEEN

"Um," Josie said, pointing at the volcano image on the screen. "What are we gonna find down there, anyway? At the bottom of the ocean?"

All eyes turned to Duane. He gave Steven a nervous glance. "I wish I knew."

"Hey."

Steven looked up. Kim stood before them, flanked by her parents. Her mother looked anxious; her father's expression was distant, vague. Kim hadn't *poofed* in as usual, Steven realized. The three of them had crept quietly into the bustling war room.

"Kim," he said. "No pressure, but . . . we could use your help."

Kim turned worried eyes to her father. He opened his mouth and started to speak, then seemed to seize up. Kim's mother took his hand, and he squeezed hers back. He grimaced, furrowed his brow, and with obvious effort turned to face Steven and the others.

"T-take care of our girl," he said.

"Absolutely not, Mom. No way."

"With respect, Steven: you do not tell us where to go. Or where not to go."

"When it's a Zodiac mission, you *bet* I do."

He strode down the corridor, picking up his pace. Mrs. Lee matched his every stride without visible effort.

Technicians bustled past, carrying supplies and equipment toward the hangar bay on the upper two levels. The entire base bristled with activity.

"Besides," he continued, "if I have to spend any more time with Dad, I won't be responsible for what happens."

"Hyperbole ill suits you," his mother snapped. "You know your father cares for you deeply."

"He doesn't respect me."

"All this is irrelevant. I am your mother. I helped you against the Dragon before, and now you must trust me—trust *us*—to help you again."

Steven stopped short. A terrible memory rose to the surface of his mind: his parents lying dead beneath the talons of the Dragon.

"You are *not* coming on the drill-ship, Mom," he said. "My team has Zodiac powers; you don't."

"As I have said repeatedly," she replied, "we have equipment that may prove useful against the Dragon."

"I'm happy to take the *equipment*—"

"We know how to use it better than—"

"I DON'T WANT YOU TO GET HURT!"

She stepped back as if he'd struck her. Trembling, she raised a hand to adjust the lapels of her suit.

"That never occurred to me," she whispered.

They stood for a moment, looking away from each other. Two grunting technicians pushed past them, lugging a heavy deep-sea buoy.

"Steven," his mother said, "the stakes here include the

survival of the human race. None of us can afford to risk that effort for the sake of one or two others. No matter how much we . . ."

She reached out as if to touch his cheek. But she lowered her hand quickly.

"We have not always been model parents." Her voice cracked slightly. "But your father is not as cold as he pretends to be."

She fished in her pocket and pulled out a tiny round object. She grabbed his arm, twisted his palm upward, and dropped the object into his hand. He looked down at a small copper disk, engraved with an image of wheat stalks.

"The 1956 penny." He looked up at her. "You kept it?"

"No. He did."

Steven blinked.

This time she did touch his cheek. Her eyes were hard as always, but there was something else behind them, some hidden reserve of emotion.

"Sometimes things are not exactly as we remember them," she said.

Then she turned and walked away.

He stood in the hallway for a long moment, turning the penny around and around, holding it up to the light. Finally, he noticed the date: 1957.

The lights had been turned down in the medical bay. Carlos lay as still as ever; he hadn't moved a muscle. A second bed had been pulled up next to his, for Jasmine. They looked like a couple who'd decided to sleep in twin beds . . . except for the maze of tubes and IV equipment taped to their motionless bodies.

"Carlos," Steven said. "Where are you right now? What are you doing?"

Carlos didn't move. A series of evenly spaced beeps issued from a machine on the table next to him. It was the only sound in the room.

"You might be able to help us with the Dragon's tech," Steven continued. "You probably helped him build it. But you're so . . . so far away."

More beeping.

"You told me about Lystria, though. That was pretty huge."

He walked around to stare at Jasmine. Her eyes were closed, her expression completely blank.

"And you," he said. "You've been a pain in my butt a lot of times. But I'm about to lead the team on our biggest mission ever. I don't know if they'll all follow my orders. I don't even know if I can trust everyone."

He took her hand. It felt warm but hung limp.

"And I . . . I just really wish you were here to help me through this."

Loud footsteps sounded behind him. Steven dropped Jasmine's hand and turned to see Malik lumbering toward him. *Great,* he thought. *Can't I even get a minute's peace without this big Ox getting up in my—*

"I wanted to apologize," Malik said.

"Oh."

"Someone has to be in command," Malik continued. "Right now it's you. I didn't respect that, and I'm sorry."

Steven looked at him, wary. "Can you take orders from a kid?"

"I don't love it, but I can do it." Malik looked straight at him, very serious. "I'm not sure if the whole pack of us can last a minute against the unleashed power of the Dragon. But I do know we *can't* if you're worried the whole time about a bunch of Maxwell's ex-soldiers running rogue on you."

Steven nodded.

"This is bigger than all of us," Malik said. "I just want you to know: we're with you."

He reached out a thick hand. When they shook, it felt like a solemn vow.

Malik gestured at Jasmine and Carlos. "No change?"

Steven shook his head.

Somewhere deep inside him, the Tiger roared. Steven raised himself up to his full height, turned away from his unconscious friends, and faced Malik directly.

"Come on," Steven said. "Let's go save the world."

LIVE

PART THREE
THE DESCENT

CHAPTER NINETEEN

"OH, JASMINE. You're not getting it. You're *really* not getting it."

Jasmine winced at the voice. She'd been walking for a very long time, across the endless sand. She wasn't hungry; she wasn't tired. She wasn't even hot. There inside the mindscape, she felt alone, detached from everything.

And yet she wasn't really alone. The sun shone bright in the sky, but it wasn't a sun. It was Maxwell's face.

"At this rate," Maxwell continued, "you'll be wandering in the desert forever."

She closed her eyes—which weren't actually eyes, she remembered; nothing in that place was real. She pictured Carlos lying helpless on his bed, and for a moment she couldn't tell whether that was happening now or in the past. Time seemed to be converging, past and present and future all jumbled into a stew of madness.

She had no idea how long she'd been in the mindscape. At first, when Steven had disappeared, she'd felt the others trying to pull her out. Trying to save her. *But I don't want to be saved,* she realized. *I need to be in here. I can't leave yet.*

I just don't know why.

An audible sigh from the Maxwell sun snapped her back to reality. Well, to unreality. Sand stretched all around, uninterrupted and unblemished, to a horizon she couldn't even see.

"Be smart," Maxwell said. "Accept my guidance."

"I've had enough *guidance* from you to last a lifetime." She glared up at the face in the sky. "Do you want me to work for you again? To study your teachings?"

"I want you to study yourself." He raised an eyebrow. "To *unburden* yourself."

"What the devil does that—"

A strong arm clamped across her windpipe, yanking her backward. Another arm, pale and thin, appeared before her eyes. The hand bore a multifinger ring reading LIVE.

"Lucky I'm left-handed," Mince said.

Jasmine let out a strangled cry. She could hardly

breathe. Her face hurt, too: a series of sharp pains, across her cheeks and nose.

I'm back in the volcano, she realized. *The moment when Mince scratched me with her poison rings and threatened my life.*

Roxanne lay unconscious on the floor of the corridor. Duane stood facing Jasmine, his expression anxious and unsure. As Jasmine watched, his face slowly transformed into Maxwell's grim visage.

"Oh." Maxwell looked around at the smooth white walls. "The volcano tech. I initiated that project, you know."

"Y-yeah?"

"It's a potent use of the Dragon's power. Ultimately, I deemed it too dangerous."

Too dangerous? Jasmine struggled, but Mince's grip held her tight. *What's going on here? Who—or what—is this manifestation of Maxwell, really?*

Mince's arm tightened against her throat. "Don't you *dare* pity me," the girl hissed.

Duane/Maxwell shook his head, disgusted. "Not good enough," he said. "You have to go further back."

Further back.

She closed her eyes, Maxwell's words echoing in her brain. Maxwell was an enigma. He seemed to be guiding her through her own history.

Is Maxwell a projection of Carlos's mind, here in the mindscape? Or is it my own unconscious mind? Am I just talking to myself?

CHAPTER NINETEEN

Or is he something else?

The pressure on her windpipe eased; the pain in her cheeks vanished. Stale air gave way to rushing wind and the sounds of battle.

She was running. Her boots tapped out a rhythm on the artificial surface beneath her feet. A small wooden shack loomed ahead; it was the only structure around.

The ground lurched beneath her.

I'm on the platform, she realized. *This happened two months ago, in Australia. Maxwell built this artificial disk and levitated it, then stole all our powers while we were trapped up here.*

She struggled to think. *I was trying to rescue the others, who were held captive inside the shack. And Steven—*

A flare of Zodiac energy filled the sky. She whirled around to see Steven and Malosi—the other Tiger—grappling with Maxwell across the platform. It was no contest. Steven and Malosi were powerless; Maxwell glowed with energy, the Zodiac power raging all around him. The *jiānyù*, the sphere containing the stolen Zodiac powers, hovered in the air near Maxwell's blazing figure, feeding him strength.

Steven lunged toward Maxwell—and froze in midair. Malosi stopped, too, his fist raised. They didn't move; they didn't even breathe. They seemed suspended in time.

The energy around Maxwell calmed. He glanced at the *jiānyù*, glowing and pulsing in the air beside him. Then he turned to Jasmine with a condescending smile.

"Well?" he asked. "Do you know what comes next?"

"I break into the shack," she said, gesturing, "and free the others. Duane, Roxanne, Liam, and Malik."

"No. Not yet."

Maxwell closed his eyes. The energy flared back to life around him; his eyes grew blank, his expression inhuman. The *jiānyù* rose higher, flaring with power.

Steven and Malosi snapped back to life. Maxwell repelled Steven's attack with a casual, savage blast of Dragon energy. Without even looking around, Maxwell grabbed Malosi by the throat and threw him to the ground.

"This is the moment," Maxwell snapped, turning to face Jasmine. "As they fell, I turned and called out to you. Do you remember?"

She stared at him. He hovered, glowing bright, above the fallen Tigers. His features, his arms and legs, were almost lost in that white glow. And there was something in his eyes. Something she hadn't seen before.

Fear.

"You called out," she repeated. "But not aloud."

"No. Through the Dragon link." His voice was urgent, even desperate. "Do you remember what I said?"

His radiance was blinding now. She raised a hand to shield her eyes.

"Yes," she replied. "You said . . . you said . . ."

He flashed white-hot, like a sun. Jasmine screamed, flinched, and dropped to her knees. She turned away—but Maxwell was still there. His face filled her mind, her thoughts, her senses. She could feel his darkness, his arrogance, the overwhelming force of his presence.

"You said, 'You were right,'" she finished.

The world seemed to explode. For a terrible moment, Jasmine remembered her time as the Dragon—the supreme, almost overwhelming power. The Dragon was greater than her, greater than Maxwell, greater than any of them. She could feel it in her hands, in her heart: the power of life and death, the ability to alter a person's mind or snuff out his breath with barely a thought.

She found herself lying in the sand, back in the desert. She spat, coughed, and struggled to sit up. A thick hand reached down, offering assistance.

Maxwell stood over her. He wasn't a sun or a god anymore, just a man in a soldier's uniform. Reluctantly, she took his hand and rose to her feet.

And then she knew.

"You're not in Carlos's mind," she said. "You're in *mine*."

Maxwell nodded. "Very good."

"That moment, up on the platform." She struggled to put the pieces together. "I saw what was happening to you. The Dragon . . ."

"I made the mistake of allowing it to draw on the other Zodiac signs," Maxwell said. "The result was staggering, overwhelming. I realized for the first time that I was in danger of losing myself . . . of being subsumed by the Dragon's godlike consciousness."

"And that's exactly what happened."

"Not quite." Maxwell smiled his arrogant smile. "You and I, Jasmine . . . we have shared a link, played our tug-of-war over the power that is our birthright. With or without that power, we are still Dragons. In my moment of crisis, I reached out to you."

"You . . . you transferred your consciousness into my brain." She reeled, coming to grips with the idea. "You've been *living* there ever since?"

"Under the surface. Deep within your subconscious mind." Maxwell shrugged. "It seemed a good place to hide."

"They all said I was acting strangely." She looked at him, horror and discovery warring in her mind. "In the volcano . . . I knew which corridors to take. That was you?"

"I built that installation—the least I could do was give you a little help. I did the same for Steven, when I showed him the image of Lystria."

"Help?" She shook her head. "Against what? The Dragon?"

"The Dragon is my problem to solve. Only I can control its power."

"You just said you *couldn't* control it!"

"You of all people should know, Jasmine: I learn from my mistakes."

"I know one thing. I've heard *that* before."

She strode away, across the burning sand. It all made sense. For weeks she'd felt burdened, as if she were carrying some terrible weight on her back. Now she knew: *It's my greatest enemy.*

She turned to see Maxwell holding out a hand to her.

"Jasmine," he said, "the Dragon's plans are not mine. It seeks the destruction of human civilization, the termination of all life not under its direct command."

She frowned.

"However," Maxwell continued, "once again, *you were right.* I cannot stop it alone."

"You want to help us?"

"Your teams are already en route to the Dragon's twin centers of power. I tell you this, as certainly as I know the Dragon: unaided, they will fall."

She straightened up and brushed sand off her leggings. *Imaginary sand,* she reminded herself.

"I don't have the power anymore," she said. "Neither do you."

"But I *can* help."

They stood together, staring at each other. *Two minds,* she thought, *facing off inside a single brain. When this is over, I'm gonna have the biggest headache in human history.*

If there's a human history left.

"All right," she said. "Let's go."

"Not yet."

She darted a look at him. *Another plot,* she thought. *Another angle. With Maxwell, nothing is easy.*

He waved his hand. The desert remained this time, but

the air between them wavered and shifted, resolving into the form of Carlos's hospital bed. He lay unmoving, eyes closed, IVs and breathing tubes reaching from his arm and nostrils to a small machine on a nearby table. He looked frail, thin, barely alive.

Jasmine turned away.

"Ah," Maxwell said. "I didn't mean to upset you. Although what you're feeling now is nothing, compared to what's coming."

She stared at the sand.

"Carlos knows more about the Zodiac powers than anyone alive," Maxwell continued. "If we're to defeat the Dragon—lock it back up in its box, once and for all—we must have his help."

"You mean we have to undo the damage *you* did to his mind."

"I admit it. Freely." Maxwell frowned. "When I held the power, there were times I used it unwisely."

"But now you can *control* it."

"Someone must." His eyes narrowed. "I am prepared to make the sacrifice."

She snorted.

"Whatever you think of me, you know I'm right." He gestured at Carlos's unmoving form. "And I know *you* would do anything for him."

Jasmine walked up to Carlos. She reached out a hand and touched his cheek. It was cold.

"What do I do?" she asked.

Maxwell took her by the arm and twisted her away from Carlos's bed. She turned, startled, and looked into Maxwell's hard eyes.

"You are not unburdened," he said. "Not yet."

She swallowed. "I don't know what you mean."

"Then this is not finished."

She tried to turn her head, to look away from his piercing eyes. But she couldn't. *He knows me,* she thought. *He knows what's inside my mind, because he's been living there for weeks. He sees the things I've forgotten, the terrors I've tried to forget.*

Horrified, she realized: *He knows my secrets.*

Once again, the world exploded into light.

CHAPTER TWENTY

THE DRILL-SHIP NOSED its way down: fifteen, sixteen, seventeen hundred meters below the surface. At first, gentle light suffused the green water, illuminating schools of fish and the occasional huge lumbering whale. Then, gradually, darkness engulfed the small craft. By the time it approached the bottom—nearly two thousand meters down—the only light came from a pair of searchlights mounted on the ship's side, sweeping across the rocky seabed.

Without those lights, Roxanne thought, *we'd be blind.*

CHAPTER TWENTY

Kim leaned over Roxanne's shoulder, eyes wide. They sat wedged in a corner of the cramped cockpit, their pressure suits crowding them even more than usual. They stared at a holographic schematic of the Shatsky Rise, the complex of underwater volcanoes spread out below the ship. The low rocky mountains stretched for hundreds of kilometers, paralleling the islands of Japan to the west.

"Is that all Tamu Massif?" Roxanne asked.

"No, just this part." Kim pointed to a large mound at the southern end of the rise. "But all by itself, it's as big as Arizona." She smiled at Roxanne.

Roxanne had been worried about this trip. She wasn't sure if she liked having her powers back; they'd caused her a lot of trouble, made her personal life extremely difficult. But she had to admit it felt good being on a mission again with her old friends—and one new one: Josie, who sat in the pilot's seat, driving the ship.

Steven brushed past in his bulky suit, elbowing Roxanne from the back. "Dude," she said, "excuse me maybe?"

He stopped in his tracks. "Sorry," he said. He seemed confused, distracted.

"Lot more crowded in here than we're used to," Kim said. "Especially in this gear." She lifted her arm, indicating the heavy sleeve covering it.

"Pressure's almost two hundred atmospheres," Josie said. "If this hull springs a leak, you'll be glad for those suits."

CHAPTER TWENTY

Roxanne stood up, stretching her cramped legs, and walked a meter or so to the pilot's chair. "I thought Vanguard built their ships to last," she said.

Josie snorted. "You willing to bet your life on that?"

As if in answer, a tremor ran through the ship. The hull creaked. The water all around churned, bubbles rising in the black water outside the viewport.

"Non," Roxanne whispered.

She turned at the sound of raised voices. Steven stood in the far corner, arguing with his parents. Roxanne wasn't sure why the Lees were there, but they'd insisted on going along. The cockpit was barely large enough for its six passengers. It didn't even have a real door, just a hatch mounted a meter up on the back wall.

"Approaching Tamu Massif." Josie frowned, working the controls. "Let me see if I can get us a visual. . . ."

A hologram rose from the small pilot's station. The ship's searchlights played back and forth along the seabed, illuminating the huge volcano. Tamu Massif stretched along the bed, rising gradually to a height of a thousand meters, then dropping off sharply. From the summit, a thin column of dark smoke rose into the swirling water.

Roxanne pointed at the smoke. "Didn't Duane say this volcano was inactive?"

"It was yesterday." Josie hissed in a breath. "I don't like this."

"It's just a little smoke."

"Not that. Well, partly that." Josie grimaced as the ship shook again. "We're approaching a suddenly active volcano, in an area plagued by tremors, in a small ship loaded with explosives. Does any of that sound like a good idea?"

"Duane said the water would help shield us from any eruptions. And, uh, explosions."

"I guess that depends how close we get. Anyway, Duane's not here, is he?"

Roxanne shook her head. At that depth, they were cut off from all communications. They'd left a remote buoy on the surface to gather readings: seismic tomography, surface deformations, Zodiac energy levels, magnetic anomalies. These would be transmitted back to headquarters, where Duane could analyze them and decide how to proceed. With luck, it would give the team a more complete picture of the Dragon's plans.

But down there in the drill-ship, they were on their own.

"You're just itchy for a fight," Roxanne said, giving Josie a playful jab on the arm. "Aren't you?"

CHAPTER TWENTY

A dangerous look crept into Josie's eyes. "I could punch something."

Then they both laughed. "Careful what you wish for," Roxanne said.

"We're two hundred meters above the summit." Josie checked a readout. "Steven? We're close enough to launch the charges now."

No answer. Roxanne turned to see Steven engaged in a tense conversation with his parents.

"Steven?"

He turned and blinked. "Right. Yes, definitely, fire the charges."

Josie shrugged. "Bombs away."

The drill-ship's searchlights narrowed, zeroing in on the lower slope of the volcano. The rocket launchers mounted on the outer hull swiveled downward, then fired. A thin missile sliced through the water, toward the area where the twin beams swooped and wavered. A school of tiny fish veered to avoid the intruder in their dark realm.

The missile struck the surface, its nose burrowing into the sodden rock. As it came to a stop, three arms swung out from hinges, forming a tripod holding the central shaft in place.

Inside the ship, Josie nodded at the holographic display. "Charge one implanted," she said. "Moving into new position along the summit now. Preparing to fire charge two."

Roxanne gave her an encouraging pat on the shoulder,

then turned toward the back of the cockpit. Kim stood with Steven and his parents, staring at a shining object in his hand. It was about the size of a lipstick tube but studded with high-tech circuitry.

"What is that?" Roxanne asked.

Mr. Lee frowned at her. "It may be difficult for you to comprehend."

Roxanne rolled her eyes. "Condescending much?"

"It is a qi disruptor," Mrs. Lee said. "A product of our company's research."

"Qi disruptor?" Steven held the object up to the artificial light, turning it around. "In Australia, you gave me a qi *amplifier*. . . ."

"This is basically the opposite principle." Mrs. Lee shrugged. "Should you encounter the Dragon, it may disrupt the entity's power for a moment."

"Disrupt the Dragon? Have you *met* the Dragon?" Kim looked incredulous. "The most powerful creature on Earth?"

"It *may* disrupt the entity," Mrs. Lee repeated, "for a moment. Possibly."

"We developed much of our company's technology under Maxwell's patronage," Mr. Lee said. "However, we managed to conceal several of our most significant achievements from him."

Steven stared at the disruptor, then shook his head. Almost absentmindedly, he stuffed it in his pocket.

Roxanne touched his arm. "Boss? You okay?"

"Rox!" Josie called. "You're up."

Roxanne cast a worried glance at Steven. He waved her toward the side of the cockpit. She walked over and touched a newly installed panel mounted on the wall. Kim followed.

The panel slid aside to reveal Duane's latest gadget. It didn't look like much: just an oxygen mask reinforced with leather straps, hooked up to a thick cable leading into the wall. Roxanne took the mask in her hands and hesitated.

Kim looked up at her. "You got this," she said.

Roxanne nodded. She fitted the mask onto her face and snapped the fasteners tight. The mask formed a complete seal around her mouth.

"Veering back into position over the first charge," Josie said. "You ready?"

Roxanne nodded. "But I fveel vidicuvous."

"What?"

She waved her hand, dismissing the question.

"Everyone grab your helmets," Josie said. "Just in case."

Roxanne closed her eyes and concentrated. She willed herself to block out the noise of the engines, the creaking of the hull, the chatter of her teammates. She focused on one thing: the Rooster energy. It billowed and grew, building all around her, shrieking with power.

Josie's voice seemed very distant. "Fire."

Roxanne screamed. The Rooster crowed. The oxygen

mask shook and bulged, but the straps held it tight to Roxanne's face. Zodiac energy flared bright, contained and channeled into the cable leading into the wall.

Before the mission, Steven had told her: *You're the only one who can do this. With Jasmine out of action, we're low on long-range powers.*

We need the Rooster!

She screamed harder. Power blasted into the depths of the ship, amplified by a dish-shaped emitter mounted on the hull. When the energy reached a critical level, the emitter flashed and fired the sonic beam, forcing it through the water toward the volcano below.

The sonic energy struck the first charge, affixed to the silty volcano by its tripod legs. The missile trembled, caught fire, and exploded.

The ship lurched violently. Roxanne stumbled into the wall, banging her head. "Ouchf," she said, the mask still muffling her words.

Mr. and Mrs. Lee approached the pilot's seat. In the holographic display, dirt billowed up, spinning and spiraling into the water. It looked like a special effect, a slow-motion capture of an explosion.

"Direct hit," Josie said, struggling with the controls. "Oh. Oh, come on, baby. Hold steady for me now."

Roxanne wrenched off the mask and sucked in a breath. "Why," she gasped, "why are we doing this again?"

"Duane said something about measuring the seismic waves," Kim said, moving up to join the Lees.

"Yes," Mrs. Lee explained. "We are hoping to determine the severity of the Dragon's coming apocalypse."

"By setting off more explosions of our own?" Roxanne shook her head. "Who came up with this plan? Some American politician?"

"It is a common technique employed by seismologists," Mr. Lee snapped. "Even now, the ship's sensors are accumulating data for later analysis."

The ship lurched again, tipping forty-five degrees to the side. Josie swore and pulled up on the control stick.

"If there is a later," Kim whispered.

"Of course," Josie said, "if the explosives damage any of the Dragon's tech, that'll be a nice bonus."

"We haven't even *seen* the Dragon yet," Roxanne protested. "How do we know—"

"Debate later. We're above the second charge."

Roxanne grimaced, cleared her throat, and donned the mask.

Once again, the Zodiac energy flowed through her, blasting out from the ship at a point near the volcano's summit. This time she felt more confident, more finely attuned to the machinery within the ship. She knew exactly how much power to draw on and how to maintain a steady flow for exactly the right length of time.

As she felt the power—as the Rooster flowed through her, shrieking and crowing—all Roxanne's doubts faded away. *This,* she realized, *is what I was born to do. This is who I am.*

After all my misgivings, all the times I've tried to run away . . . I guess I'm a Zodiac.

The second charge exploded, high on the volcano's peak. Another shock wave struck the ship, much closer and stronger this time. The vessel rolled up through the water, briefly turning completely upside down.

"Hang on!" Josie yelled.

Kim slammed into Roxanne. The Lees shot up toward the ceiling—except it wasn't really up, Roxanne realized. The ship was turning again, slowly righting itself.

Mr. and Mrs. Lee landed on the floor with a thud. Mrs. Lee picked up her helmet and motioned for her husband to do the same.

"We're okay," Josie said. "Hull integrity is holding. Moving into position now for third detonation. . . ."

"Look," Kim said.

Roxanne yanked off the mask and rose to her feet, following Kim's pointing finger. The hologram showed the volcano, with two blast points marring its surface. The second explosion had cleared away an area of rock, leaving a flat crater halfway up the gradual slope.

"That's a caldera," Kim said, "a kind of crater formed by an ancient eruption. It must have been covered up by centuries of sediment."

Roxanne nodded. "It might be a way inside."

"Inside to what?" Josie asked.

Mrs. Lee stared intensely at the crater. "To whatever the Dragon is doing in there," she said.

CHAPTER TWENTY

"That smoke seems to be getting thicker, too," Roxanne said.

"Hey," Kim said. "Where's Steven?"

They all looked up. Roxanne cast her eyes around the small cockpit, across the pilot's chair, the Zodiac amplification mask, the smaller hologram stage in back. Steven was no longer in the vessel.

Three holograms flared to life all at once: the small one in the corner, the larger display at the pilot's station, and a third one against the back wall. They all showed Steven's face.

"Um," Steven's image said, his voice echoing in triplicate. "So."

His eyes, Roxanne thought. *I've never seen him look so grim.*

"I'm recording this before we take off," he said, "because this mission—well, there's a part of it you guys weren't told about."

Mrs. Lee moved close to her husband, staring at the hologram. Her mouth silently formed the word *son.* Mr. Lee turned to her and whispered a few words in her ear.

"I'm sorry I had to lie to you," the recording continued. "But I knew you'd never go along with this. . . ."

"Hey," Josie said, an edge of panic in her voice. Roxanne turned to look. From the viewport in front of the pilot's chair, a bright light shone in through the darkness.

"Where's that coming from?" Kim asked. "Is there something else down here?"

"Shut off that hologram and bring up an external

view," Roxanne snapped. "We've gotta see what's happening outside."

"No matter what happens," Steven was saying, "you must continue setting off the charges. . . ."

"But he's telling us something important," Kim said.

"We'll hear it later!"

Steven's image froze midsyllable and flickered off, replaced by an external camera view of the seabed. The volcano seemed angrier, pockmarked and smoking—and a bright glow suffused the entire area. It seemed to radiate from *inside* the mountain, filling the ebon-black void with a godlike radiance.

Roxanne recognized it immediately. "Dragon energy," she breathed.

"Look!" Josie said.

Roxanne peered at the hologram. Above the volcano, tiny against its unearthly glow, a small pressure-suited figure swam through the churning water. It moved like an arrow, speeding straight toward the exposed caldera on the mountain's surface.

Roxanne shook her head in disbelief. "Steven Lee," she said. "Are you *insane*?"

Am I insane?

Steven shot through the darkness, angling downward. He swam furiously, sucking in deep, regular breaths from his oxygen tank. Even with the Tiger's enhanced senses, he could barely make out the shape of the smoking mountain below.

It's so huge, he thought. *I can't see the far side of it.*

Tiny spotlights from the drill-ship above fanned across the seabed, illuminating the volcano's vast expanse. At its peak, a thin column of smoke hissed upward into the water.

He felt a jolt of panic. *This is the only way,* he told himself. *I have to do this. No matter what happens to me.*

The drill-ship's lights swung away, leaving him in blackness. Immediately, the voices rose in his mind: the Tigers, the Zodiac users from times past. *They've always been with me,* he realized. *I just got better at tuning them out.*

The darkness was complete. Ghostly faces appeared, just as they had inside Mount Merapi. A slim man in elegant robes. A farmer with tired eyes. An old woman with teeth filed into sharp fangs.

"The choice," the Tigers said. "The choice is coming."

Steven tried to speak, then remembered the breather in his mouth. *No,* he thought.

"You cannot avoid it."

I won't do it. I won't make that choice.

"We warned you," they said. "You refused to listen."

I can do this. I can save them all. My friends, my parents . . . all of them.

He looked down, reaching out with his Tiger sense.

He could barely make out the mountain as it drew closer, its gradual slope flattening out near the top. He kicked, aiming at the flat area unearthed by one of the explosions.

The caldera, he remembered. He studied it, searching for a way inside the mountain.

He felt cold, numb. *I'm probably not coming back from this. I knew that the minute I swam through the hatch. But we can't trust the missiles to finish off the Dragon's machinery—and I can't risk anyone else's life on this. Not my team, not Malik's team, not my parents.*

It's up to me. I've got to break the cycle.

All at once, a bright glow flared up from the mountain. Darkness turned to light; the Tigers retreated inside Steven's mind. A swarm of eels twirled away, frightened by the sudden radiance.

Above Steven's head, the Tiger flashed to life. It roared silently, raging in protest at the hostile environment. It turned its head to snarl down at the vast, smoking volcano.

It knows, he thought. *It knows we're going to fight the Dragon.*

He looked down, shielding his eyes as his vision adjusted. The volcano spread out below, hundreds of kilometers wide. There was no doubt; he'd seen that glow before. It was the Dragon.

We have to do this, he told the protesting Tiger. *We're the only ones who can. It's crazy. It might be our last battle. But there's no choice.*

The Tiger, he realized, wasn't listening. Its senses

tingled in alarm. Frowning, following some strange instinct, Steven turned to look upward.

The drill-ship was a tiny oval in the distance, its spotlights visible as two dots along the hull. Below it, two small figures in pressure suits moved swiftly through the churning water. Even before they drew close enough to make out clearly, Steven knew who they were.

Mom and Dad.

No, he thought. *Not them. I won't risk their lives. That's the whole point of this. Dammit, Dad!*

He closed his eyes—and saw the wheel, the circular representation of the twelve Zodiac symbols. The wheel began to spin, just as it had done inside Carlos's mind. It moved faster and faster, the images along the edges blurring.

It's all spinning out of control, he thought. Again he heard the words of the ancient Tigers: *None among us may escape this destiny.*

He opened his eyes. His parents were closer now, moving straight toward him. Mr. Lee's expression was grim as always. Mrs. Lee's eyes were wide above the breather in her mouth.

He wanted to scream at them. *Why? Why are you doing this?* But at that depth, his radio wouldn't function. All he could do was watch them approach.

The Tiger roared in Steven's mind, an edge of panic in its voice. *It feels caught,* he realized. *Like it's being drawn into an inescapable trap, a web of destiny. A cage.*

Steven twisted and kicked hard, bringing himself to a near stop. The caldera lay directly below. In the eerie Dragon-glow, he could make out a small opening in its rocky surface.

Mr. and Mrs. Lee drew up beside him. They didn't speak; they couldn't speak. They just stared at him. Then his mother lowered her eyes, jerking her head in a downward motion.

Steven looked down again at the volcano, at the smoke hissing up into the water. *There's no choice now,* he realized. *No escape.*

Maybe there never was.

He swept his arm around and pointed down at the caldera. Then he kicked hard and resumed swimming toward the opening. He didn't look back.

His parents exchanged dour looks, then turned to follow.

CHAPTER TWENTY-ONE

THE STEALTH PLANE rocketed through the air, flying low above the vast desert. Its engines purred along, whisper quiet; specially built dampers kept it hidden from infrared and radar scans.

"Slowing to three hundred fifty kph," Malik said, pulling up on the stick. "All systems normal."

In the copilot's seat, Liam studied the radar screen. It showed no blips, barely any blemishes on the flat landscape. The desert, less than thirty meters below, was almost featureless.

"Snake?" he asked. "You sure this disaster site is out here?"

Before he could turn, Snake was at his shoulder. She was quiet and slinky, and she seemed to enjoy unnerving the members of Steven's team.

"Trust me, little Ram." She laughed. "Just a bit farther."

"Trusting you ain't my first instinct," he said, an edge creeping into his voice.

"If you want, I could convince you."

Her eyes glowed green. The outline of a hissing snake appeared over her head.

"Knock it off," he said, "before I head-butt ye out the hatch."

Malik cleared his throat. "Play nice, you two."

Nicky, the fourth member of the team, crossed the large cockpit to join them. He was in human form; his only yellow fur was the hair on his head. But even so, his power made him a strong, imposing figure. When he clapped Liam on the back, the Irishman lurched forward in his seat.

"You glad t'be back with the *team*, Rammer?" Nicky laughed. "Bet this ain't the group you thought you'd be fighting with."

Liam shot him a glare and turned away. Nicky was right. When he'd returned to the Zodiacs, Liam had assumed his next mission would be alongside Steven, Roxanne, Duane, and maybe Kim. The five of them had trained together, fought side by side, and stopped Maxwell's plans several times in the past. They knew each other's moves, trusted each other absolutely.

But Malik had requested Liam's presence on the mission. "Steven's team is armed with missiles. They're making a remote assault," Malik had explained. "But *our* fight is gonna get messy—maybe even hand to hand. I need all the muscle I can get."

Liam couldn't turn him down. But now, as they approached an unknown spot deep in the Sahara, he started to have doubts. *I trust Malik,* he thought. *I think. But all three of these guys have worked for Maxwell in the past. What if . . . ?*

He hated to even consider the possibility. *What if they're still secretly loyal to him?*

He stood up and walked down the steps toward the large area in the back of the cabin. Nicky and Snake watched him go; he could feel their eyes on him. When he reached the big table in the center of the room, he figured he was far enough away to speak privately.

"Duane?" he said, touching his earpiece. "Ye read me?"

"Yes." Duane's voice was faint, crackly. "I'm receiving your telemetry. Still no Dragon energy in your vicinity, but I'm getting some strange EM readings."

"How 'bout the tremors?"

"Still increasing." Duane sounded worried. "In fact, the timetable seems to be accelerating."

That doesn't sound good, Liam thought.

"Are you approaching your position?" Duane asked.

"That's what they tell me." He cast a suspicious glance at the cockpit. "What about Steven's team? They getting anywhere?"

"They're out of contact, as expected. Seismic activity in their vicinity has spiked."

"Seismic activity . . . that could be good or bad, aye? Either the Dragon is settin' off even more earthquakes, or Steven and Rox are blowing the devil out of its secret base."

"Yes," Duane replied. "Until their team surfaces, there's no way to know."

"Yo, Rammer!" Nicky called, tapping his ear. "Time for radio silence."

"Stop bloody calling me that!" Liam walked a little farther away and touched his ear again. "Hey, Duane?"

"Yes?"

"Wish you were here."

There was a pause. Liam thought they'd been disconnected.

"Me too," Duane said.

Liam cut the connection, turned around, and gasped.

Nicky and Celine stood at the large table, which was covered with a holographic display showing an exterior view of their destination. The desert landscape seemed to stretch forever, uninterrupted—except for a deep hole blasted in the ground. Readouts described it as almost five kilometers in diameter, and less than twenty kilometers away.

But as the image zoomed in, Liam realized the hole wasn't empty. Curving metal arms, gray and grimy, stretched over the gap like the legs of a spider. They met at a central building, a featureless block whose base disappeared into the abyss and whose summit rose half a kilometer above its mouth.

"Someone's been busy." Nicky whistled. "Or some*thing*."

Liam walked around the hologram, peering up and down. "This is the control machinery? For the whole worldwide seismic craziness?"

"That's what they tell me," Celine said.

"It stretches way down into that hole." Nicky shook his head in confusion. "Down to the . . . what did the brainiac kid call it? Lithosphere."

"The tectonic plates," Liam said. "Like Steven and Kim described. The Dragon is using what it learned in Indonesia."

Celine nodded. "The kid, Duane, he says there's one of those ley lines below this spot. Sends the seismic commands all over the world."

"Lystria. From the ashes," Liam said. "I'll say this for Maxwell: he's big on recycling."

Nicky pointed at one of four large spires rising from the edge of the hole. "What are those tent pole things?"

"Control towers," Malik called from the pilot's seat. "At the edge of the hole, forming a perfect square. They probably coordinate the seismic machinery, and who knows what else."

Liam studied the complex. "If we can take 'em out, the struts should collapse."

"Taking a lot of Dragon tech with 'em," Nicky agreed.

It's like some nightmarish techno vision of the future, Liam thought. *There's not a trace left of what used to be here: a vibrant city where people lived their lives.*

Is that what the Dragon wants? A planet cleansed of humanity, with nothing but machines obeying its will?

A shiver ran through him. But it wasn't just the horror of the Dragon's plan. Some danger instinct, honed in the seedy pubs of Dublin, was pricking at his neck.

"This is too easy," he said.

"I was thinking the same thing," Malik replied. "The complex is shielded from satellite surveillance. But now that we're close, those towers are begging to be hit."

Liam reached out with both hands, into the hologram, and spread his arms. The image zoomed in on the central building. A walkway led out from it, crossing the gap like a plank over a moat, connecting to the charred sand beyond.

"Are there weapons?" he asked. "Is it even *manned*—"

"Look," Nicky said.

Liam zoomed in further. At the base of the walkway, a doorway had opened in the wall of the central building.

CHAPTER TWENTY-ONE

Two Vanguard soldiers, armed with large energy rifles, marched out in formation. Two others followed, and then four more. They strode across the walkway under the blazing sunlight, over the gaping abyss.

"Any more questions?" Celine asked.

Plenty, Liam thought.

A hundred soldiers—possibly more—poured out of the building. As they reached the end of the walkway, they fanned out across the desert sand. They looked like ants crawling from a mound, each taking up its appointed position. Their movements were precise, unhurried.

And they kept coming.

"That's a lotta soldiers," Nicky said. "And a lotta guns."

"We're almost directly overhead," Malik called. "We're shielded from radar, but I'm taking us up a bit to make us a tougher target."

The plane lurched, its nose tipping upward. Liam stumbled for balance, staring at the hologram. The soldiers were still fanning out, but they held their energy rifles loose at their sides. They made no aggressive moves.

"I count almost a thousand troops now." Nicky shook his head. "That's almost everyone in Vanguard."

"Yeah," Celine said, pointing. "But only one of 'em matters."

Liam followed her sharp-nailed finger. A figure in a gray jumpsuit ran out of the building, leaping across the walkway over the soldiers' heads. He had jet-black hair and a beard, elongated arms and legs—and bare prehensile feet.

Malik rose from the pilot's seat and moved to join them. "Monkey," he said, glaring at the hologram.

"I knew it." Celine shook her head. "That guy's my own personal curse."

Monkey dodged and jumped, forward and side to side, leapfrogging over and around the soldiers. They didn't seem to notice. As the last of them poured across the walkway, they settled into a rainbow formation several rows thick, fanned out in front of the hole in the earth.

Monkey landed on his hands and feet, facing the soldiers. His eyes rose, briefly, to regard the spires, the metal spider legs, and the central block towering over the entire complex.

Then his face whipped up. His cruel eyes seemed to look straight out of the hologram. He touched his earpiece and smiled wide.

"Hey, dudes!" Monkey's voice echoed in the cabin. "Who's up there? Celine, I hope?"

Celine started to speak—but Malik motioned her back, away from the hologram. She retreated to a corner of the room.

"It's me, Vincent," Malik said.

"Malik! Looks like it's payback time." Monkey's grin grew wider; he seemed to have an infinite number of teeth. "But I know you didn't come alone. Who else you got up there?"

"Just the Ram. And your old friend Nicky."

CHAPTER TWENTY-ONE

Monkey snorted. "Friend? He's just another traitor, like Celine."

"Dude. That hurts." Nicky touched his heart. "You know I got mad love for you."

Monkey loped across the sand. He paced back and forth in front of the rigid soldiers.

"Tell you what," he said. "Land your plane right now, and we'll talk about stuff."

"Stuff?" Malik asked. "What stuff?"

"Power. Death. The future." Monkey stopped to caress an energy rifle in one of the soldiers' hands. *"Loyalty."*

Malik frowned. "You think you can knock us out of the sky with those little guns?"

"Oh, *no*, Malik. We're not going to fire on you."

"Then give us one reason not to burn yer Tinkertoy city to the ground," Liam snarled.

"I'll give you a thousand reasons."

In the hologram, Monkey gestured. Behind him, two soldiers turned to face each other. A clatter of movement came over the radio.

"What are they doin'?" Nicky asked.

Liam reached out and widened the view. As the image zoomed out, he saw that the soldiers had paired off, each facing his or her closest neighbor. Slowly, their mouths grim beneath their helmets, they raised their energy rifles and aimed them straight at each other's heads.

"Land the plane," Monkey said, "or they all die."

"Is he serious?" Liam looked at Malik, then Nicky.

"Can he do that? Make them shoot each other?"

Malik looked unsure. Nicky shrugged, his eyes wide.

"He can do it," Celine whispered from the back of the room. "The Dragon . . ."

Malik paced around the hologram, studying the rows of soldiers poised to shoot each other. They held their rifles steady; their hands didn't quiver at all. The tips of their guns glowed with charged power.

"Mind control," Malik said. The Ox flashed above him, snorting in helpless anger.

"Land. The plane," Monkey repeated.

"He's bluffin'," Nicky said.

"There are people down there we used to work with," Malik said. "Friends."

Liam watched Monkey, studying the cruelty and triumph on his hairy face. "Aye," he said. "We can't take the chance."

"Stand by for landing," Malik barked. He switched off the hologram with a savage swipe of his hand.

Celine and Dog moved toward landing couches along the sides of the cabin. They looked like sleepwalkers: helpless, defeated. Malik cast a grim look at Liam, then walked back to the pilot's seat.

Liam turned and followed, taking the copilot's position for landing. "The odds seem t'be in that ape's favor," he observed. "Ye think we're beat?"

"Not yet," Malik replied.

CHAPTER TWENTY-ONE

Things went bad the moment they stepped off the plane. Nicky broke ranks, running forward to confront Monkey. Yellow fur spread across his body, covering his scarred face. The spectral Dog appeared, howling, above his head.

"I'm givin' you one warning," Nicky growled. "Let those guys go."

Liam watched, shaking his head. Malik followed.

Monkey was crouched, ready to meet them. The lines of Vanguard troops stretched out behind him, almost as far as the eye could see. There were well over a thousand of them now; they had lowered their guns but faced straight ahead, eyes glassy and blank. In the distance, the metal spires of the Lystria complex rose into the sky.

Monkey loped forward on hands and feet. He raised his head slowly, like a shark rising out of the water.

"You," Monkey said, "are as ugly as you are disloyal."

Nicky roared and wielded his claws. Malik grabbed his arm, yelling, "No!"

Monkey whirled around and gestured. Two soldiers stepped out of the group: a small woman and a large muscular man. They wore standard Vanguard uniforms, helmets shielding their eyes.

Monkey flashed a nasty smile at the Zodiacs. "Watch this." He turned to the big male Vanguard agent. "Alpha, how long have you worked with Beta here?"

"Four years," the man rumbled. He stood rigid, barely moving.

"Is she your friend?"

"Sometimes she ain't so nice to me. But mostly, yeah."

"Beta," Monkey said, turning to the woman, "would you risk your life for your partner?"

The small woman, Beta, hesitated for a moment. "Yes," she said.

Monkey took a step back.

"I want you to raise your guns and aim them at each other."

The two soldiers stared straight at each other. Slowly they lifted their energy rifles.

Nicky and Malik exchanged alarmed looks. Again, Malik jerked his head at Nicky, silently ordering him: *Don't do it.*

"Mate," Liam said, stepping forward. "There's no need for this."

"Actually, there is," Monkey replied. "Alpha. Beta. If I order you to shoot . . . will you do it?"

The two Vanguard soldiers replied simultaneously. "Of course." "Without question."

"Why?"

They turned to face him, speaking in unison. "Because *the Dragon is our future.*"

Liam glanced at the mass of Vanguard soldiers, arrayed across the sand. *Mind control,* he thought. *And there's hundreds of 'em. . . .*

CHAPTER TWENTY-ONE

"This is what you want?" he asked, turning sharply to Monkey. "Is this the Dragon's ideal world, the future of the human race? 'Cause it looks pretty bloody grim to me."

Monkey loped over to Liam. The Irishman stood still, one eyebrow raised, as Monkey sniffed in a circle, moving his head around to study Liam from every angle.

"You won't win," Monkey said, the grin returning to his face. "You and Jasmine, and that yappy little Tiger of yours. You *can't* win. Do you know why?"

"Too handsome?"

Monkey threw back his head and laughed. "You won't win because you're not willing to make sacrifices."

"Sir?" Alpha asked. His gun was still aimed at his partner, and hers at him. "Sh-should we fire?"

Monkey turned slowly on one foot. He tapped a long finger on his chin, over and over, as if considering his answer.

"Vincent," Malik said. "Please."

Monkey whirled and flashed Malik a smile. "I like hearing you beg." Then he turned back to Alpha and Beta with a casual wave. "Nah," he said.

The two Vanguard soldiers lowered their weapons. Liam sighed in relief.

"But you *would* have sacrificed yourself if I asked you to," Monkey continued. "Because *the Dragon is our future.*"

"The Dragon is our future," Alpha and Beta repeated.

Monkey raised his arms high, like a conductor

addressing his orchestra. With a quick clatter, the Vanguard troops raised their energy rifles.

"The Dragon is our future," they rumbled, the phrase echoing down the rows of helmeted soldiers.

Liam stared grimly at the framework of the Lystria complex, the strange metal arms and towers rising out of the pit. *Take out the control towers,* he thought, *and the machinery should collapse. But how do we get through a thousand-plus brainwashed soldiers to do it—without hurting 'em?*

Monkey was still facing the soldiers. At his command, they began to recite a chant in perfect unison.

"The Dragon is our future," they said. *"The earth will shake; the earth will burn. When the work is done, ten percent of humankind shall remain. We are the worthy. We are the ten percent."*

A chill ran through Liam. "Ten percent?" He turned toward his allies. "Mates, I think we better—"

He stopped. Nicky was staring at Monkey with blank eyes. As Liam watched, the Dog fur receded from Nicky's body, leaving him pale and human.

"The Dragon," Nicky said in a quiet voice.

"Malik?" Liam said. "You said somethin' about mind control?"

Malik's eyes were equally blank. *"The Dragon is our future,"* he said.

Liam's heart sank. *I'm all alone,* he realized. And for just a moment, the terrible doubt returned: *Was this their plan all along? My so-called partners—Malik, Nicky, Snake—have they* always *been loyal to the Dragon? Was this mission doomed before we even started?*

Am I all alone?

He shook his head. *Get ahold of yerself,* he thought. *It's not Malik and Nicky; it's the mind control. It's the bloody Dragon!*

He glanced at the nearest tower. *I could ram it,* he thought. *Just take a flying leap, vault over the soldiers, and—*

Monkey laughed loudly. He danced around, capering in the sand, and came to rest with his face centimeters from Liam's.

"This is what happens," Monkey hissed, gesturing at the machines of Lystria, "when you invade the Dragon's domain."

"The Dragon," Liam sneered.

"Yes?" Monkey twisted his face around, peering into Liam's eyes. "What about it? What are you trying to say?"

"The Dragon is our future," Liam said. The words were out of his mouth before he knew it.

Monkey grinned. "Yeah, it is."

Liam looked around, reeling slightly. The bizarre metal arms still rose above Lystria, but now they seemed symmetrical, orderly. Their strength held the complex together. And the soldiers, spread across the sand: they were his comrades. They were the future.

The survivors. The 10 percent.

A warm feeling ran through him. *Maybe there's hope,* he thought. *Maybe I don't* have *to be alone—*

Something buzzed in his ear. He heard a voice, as if from a long way away. "Liam?" Duane said. "I'm reading some strange telemetry on your—"

Liam reached up and clicked off his earpiece.

Dimly, he became aware of Malik and Nicky, moving up beside him. *We're brothers now,* he realized. *Brothers in the Dragon.*

The thought made him happy.

Their three faces rose to stare into Monkey's waiting eyes. *"The earth will shake,"* Liam chanted, the others echoing his words. *"The earth will burn. . . ."*

CHAPTER TWENTY-TWO

"LIAM? LIAM, come in, please. Liam?"

Silence. Duane looked up at the screen directly in front of him, which showed an ID photo of Liam's smirking face. The text overlaid on it read CALL TERMINATED.

Frustrated, Duane yanked his earpiece out and threw it across the room. It sailed slowly through the zero-gravity chamber and bounced harmlessly off one of the hundreds of screens lining the Infosphere. He kicked off and swam through the air, fists clenched, and managed to grab the earpiece just before it could strike another screen.

CHAPTER TWENTY-TWO

most of the Zodiac complex, had been It measured five meters in diameter, which was packed with sophisticated ıent. The screens showed security foot- ac complex, maps and schematics of the earth, Zodiac [illegible]ver scans from around the world, transmissions from the two active mission teams, seismic and tomographic readings from the volcano institutes, and status readouts on every currently active Zodiac-powered individual.

None of which, Duane thought, *is going to make this mission succeed.*

Using handholds, he pulled his way to a complex of screens monitoring the Lystria mission. One, labeled SATELLITE VIEW, showed nothing—just a featureless sandy landscape. The one reading STEALTH PLANE VIEW showed a shaky camera image of the same spot. But the inhuman, metallic Lystria complex was clearly visible, reaching out over that hole in the desert. A small army of Vanguard soldiers stood just outside it, facing three dots that Duane assumed were Liam and his party.

Duane reached for the screen and pinched, trying to zoom in on the image. The three dots grew larger but no clearer. The team hadn't had time, he remembered, to rig a remote control from the plane's camera. Duane could manipulate the image but not the view from the camera itself.

"Blash-dast it," he said.

When Duane was nervous, he tended to make u swear words.

Frustration built up inside him. He felt the Zodiac energy rising all around, the raging Pig snorting and pawing above his head. The screens began to spark and flicker in response.

No, he told himself. *Stay calm. If I don't control my power, I could short out the whole Infosphere!*

And they're counting on me. They're all counting on me.

He closed his eyes and forced himself to breathe regularly. His power had first manifested back in Cape Town, his home city. He'd shorted out a network of government computers and been branded a dangerous hacker. After Carlos and the others had rescued him from that mess, Jasmine taught him how to keep his power from running wild.

Now they're counting on me. And I can't save them.

He forced himself to remember the techniques Jasmine had shown him. "When things get overwhelming," she'd said, "do not try to solve everything at once. Focus on one problem at a time, and see where it gets you."

Okay. Problem one. He opened his eyes and scanned the row of screens. Below the image of Lystria, a long line of numbers and statistics scrolled by. The plane was still transmitting data from the site.

Duane noted a slight surge in Zodiac energy, enough to confirm that the team was in the right place. But the EM output from the complex was still growing. That meant

CHAPTER TWENTY-TWO

Liam and Malik hadn't accomplished their mission—and now they weren't answering Duane's calls.

Problem two. He shot across the Infosphere, coming to rest before a cluster of screens assigned to cover Steven's team. At two kilometers beneath the surface, that team was cut off from radio contact, as planned. On one screen, the data buoy they'd left on the surface bobbed up and down in the choppy waves, lights blinking across its surface.

The next screen displayed that data. Seismic readings, long-range radar/sonar scans of the deep ocean. Magnetic readings. All higher than usual.

As Duane watched, the Zodiac energy level spiked, rising a thousand times higher than it had been. He sucked in a breath. Only one entity on Earth could command that level of power: the Dragon.

The team, he thought. *They're right in the middle of that power storm. And Steven . . .*

Steven had shared his plan only with Duane. When they reached the bottom of the sea, Steven intended to split off from the others and swim alone into the heart of the volcano. He felt a responsibility, he'd said. He'd also said that he wanted to avoid a choice and break a cycle. But he hadn't explained what he meant by that.

Reluctantly, Duane had agreed to the plan. Now he felt guilty. *I could have warned Roxanne and Kim,* he thought. *I should have told him not to do it.*

But he knew: *You can't tell Steven Lee what to do.*

A series of beeps rose from another quarter of the

sphere. Duane pushed off and shot toward a grid of screens, each of which showed a piece of a world map. Between the Eastern and Western Hemispheres, a long blurry line showed the curved pattern of the Ring of Fire—the worldwide map of underwater volcanoes. That line was pulsing, glowing. Little dots sprouted along it like buds on a rosebush, indicating new centers of volcanic activity. The line grew thicker, spreading into the vast ocean between the continents.

"Oh, mashed potatoes," Duane said.

He touched an adjacent screen and scrolled through a series of bulletins from the volcano institutes. Seismic alerts, rising sea levels, underwater and land-based volcanoes suddenly becoming active. *I've got more data than anyone else,* he thought. *This is up to me.*

He consulted a newsfeed, a summary app he'd designed for rapid skimming. Unpredicted earthquakes had just struck California, Afghanistan, and eastern China. Volcanic islands were being evacuated in Russia, the Philippines, and New Zealand. A flashing alert labeled SENDAI, JAPAN caught his eye; he clicked on it. A photo filled the screen, a horrific image of fire raging across a line of low buildings. A translated headline read WORSE THAN TOHOKU?

So far, the authorities were downplaying the worldwide pattern. Some countries had dispatched diving teams to underwater activity sites; others were just denying the phenomenon. But they wouldn't be able to deny it for long.

The Pig roared and sniffed above Duane's head as he

concentrated, using his unique Zodiac power to absorb and process the data from the screens all around him. The control machinery in Lystria. The off-the-scale Zodiac readings above Tamu Massif. The line of worldwide volcanic activity, bulging and thickening before his eyes.

Ninety minutes, he realized. *That's how long before the chain reaction becomes irreversible. Before the earth cracks open, flooding the atmosphere with deadly volcanic ash and fire.*

The Lystria team could destroy the machinery, but its members had gone off the grid. The team at Tamu Massif had an even harder job—stopping the Dragon—and that group, too, was cut off from radio contact. This plan had started off with too many variables, and things had gone progressively downhill since then.

Stopping the Dragon. That was the real trick, the major problem—the reason, ultimately, why Duane felt so hopeless. Even if the Zodiacs could destroy the Dragon's machinery—even if they prevented the Tamu Massif eruption and stopped the volcanic apocalypse—the Dragon itself would survive. Worse, it would be very, very angry. And nothing they could do, no technology in either team's possession, could even put a dent in the Dragon's power.

He glanced at a screen on the other side of the sphere. Carlos and Jasmine lay side by side in matching beds, hooked up to blinking machines. Their eyes were closed, their bodies perfectly motionless. Dr. Snejbjerg hovered in the background, watching them with concern.

Carlos, Duane thought. *You could help. You worked with*

the Dragon; you helped develop the volcano tech. You're the only one who might be able to stop this.

If you'd only wake up.

"Open your flib-gibbering eyes!" he said.

But Carlos didn't move. So Duane turned away and resumed monitoring, collating, and sorting the data before him—waiting, with gritted teeth, for the end of the world.

Jasmine flinched as a blast of frigid wind struck her. She shivered and let out a strangled noise.

Carlos laughed. Embarrassed, she punched him; her gloved fist sank into his heavy parka. She snuggled against his warm chest.

"Jaz," he said, pointing. "You don't want to miss this."

A huge cement mixer rumbled loudly as its drum began to spin. It sat, along with a few other all-terrain vehicles, on a carpet of snow that seemed to stretch on forever—except for a huge circular trench, almost half a kilometer in diameter, that had been cleared away and dug to a depth of two stories. Workers in heavy coats stood nearby, directing the operation, shivering in the extreme cold. The sun beat down, glaring brightly against the snow.

With a grinding noise, the cement mixer's chute swung over the trench. As the gray cement began to flow, Jasmine's breath caught in her throat.

"Zodiac headquarters," she whispered.

CHAPTER TWENTY-TWO

Carlos smiled and pulled her closer. He smelled of sweat and hard work. She closed her eyes, drinking in the feel of him.

For a moment, she forgot it was only a memory.

"This was the time," she said. "After all our planning, this was when the dream became real. When I realized we actually *could* make the world a better place."

"Oh, Jasmine. Really?"

She opened her eyes. Carlos had turned rigid and cold, his arms frozen in place around her. The cement mixer had stopped turning; the thick stream of cement hung over the trench like an abstract sculpture. The workers were gone.

She turned, knowing whom she would see. Maxwell wore his usual uniform, with no snow gear over it. He didn't seem cold.

"'Make the world a better place'?" He grimaced. "I believe I just threw up in my mouth."

Furious, she disengaged from Carlos and stalked over to Maxwell. She reached up and slapped him across the face as hard as she could. Her hand passed straight through his body; she stumbled and almost fell.

"Mindscape. Remember?" Maxwell laughed. "You really have to get better at this."

"Actually, I think I've had enough."

"And yet you're still here. Your friends have tried several times to extract you."

"You. You're preventing that. Keeping me in here."

"I'm not keeping you anywhere."

She glared at him. She couldn't trust Maxwell; she knew that. Yet his words rang true.

"Are you just torturing me now?" She gestured at the cement mixer, at the clearing that would become Zodiac headquarters. "This was the coldest I've ever been in my life. And . . . and the happiest."

"I'm not picking these flashbacks. You are."

She spat in the snow. *Riddles,* she thought, *nothing but riddles.* "How do I get rid of you? How do I get you out of my head?"

His face grew serious. "Wrong question."

"*You* don't get to decide what questions I—"

"The right question," he continued, "is how do you get *him* out of *his* head?"

Maxwell gestured at Carlos. The scientist remained completely still, his arms wrapped around the space where Jasmine had stood a few moments before. He looked happy, content, watching the dream they'd shared become a reality.

Just like I was.

"Okay," she whispered. "What do I do?"

He walked up and took her by the shoulders. "I've told you. Twice now." His eyes bored into hers. "You must unburden yourself."

All around Maxwell's figure, the landscape began to shift. Snow flattened into sand; the cement mixer wavered and vanished. Cold, biting air turned to dry, searing heat.

Jasmine found herself back in the desert. She pulled

away from Maxwell and turned, knowing what she would see. Once again, Carlos lay in his hospital bed, surrounded by the endless sand.

"The world needs him," Maxwell said. "And you claim you love him."

"I do. More than anything."

"Then tell him."

She grabbed Carlos by the shoulders. "Wake up," she said, shaking his limp body. "Wake up!" But Carlos's eyes didn't open.

"Tell him."

She whirled to face Maxwell. "Tell him *what*?"

Maxwell shot her a look of disappointment. Then, all at once, he started to glow. Not with Zodiac energy, she realized. This was red, electrical—more like the discharges given off by the Vanguard energy rifles—

The blast knocked her off her feet. She skidded across the ground—which seemed to have transformed into some sort of hard stone surface. She bounced off a railing and tumbled to the floor.

She scrambled to her feet. She stood on a narrow walkway—an observation deck, she realized. She leaned over the railing; beyond about a meter of safety netting, a beautiful city lay stretched out below. A calm river wound through close-packed old buildings bordered by high trees.

Oh, no.

A glance back confirmed her suspicions. A distinctive arch of riveted girders stood in the center of the deck,

obscuring the other side of the walkway. There was no doubt: this was the Eiffel Tower, in Paris.

"Oh," said a woman with a deep voice, as if echoing Jasmine's thoughts. "Oh, no."

Ice ran through Jasmine's veins. She hadn't heard that voice for years.

She crept around the arch, toward the sound of the voice. She wanted to flee, to avoid this moment from her past, to banish it forever from her memory. But that was impossible. Now that she was there, she had to see.

A tall woman in a trench coat knelt over a man in a Vanguard uniform. The man lay on the deck. He had a hole in his chest.

"Oh," the woman said, running her hand along the man's face. "Oh, Liang."

The man didn't move. Smoke rose from his wound, but he was clearly dead.

Mom and Dad. Jasmine couldn't move, couldn't even breathe.

This is the day they died.

The woman cast a quick glance up at Jasmine. A dozen expressions crossed her face: fear, anger, sadness, worry. Her mouth silently formed the words, *I'm sorry, Jaz.*

Then she whirled to her feet. Her trench coat flipped open, revealing a matching Vanguard uniform. "You killed him," the woman said.

Jasmine forced herself to look up. Again, she knew

what she would see. She'd lived this moment already, many years before.

Maxwell stood at the far end of the walkway, his eyes shining with fury. He held an energy rifle, its barrel still glowing red-hot. They were alone; the rest of the tourists had fled at the first sign of violence.

Maxwell, Jasmine realized, was more than a phantom there. He wasn't the Dragon yet; this had happened before the Zodiac Convergence, before the powers had exploded into the world. But he wasn't just a hitchhiking presence in her mind, either. He was an active participant in this event.

And he just murdered my father.

Jasmine glanced quickly at the dead body. *He used to like dogs,* she thought, *and watching movies in the middle of the night.*

The sorrow was almost unbearable. But that wasn't the worst of it, she knew. There was more to come.

"I killed him," Maxwell acknowledged, "as I would eliminate any traitor to my organization."

"Traitor?" Jasmine's mother took a step toward Maxwell. "What are you talking about?"

"Really, Mu Ning." Maxwell's eyes were hard, unmoving. "The deception is over."

"You've gone mad."

Mu Ning, Jasmine's mother, reached into the pocket of her trench coat. *No,* Jasmine thought. *Don't do it, Mom. Don't do it.*

Maxwell raised the energy rifle. "Did you lie this way to your superiors in the American CIA? When you met with them at the—"

No. No no no no no.

"—at the Saint Maurice Banquet?"

Mu Ning charged. Maxwell stepped back, surprised, and raised his energy rifle. But before he could aim, Mu Ning whipped out a charged energy knife and slashed it across his chest.

Maxwell let out a loud, inhuman howl. He stumbled back and lost his grip on the energy rifle. His uniform fell in tatters from his chest; blood dripped to the floor. As he staggered back, Mu Ning tackled him and raised the knife for another blow. Their eyes locked together.

Mu Ning pressed her knee into Maxwell's chest, pinning him to the observation deck. Jasmine couldn't move; all she could do was watch.

Everything seemed to freeze. Maxwell's head whipped sideways, his eyes staring straight at Jasmine. "*Now* do you understand?"

Before Jasmine could react, the world snapped back into motion. Mu Ning spat down at Maxwell, spraying his face. Her knife's blade crackled with energy as she plunged it down, aiming straight at his chest.

Maxwell's arm shot out, almost too fast to see. He grabbed Mu Ning by the throat and lifted her up, off the observation deck. She flailed, struggled, and made a choking noise.

CHAPTER TWENTY-TWO

Almost casually, he reached out and twisted her wrist. The knife slipped from her fingers, landing on the deck with a sizzle.

"I hope your daughter," he hissed, "proves more useful than *you*."

He swung his arm back, lifting Mu Ning high. Then he lunged forward and hurled her off the deck.

Jasmine ran to the railing. Mu Ning's flailing body soared through the air, over the protective netting. As Jasmine watched in horror, her mother began the long drop toward the city below.

Mu Ning's form grew smaller and smaller. Before it could strike the ground, it disappeared into a grove of trees.

Jasmine whirled. Maxwell stood facing her. His uniform was torn, his chest bleeding. He looked like a wounded animal.

"You killed them," she said. "You did this."

To her surprise, he shook his head. "You *still* don't understand."

He reached out a hand and swept it sideways—and they were sitting at a sidewalk café. Jasmine glanced in surprise at the tattered banner above them, then at the cobblestoned street. A river flowed just beyond it, serene and peaceful.

Across the table, Maxwell leaned back in his chair, frowning at something on his phone. He wore casual clothes; there was no evidence of his knife wound.

Jasmine picked up a huge croissant and took a bite. Jelly filled her mouth, the taste of warm fruit mixed with butter.

"I love Paris," she said.

Maxwell raised an eyebrow, then flashed her an indulgent half smile.

I know when this was, she thought. *Just two days before the murders—before the day he killed my parents. I'm . . . how old am I? Sixteen?*

And I'm already working for him, she remembered with horror. *I begged him to let me join Vanguard.*

Jasmine leaned across the table, smirking. She felt numb, detached. All she could do was let things play out as they had, with her teenage self calling the shots.

"I'm sick of going over reports," she said. "When you gonna give me a *real* job? Something with a little wetwork?"

Maxwell chuckled.

"I'm *ready*," she insisted.

He laid down the smartphone and studied her. "You think you can follow in your parents' footsteps?"

"My parents?" Young Jasmine snorted. "They don't know what they're doing."

I was a cocky little brat, she thought. *Never satisfied. Never appreciated them.*

"I can't argue with your assessment," Maxwell replied. "They certainly let me down on the Johannesburg mission."

"They're never around anymore," Jasmine said. "All they do is go to parties."

Something hard entered Maxwell's eyes. "Parties?"

No, Jasmine thought. *No, you little fool. Don't say it. Don't say it!*

"Yeah," she said. "Tonight they're going to something . . . the Saint Maurice Banquet?" She made a *pffft* noise. "Of course, they're not takin' *me*."

Maxwell stared at her. She remembered the sudden queasiness that look had triggered. Somehow young Jasmine had known her world was about to be turned upside down, though she hadn't understood why.

As Maxwell turned to type something on his phone, she leaned forward again. "So you gonna give me a mission or what?"

"I promise," he said, not looking up, "you'll see action very soon."

But Jasmine was barely listening. She forced herself to look at Maxwell—at the man who'd killed her parents, murdered thousands of people, kidnapped and wounded members of her team. The man who'd led her back in time to this moment.

"I told you," she whispered. "*I* gave you the information."

He nodded. A smile crept around the corners of his lips.

"The banquet. That's how you knew my parents were . . . were spying on you." She stood up, squeezing her eyes shut to hold back tears. "I didn't know. I didn't know about them or . . . or what I was telling you."

"I told her I hoped you'd be more useful." Maxwell's voice was hard. "She never knew: you already were."

"It's my fault. My fault you killed them." She couldn't stop the tears; she raised both hands to wipe them away.

"I've known it for a long time. Carried it around with me like an anvil."

"And you couldn't tell anyone. Not even those closest to you."

"Why did you do that?" She opened her eyes wide, glared at Maxwell. "Why did you make me relive it? To torture me, force me to admit it to you?"

"Not to me," he replied, his voice even. "To him."

They were back in the desert. Maxwell stood on the other side of Carlos's hospital bed, gesturing at the unmoving body between them.

"I can't heal the damage," Maxwell continued. "I can't make him live with what he's done. Only you can do that."

Maxwell stepped away, a strange expression on his face. *He's in my mind,* she thought. *He feels what I'm feeling.*

"I'm sorry, Jasmine," he said. "For some of it, anyway."

She turned to look down at Carlos. His face seemed thin, drained of life. She took his withered hand and leaned close to him.

"I know what you're feeling," she said.

She stopped and caught her breath, bracing herself.

"Sometimes we do things," she continued.

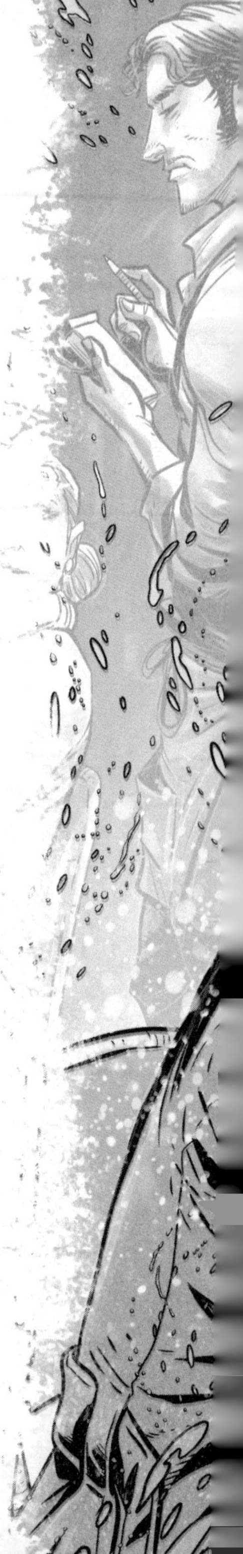

"And . . . and afterward we feel like we can't live with ourselves. Like we've ruined our whole lives in one moment, become someone else entirely. Not even a person—a *thing*, something too horrible to face in the mirror. And it feels like there's no way we can ever get back to the person we used to be."

He didn't move. She clutched his hand tighter.

"You felt that way," she continued. "I know you did. When you helped Maxwell, when you turned against me and stole all our powers. It wasn't your fault. He brainwashed you . . . the Dragon did. He saw something inside you, drew it out and played on it, made you feel like you were doing the right thing. But it wasn't your fault."

His hand twitched. She leaned closer.

"I know. Because I've felt the same way. I wanted to work for Maxwell so bad . . . I told him things I shouldn't. And those things led directly to the death of my parents. I've never told you that, never told anybody. Because I, I, I didn't want you to think of me like that. Because I blamed myself *so much*.

"But you know what? I was a stupid kid. And I didn't know, couldn't have known, what I was doing. I'd give anything if I could take it back, if my folks could be alive right now. But I can't do that. It doesn't matter what kind of superpowers you have. . . . That's just not the way the world works.

"So I have to forgive myself." She wiped a tear from

her eye. "And you know what? You have to forgive yourself, too."

He stirred. A small restless noise came from his mouth.

"We need you," Jasmine continued. "*I* need you. You big dumb nerd."

Again the noise. This time it was clearly a laugh.

"Jaz," he croaked.

She couldn't help it. She broke into tears and fell over his bed, burying her head in his chest. He smelled good, just as he had that day in the snowy wastes of Greenland. He smelled like home.

"I had no idea," he continued, his eyes still closed. "No idea you were carrying that around."

"Yeah." She smiled. "It kind of sucked."

"Not as bad as . . . eating applesauce through a tube for a week."

She laughed, then cried a little more. At last she straightened herself up and wiped away her tears.

"The team needs your help," she said. "Things are pretty bad, I think. And believe it or not, Maxwell isn't the—"

She looked around, startled. Maxwell had gone, retreated somewhere back inside her mind. She and Carlos were the only two people in the world, alone under the blazing sun.

Carlos's finger rose, beckoning to her. He said something she couldn't make out. As she leaned in closer, he opened his eyes for the first time.

"Duane," he gasped. "Take me to Duane."

CHAPTER TWENTY-THREE

STEVEN SWAM FURIOUSLY, trying not to think about a lot of things: His team, being buffeted in a tiny ship somewhere above his head. The explosive charges planted along the volcano below him. His parents, who might very well be following him to their deaths.

The end of the world.

The caldera, the crater exposed by the drill-ship's first detonation, loomed below, lit by the Dragon-glow from inside the mountain. Steven reached out with his Tiger senses, scanning the area. The crater was the size of a small lake, with gray stone walls surrounding a surprisingly flat floor. On the far side, along one wall, a jagged hole led inside the mountain. *That's it,* he thought. *That's the way in.*

CHAPTER TWENTY-THREE

He turned to check on his parents. They were still trailing him, thirty meters or so behind. They couldn't match the Tiger's speed, but their suits were equipped with specially designed underwater jets.

He pointed at the hole in the rock wall. His mother waved in acknowledgment, then activated her jets and shot toward him. Mr. Lee followed.

The entrance was round and barely a meter in diameter, with jagged edges. By the time Steven reached it, his parents were right on his heels. He eased his way inside, clicking on his suit light to illuminate the winding passageway.

A flurry of bubbles washed over his shoulder. He turned to see his mother struggling with her air hose, which had caught on a jagged wall protrusion. Air bubbles fanned out from the point where the hose touched the rock.

Mom!

He kicked off the wall and started swimming, but his father was already there. Mr. Lee grabbed hold of his wife's air hose and twisted it free. Mrs. Lee swam away—but the bubbles continued to flow.

Mrs. Lee's eyes were wide. *She's sprung a leak,* Steven thought. *Her air supply won't last another minute!*

He glanced back at the tunnel entrance. The drill-ship was too far away. His mother would never make it back there.

Mr. Lee wrapped an arm around his wife's shoulder. He turned and locked eyes with Steven, then pointed forward down the tunnel. Steven swallowed, nodded, and resumed swimming.

Now he had another thing to not think about.

The tunnel seemed to stretch on forever, winding and curving all around. Its walls ranged from jagged and unfinished rock to smooth tiles with the same Vanguard designs as in the Mount Merapi complex. Steven swam as fast as he dared, aware that his parents couldn't negotiate the twists and turns as quickly as he could.

He felt a kick on his back. He turned to see his father gesturing frantically. Mrs. Lee had fallen behind, flailing. Her eyes looked glazed, unfocused.

Her air hose hung free, completely severed.

Swimming furiously, Steven took one of his mother's arms while his father grabbed the other. Together they guided her forward, around a bend.

Hang on, Mom, he thought. *Hang on!*

A huge steel door, swung partway open, filled the passageway. They swam through it, into a small chamber surrounded by metal on all sides. Steven handed off his mother to his father and swam back to the door. Even with the Tiger's strength, he could barely move it against the water pressure. But he managed to push it shut and hurriedly turned a crank to seal it.

Mr. Lee had already found the pressure controls. Water began to drain out of the chamber as air hissed in from jets mounted on the ceiling. When the water level reached their necks, Mrs. Lee wrenched off her helmet and yanked the breather out of her mouth.

"I'm—" She coughed water. "I am all right. Thank you both."

As the water continued to drain away, Mr. Lee pulled off his own helmet. He took his wife in his arms and clasped her tight. She mumbled "I'm all right" again, but he still held her for a very long time.

Mr. Lee's face barely showed any expression, but it was still the most emotion Steven had ever seen the old man display. He felt cold, detached from the warmth of the moment.

They're always in sync, he thought. *A perfect unit, helping and supporting each other. A unit that doesn't include their son.*

Again he felt the web tightening. The inescapable destiny of the Zodiacs closing in on him like a shroud of death.

"Why?" he asked.

They turned in unison. Mrs. Lee stepped forward, started to speak, and coughed again.

"Why what?" she asked.

"Why are you *here?*"

"We slipped away from the ship. While your teammates were busy watching your little video."

"I don't want you here." Now that the emergency was past, Steven felt himself losing control. "I didn't want you on this mission at all. You never listen to anything I say!"

Mr. Lee brushed past his wife, glaring at Steven. "Perhaps we should be asking *you* the same question." He seemed cold again, his imperious mask completely restored. "What were you thinking, swimming off by yourself? Abandoning the mission?"

"*Abandoning?* Dad, this *is* the mission—"

A grinding noise interrupted him. On the far wall of the chamber, a second hatch began to cycle its way open. The water had almost vanished, reduced to a trickle flowing into drains set into the tiled floor.

Mr. Lee shot Steven another glare, then turned and strode through the door. Mrs. Lee followed him.

Steven stood in the pressure chamber, fuming in helpless panic. *I can't have them here,* he thought. *I'm going to destroy this place. I'm probably not getting out alive!*

Again, in his mind, he saw the vision from Mount Merapi: his parents lying dead in a pool of blood.

"Son?" Mrs. Lee called. "Come in here, please."

He stepped through the hatch into an enormous, high-ceilinged lab. Computers, sinks, refrigerators, autoclaves, and cryogenic chambers filled the space along the walls. Ladders reached up to the ceiling, nine meters or higher, allowing access to mounted storage compartments. The air smelled sterile, unnaturally clean, with just a hint of ammonia.

The lab was neat yet cluttered, stocked with every imaginable form of scientific equipment. It felt like a grown-up, unbelievably expensive version of a child's playhouse. Energy hummed all around, rising and falling, like ghosts in the walls.

Steven's parents stood at a high table. An intricate white crystal sat atop it, gleaming in the artificial light. It was multifaceted, with arms reaching up and out like the branches of a tree.

"One of ours," Mrs. Lee said.

Mr. Lee nodded. "A Sha Qi crystal." His eyebrows rose in alarm. "It's active."

Steven approached. "You guys built that thing?"

"Developed it. Under Maxwell's supervision." Mrs. Lee peered at the crystal. "I have never seen one so large."

"Okay." Steven concentrated, willing the Tiger to appear above him. "One Shocky Crystal, about to be ripped apart—"

"STOP!" Mrs. Lee held out a hand, startling him. "Sha Qi energies are extremely volatile. Until we know this crystal's function, it would be unwise to damage it."

"You asked why we came," Mr. Lee said, turning to address Steven directly. "This is why. We have specialized knowledge that your team lacks."

"Really?" Steven couldn't help feeling furious with them. "Or maybe you just feel guilty that he's using *your stuff* to destroy the world?"

Mr. Lee glared at him. "There are tens of thousands of volts running through this crystal," he said. "Perhaps enough to clip even a Tiger's claws." He turned away, walked over to a computer display, and started poking at the keyboard.

Mrs. Lee glanced at the crystal. She took a step toward Steven—then flinched, jumping to the side. A huge gray boulder, flat and slatelike, swung through the center of the lab, passing through the spot where she'd been standing. It seemed to have appeared from nowhere, out of the air itself.

Steven whirled to see another large boulder slicing through the air in the other direction. The two rocks were headed toward each other, on a collision course—straight for him.

Yet he didn't move. The Tiger was quiet, not at all alarmed. Steven stood stock-still, ignoring his mother's alarm, as the boulders approached. When the rocks collided, they passed right through him.

"Ah," Mr. Lee called from the far side of the room. "I seem to have activated some sort of holographic display."

Mr. and Mrs. Lee converged on their son, standing with him in the center of the room. All around them, flat boulders swooped and soared through the air. Some pairs passed harmlessly side to side; others collided and ground above or beneath each other.

"The tectonic plates," Steven said. "This is another simulation, like the one inside the Indonesian volcano."

"No." His father shook his head. "It's not a simulation. It's—"

CHAPTER TWENTY-THREE

"It's a monitoring program," Mrs. Lee finished.

Steven turned to them, his eyes wide. "You mean . . . all this . . ." He gestured at a pair of spectral boulders, colliding spectacularly in midair. "This is what's *actually happening* in the tectonic plates beneath our feet? Right now?"

His parents exchanged smiles, so quickly Steven wasn't sure he'd really seen it. "That is our best guess," Mrs. Lee said.

He studied the collisions. Looking close, he could see Dragon energy shimmering in the space between the rocks. Every time one plate struck another, a small burst of energy flashed into the air.

"Maybe—maybe we can use it somehow," he said. "To stop the reaction—"

"OH! SMART IDEA!"

The rock hologram abruptly vanished—replaced by a huge grinning face, almost five meters high, in sunglasses. Steven stumbled backward, surprised.

"Mince," he said.

The Lees edged their way around the giant Mince hologram. Wherever they moved, her gaze seemed to follow. She looked like a little girl about to step on some insects.

"OH, WAIT," she said. "I MEAN *STUPID*. STUPID IDEA."

"Steven," his father said sternly, "who is this person?"

"You don't want to know," Steven replied.

"I'M THE SMARTEST SIXTEEN-YEAR-OLD IN THE WORLD, OLD MAN." The Mince hologram turned to smirk down at Steven. "I GOTTA GIVE YOU CREDIT, KID. YOU REALLY THINK YOU CAN COME INTO *MY* LAB, TAP INTO *MY* COMPUTER SYSTEM, AND OVERRIDE *MY* PROGRAMS?"

"I didn't come alone."

"NO, YOU DIDN'T! THAT'S WHY THIS IS GONNA BE SO MUCH FUN."

He felt a sudden chill. The web of destiny, tightening . . .

"What do you think's going to happen to *you*, Mince?" he asked. "After the Dragon destroys, cleanses, whatever—after it spreads ash and fire all over the world? Where do you think you'll wind up?"

"I'LL BE RIGHT HERE, STUPID. IN MY LAB. I GOT ALL THE TOYS AND SPECIMENS I NEED. AND NO PEOPLE TO SCREW THINGS UP."

There was a loud rumble. The lab trembled and shook. Glass beakers rattled; a ladder clattered against the wall.

"You hear that?" Steven asked. "That's my team, setting off explosives all over this volcano. They're gonna keep doing that until this lab of yours is just a pile of scrap."

"HUH. THEY MIGHT." Mince seemed to consider for a moment. "OR THEN AGAIN . . ."

She wavered and disappeared. In her place, filling most of the two-story room, an exterior image appeared. The mountain shone brighter than before, lit by some unseen fire within. The drill-ship churned through the water, moving closer to the mouth of the volcano.

Uh-oh, Steven thought.

As the drill-ship approached, the volcano's mouth seemed to light up. Something poked into the water: a thin, jagged shape, crackling with energy.

"That," Mr. Lee said, "is not an eruption."

"No," Steven whispered. "It's a horn."

Mrs. Lee frowned. "A wind instrument?"

"No. An *animal's* horn."

The horn continued to rise, like a lightning bolt moving in slow motion. It sparked with power, illuminating the deep water. A second horn crackled into view next to it, followed by the tip of a head made of the same eldritch energy.

The horns jutted into the water, revealing themselves as twisted, curving antlers knotted with deadly sharp hooks. Below them, a pair of glowing malevolent eyes rose above the lip of the volcano.

"The Dragon," Steven said.

"Yes," his father replied. "But not precisely the Dragon you've known."

The creature paused, the bulk of its head still concealed within the mountain. Its horns and forehead appeared to be composed entirely of energy, sparking and wavering in the water. As soon as Steven focused on one part of it, that part seemed to shift and change.

Only its eyes were solid. They seemed to stare straight

at him for a moment. Then the Dragon turned to glance up at the drill-ship, hovering dangerously close.

"No," Steven whispered. "Oh, no."

He didn't even see its mouth open. But a stream of fire surged upward, cleaving the water. The flame struck the drill-ship, knocking it on its side.

"HARD CUT!" said Mince. She sounded delighted.

The image wavered again and shifted to an interior view of the drill-ship's cockpit. The little ship lurched; Roxanne and Kim flew through the air, striking a wall hard. Josie rocked back and forth in the pilot's seat, struggling with the controls.

Kim stumbled to her feet and shook her head to clear it. She grabbed Roxanne's arm and pointed down at the floor.

Water was gushing in. A steady stream, as if a garden hose had been switched on. As Roxanne knelt down to examine the hull, Steven saw a thick vertical crack stretching up from the floor.

The ship tumbled again, more violently than before. Roxanne rolled over and struck her head—

—and the image vanished.

Steven stood, shaking, his eyes wide. *Roxanne, Kim, and Josie,* he thought. *Rooster, Rabbit, Horse. None of their powers are suited to that kind of attack. None of them can survive—*

"AW! YOU WANT TO GO HELP 'EM?"

Footsteps, coming from the pressure chamber. Steven turned to see Mince herself striding into the room. She was a fraction the size of her holo-image but every bit as imperious and cruel.

Mince gestured toward the open hatch. "Go ahead."

Steven considered for a moment. *My mission is to blow this place up,* he thought. *But my team—they might be drowning right now. I can't abandon them!*

"Mom," he said, starting toward the hatch. "Dad. Come on."

"No, Son."

He whirled, thinking: *Are they* really *arguing with me now?*

But his heart sank as he saw his mother, holding up the mangled end of her severed air hose.

"Whoa!" Mince strode through the chamber, keeping her distance from Steven. "This is a tough one. You can stay here and protect Mummy and Daddy like a good little Tiger cub . . ."

She gestured. The exterior view appeared again, focused this time on the drill-ship. A second fireball struck it, engulfing the tiny craft in flames.

". . . or you can swim to your pals' rescue."

CHAPTER TWENTY-THREE

Mince stopped to lean against the table with the Sha Qi crystal on it. She turned and stared at the Lees with a predatory smile.

"Of course," she continued, "you'll have to leave *them* with me."

She held up her hand. Mince wore only one set of rings now: the ones that read DIE.

Steven glared at her. Mince stood equidistant from him and the Lees—no, not *quite* equidistant. She was a little closer to his parents than he was to her. He might be able to cover the distance, to leap over and reach her before she could harm them. But maybe not.

With a shock, he realized: *This is it. The choice. The doom the Tigers predicted.*

His team faced mortal danger outside. But his mother couldn't leave the mountain, and Mr. Lee would never go without his wife.

The Tiger roared, a scream of frustration. In response, its ancestors echoed the words they'd spoken before: *Your friends, your teammates, your duty—or your family, the people who gave you life.*

"No," he said aloud. "I can't make that choice. It's impossible."

We all made it. Every one of us. And the result was always the same.

Mince laughed. The Lees stood together, watching their son. In the hologram, the drill-ship tumbled over and over, slowly filling with water.

There'd been water in Steven's vision—the one he'd seen back in the Mount Merapi installation. His team had stood in a circle: Roxanne, Duane, Liam, and Kim. Their eyes had risen and fallen, watching as water dripped from some unknown brightly lit source. *Drip. Drip. Drip.*

He remembered what came next. His team, dead and bloody on the ground. Mr. and Mrs. Lee, too—sprawled hand in hand, together in death as they had been in life.

Oblivion.

And the Dragon filling the sky, filling the world, spreading its breath of fire over land and sea, friend and foe. Over anyone and anything who dared challenge it—including a foolish young Tiger whose cycle, at last, had come to an end.

CHAPTER TWENTY-FOUR

LIAM DRIFTED through time and space, lost in one of his earliest memories: a visit to a very old church. A gray stone building with arched windows, locked in the past beneath the blue skies of Ireland.

Little Liam stood in the roomy sanctuary, staring at an old chipped tub. He asked his mum why there was a tub inside the church and why there were no water pipes connected to it.

His mother laughed. She had gray hair, beige clothes, and a nice laugh. "It's not a tub," she said, mussing Liam's hair affectionately. "It's called a font."

An ancient carving wrapped around the outside of the font. In the image, a man faced off against a fearsome serpent: a creature from fairy stories, with the body of a snake, huge jaws, and swept-back ears. Liam knew that the man was brave. A horrific beast had invaded his home, and the man had no choice but to defend himself and his family. He was a fighter.

That's what little Liam wanted to be. A fighter.

But as he relived the moment, he found himself staring at the beast. Its jaws were wide and strong, its eyes fierce with power. To his younger self, it had been an abstract, frightening monster. But now he knew: *It's the Dragon.*

And the Dragon was linked to the land. Its energy reached deep below the grass, past the roots of the oldest trees, to the living core of the earth.

The Dragon is our past.

The words echoed in his mind, accompanied by lilting strains of Celtic music. They struck a chord in his subconscious mind, spoke directly to his Irish heritage. The power called to him, welcoming him into its embrace.

The Dragon is our future.

"Ram?"

He turned to look at his mother. She was staring at him, an intense expression on her face.

"Mum?" he asked. His voice sounded squeaky. "What did you call me?"

"Ram. Liam." Her voice was low, urgent. "Snap out of it."

"Mummy, I don't understand."

CHAPTER TWENTY-FOUR

He glanced nervously at the carved Dragon on the font. It felt warm, comforting. Would it protect him?

His mother slapped him.

Liam yelped and toppled over. The floor of the church should have been cold stone, but it felt like sand.

"Mummy!" he cried. He was stunned; his mother had never, ever hit him before. "Why did you do that?"

She towered over him, staring with hard eyes. Now he noticed: her eyes were glowing.

"Mummy?"

He struggled to his feet—and whirled, panicked, toward the Dragon carving. But he couldn't see it anymore.

The earth will shake, he thought. *The earth will burn. . . .*

"Ram! Focus on me!"

Hands grasped his shoulders, turning him around. Filled with dread, he looked up toward his mother—his mother who'd slapped him, betrayed him, betrayed the Dragon. The Dragon that had given him back his past, taken him home, welcomed him into its new world.

But it wasn't his mother who stood before him. It was Snake. Her eyes shone bright, boring into his mind.

"I can't keep this up," she said. Sweat beaded on her furrowed brow. "The Dragon's mind control—it's on a whole other level than my hypnosis. I can poke a hole in it, but you've got to shake it off yourself."

Liam stared into her eyes. Her power burned through him, presenting him with a lifeline back to reality. But the Dragon offered brotherhood, togetherness, love. It promised freedom from thought, from obligation, from all the hard choices of life. *I can't,* he thought. *I can't leave all that behind. . . .*

Then he remembered the man in the carving. The man who fought back against overwhelming odds, who risked his life to slay the monster. The man who loved his friends, his family, his homeland.

That, he thought. *That's who I want to be.*

The hero.

The fighter.

"I'm all right," he said. "Thanks."

He was back in the desert; the sun glared in his eyes. Malik stood behind Snake, looking dazed. And Monkey's legion of Vanguard soldiers remained completely still, lined up in perfect rows behind their leader. The strange towers of Lystria loomed beyond, the pit crisscrossed by the web of machinery.

"So," Monkey said, "my old partner *is* here, after all." He loped over to sneer at Snake. "Malik's little secret weapon."

"Vincent," Snake said, using Monkey's real name, "listen to me. The Dragon is using you."

"The Dragon rewards loyalty," Monkey said. "But then, you wouldn't know anything about that. You work for *Steven Lee* now."

"I work for myself," Snake hissed.

Monkey dismissed her with a sniff and capered over to Malik. "Ox, baby. You're loyal, right? You don't want to fight us?"

"I . . . don't know," Malik said. "Can't seem to think straight."

"We're your friends," Monkey continued. "Your buddies in Vanguard. Remember that?"

"Vanguard," Malik repeated. "I work for Vanguard. Or . . . I used to?"

"He's fighting it," Snake said. "They both are."

"You can't fight the Dragon," Monkey said, gesturing. "Ask *him*."

Liam studied the line of soldiers. His heart sank as he noticed a new addition to their ranks: Nicky—Dog—stood with the Vanguards, his eyes glassy and staring.

The Monkey's right, Liam realized. Snake had shocked Liam back to his senses—for now. But he could still feel the Dragon's lure, its tempting warmth. It danced around the edges of his mind, pushing and probing, searching for a way back in.

"Vincent," Snake said. "Maxwell betrayed you, remember? He stole your powers."

Monkey shrugged. "They came back."

Liam studied his teammates, thinking furiously. *Nicky's completely compromised,* he thought. *Malik is fightin' the mind control, but he's wavering. Snake is busy with Vincent.*

Looks like it's up to me.

"Maxwell stood over you," Snake continued, staring into Monkey's eyes. "Over both of us. He drained your power with his bare hands, and you asked him, 'Why?' Do you remember that?"

Monkey looked into her glowing eyes. "'Why?'" he repeated. "I asked him, 'Why?'"

She's hypnotizing him, Liam realized. *Using her power. But it won't last long.*

Liam glanced up at the nearest control tower. It was eighty, maybe a hundred meters away, at the edge of the pit. *Trouble is, there's at least a thousand soldiers between* it *and* me. . . .

Snake stepped closer to Monkey. "And Maxwell? What did he say?" Her eyes glowed brighter. "When you asked him why he was doing that to you?"

A look of fear crossed Monkey's face. "He . . . he said . . ."

They spoke the words in unison. "'Because I can.'"

Liam stared at the tower. *That's it,* he knew. *That's where the mind control is coming from. The Dragon isn't here, not in person; it's busy someplace else, probably fighting Steven's team. So its power is being broadcast through that machinery.*

As he thought of the Dragon, Liam felt a wave of doubt. He remembered the warmth, the security of the creature's dark embrace. He thought of the ancient carving, the power that seemed to reach down to the very roots of his homeland.

If I don't move now, he thought, *it'll snare me again.*

He took off running.

"Hey!" Monkey yelled. He pulled away from Snake, shaking off her hypnotic power. "Stop him! All of you, stop him!"

CHAPTER TWENTY-FOUR

Four soldiers converged on Liam's charging figure. He laughed and swung a fist, knocking one man away. He zigzagged to one side, then the other, jabbing out with both elbows. The soldiers toppled, offering barely any resistance.

These guys are stiff, he realized. *Looks like mind-controlled drones don't make the best fighters!*

A wall of soldiers blocked his way—eight, maybe nine. Liam hesitated. Even with his powers, he could be taken down by superior numbers. And he hadn't had time to work out a plan.

Grimacing, he lowered his head. The snorting Ram appeared above him, scraping its feet, eager to charge. As he barreled forward, the soldiers raised their energy rifles.

Before Liam could reach the soldiers, a thick fist bashed into the nearest man's helmet, knocking him to the ground. Liam looked up, amazed, to see Malik wading into the line of men. The Ox flared bright as Malik punched and kicked, expertly slapping away weapons and fists.

In less than a minute, nine Vanguard soldiers lay still on the ground.

Liam cast a glance back. The rest of the soldiers watched, unsure of their next move. Snake had retreated behind them, out of sight.

"Mate," Liam said, clapping Malik on the back. "I knew ye'd come through!"

Malik looked down at the unconscious bodies. "So much for my triumphant return to Vanguard."

"Yer better off," Liam said. "Uh-oh—incoming."

Monkey approached, leading the soldiers. "Surround 'em!" he yelled, pointing at Liam and Malik. "Bring 'em down!"

Malik turned to Liam. "You got a plan?"

"Aye," Liam replied. "I do now."

He pointed at the charging Vanguard agents—hundreds of them, converging on Liam and Malik. Then he lifted his finger up, toward the tower behind them.

"Got it," Malik said.

In one quick motion, Malik lifted Liam and threw him toward the mass of soldiers. Liam ducked and rolled, then reached forward and grabbed on to the lead soldier's helmet. The man yelped and scrabbled at his head—but Liam just bounced off, laughing and twisting in the air.

"Go, you crazy cannonball!" Malik yelled.

Liam reached out feetfirst and kicked off another soldier's helmet. Liam bounced up; the soldier went down. The others, the soldiers nearest him, pointed and aimed their weapons.

"Shoot him!" Monkey screamed. "Blast him out of the air!"

As Liam landed, a volley of energy beams seared past him. He felt a jolt of panic: *Maybe this wasn't such a great plan!* He glanced up at the tower. *Still at least forty meters away. Those beams will fry me before I can . . .*

CHAPTER TWENTY-FOUR

Wait a minute, he thought. *I've been fighting defensively, because I'm not used to having my power. But I'm invulnerable again!*

One of the soldiers had Liam in his sights, aiming his rifle carefully. Liam grinned straight at him.

"Gimme all you got," Liam said, and leaped.

The beam struck him in the chest, propelling him into the air. His jacket ripped; a burn hole appeared in his shirt. He laughed.

"Again!" he cried.

The soldiers frowned, blinked, and kept firing. In the distance, Liam could hear Monkey's angry shouts.

Liam rode the energy beams, using them to blast up and around, left and right. He angled and aimed his body carefully, bouncing and caroming off the ground and the soldiers' heads, leaping closer and closer to the deep pit of Lystria.

He'd almost reached the tower when he miscalculated. A full-strength energy beam sent him flying sideways, over the gaping abyss of the pit itself. He flailed, reached out, and grabbed hold of one of the long arcing struts that stretched from the central building to the edges of the pit.

That close to the heart of the complex, the hum of machinery pulsed and throbbed. Liam gazed into the pit. Even in the bright sunlight, he could see only a meter down. Beyond that was blackness, deep and total.

Monkey stood at the edge of the pit, backed up by his remaining soldiers. "Don't!" he called out. "Don't touch anything!"

Liam studied the control tower. He could feel the mind-control energy emanating from it. The Dragon's iron will, processed and delivered by remote control.

"Get down from there!" Monkey screamed. His soldiers held up their weapons, aiming tentatively. But they couldn't risk a shot so close to the machinery.

Liam lowered his head and braced himself against the machine strut. The Ram raged and snorted, louder and fiercer than ever before. It leaned forward, aiming its coiled horns at the control tower.

"Never send a machine t'do a Dragon's job," he growled.

Then he jumped.

When he struck the control tower, all hell broke loose. As his indestructible head rammed through the outer wall, Liam caught a quick glimpse of circuitry filling a tall chamber. Then the chamber burst apart; sparks flew, fires broke out. The tower cracked, broke in half, and toppled into the pit.

By the time Liam burst out the far side, he was laughing again.

When he landed on the ground, the soldiers were already scattered. With the Dragon's mind control disrupted, they seemed confused. They milled around in groups of four or five, comparing notes, discussing possible courses of action. Some of them had already started marching off across the desert.

CHAPTER TWENTY-FOUR

"Nice work," Malik said, clapping Liam on the back. "Mate."

"Aye, thanks." Liam looked around. "Where's Monkey?"

"I tried to stop him." Snake walked up, rubbing the back of her neck. "He clocked me and ran off."

"Brute force," Liam said. "The surest way t'beat hypnosis."

"We're not done yet." Malik pointed out over the pit. "There are still three control towers standing."

Liam studied the complex. The tower he'd struck sparked and crackled, little fires burning along its exposed stump. A few of the large struts had buckled, but most were still standing, connecting the central building to the remaining towers.

"Yeah," Liam said. "Take those out, we might knock out the Dragon's whole plan."

Malik clenched his fists and flexed. The raging Ox rose above him, snorting and stampeding in the air.

"One for you," Malik said. "And one for me. That leaves—"

"One more for me."

They turned to see Nicky. He looked sheepish—as sheepish as a man covered with yellow fur could look, anyway.

"Three of us," Malik said, nodding. "Three towers. And a thousand half-brainwashed soldiers."

Snake smiled. It wasn't her usual smirk. It seemed genuine, an expression of honest delight.

"I'll make the popcorn," she said.

"Duane? Duane, ye crazy Pig, are ye there?"

Duane whipped his head toward the screen. He shot across the Infosphere, bringing himself to a halt before an image of Liam's face.

"Liam! You're alive. Well, obviously you're alive." Duane blinked. "What's your status?"

Liam grinned. "Our status?"

The image changed to a wide-range view. The complex of Lystria lay shattered, in ruins. All four control towers had been smashed. The central building had been cracked open like a nut; it listed at an angle, leaning against the inside walls of the pit. Metal struts lay jumbled all around, like sticks thrown into a pile. Smoke rose from two of the towers and from inside the pit itself.

"Let's just say," Liam said, "the dead of Lystria might rest a little easier today."

The image panned out across the desert. A long line of soldiers, wearing the distinctive Vanguard uniforms, trudged off into the wasteland. They looked like refugees from a war.

"So did it work?" Liam asked. "We stop the Dragon in its scaly, slimy tracks?"

"Hold on a minute."

CHAPTER TWENTY-FOUR

Duane punched up a readout on an adjacent screen. The Dragon energy was indeed reduced at the Lystria site—almost nonexistent, in fact. But . . .

"Rammer?" Nicky's face crowded in next to Liam's on the screen. "How'd we do?"

Duane ignored them. He called up a range of worldwide readings: seismographs, energy levels . . . eruption frequencies. . . .

"No," he said. "You haven't stopped the Dragon."

Their faces fell.

"You've *reduced* its power," Duane added, hurriedly. "Tremors have subsided around the world. But everything within . . . approximately four thousand kilometers of Tamu Massif, in all directions, is still about to blow."

Liam sighed. "So the world won't catch fire. Only about a quarter of it."

"That's about right." Duane frowned. "The Tamu Massif complex . . . it must contain a backup system for the region in its vicinity. And judging from the readings I'm getting from the buoy left on the surface by Steven's team—"

"That's where the Dragon is." Liam grimaced. "I kind of figured that."

The image swiveled to Malik's somber face. Snake stood with him. "There's nothing more for us to do here," he said, gesturing at the smoking pit. "We're returning to base."

"Looks like it's up to Steven now," Liam said.

"Yes. Steven." Duane cut the connection. "And possibly . . ."

An impatient noise caught his attention. He turned to the far side of the Infosphere. "Yes, yes. I'm coming."

Carlos floated in the sphere's null gravity, still wrapped in a blanket. His eyes were barely open, but his hands sketched out a design on one of the screens. Duane swam over and studied the image.

"Interesting," he said. "Do you think we can build it in time?"

With great effort, Carlos turned to look him in the eye.

"We'd better," he said.

CHAPTER TWENTY-FIVE

THE DRAGON THRUST its head out of the volcano, snarling with wrath. Primal energy, the forces of nature itself, pulsed through the creature's protean form. The sea churned at the Dragon's command; the earth coughed and spat fire.

The Dragon was changing. Evolving, growing stronger with every passing minute. Electricity, magnetism, gravity—all the elemental forces danced along its skin, sparking and radiating from its form. Its wings tingled with power, itching to break free of its mountain base. But not yet. Not yet.

CHAPTER TWENTY-FIVE

The world was changing, too—bending to the Dragon's will, to its inhuman dream of a perfect future. All along the seabed, in the dense rock that partially formed the planet's crust, plates collided, heated, transformed. Very soon *everything* would change.

A mote, a speck of matter, caught the Dragon's eye: the metal vessel, still limping its way through the dark water. It was badly damaged, its air steadily leaking out. But it managed to fire off another burst of sound, detonating yet another explosive charge along the volcanic mountain below.

The resulting quake barely registered on the Dragon's superhuman body, but some instinct—possibly left over from its human host—made its neck scales prickle in alarm. The ship and its puny explosions couldn't harm the Dragon. But they might damage the machines, the postorganic constructs that were crucial to building the Dragon's new world.

The Dragon whipped its head upward, opened its jaws wide, and spat fire. Just a tiny flame, enough to bathe the vessel. The ship tipped, listed, and rolled end over end.

Inside, the water had risen to waist level. Josie half sat, half floated in the pilot seat, a dazed expression on her face. Kim leaned over her, tending to an open gash on her forehead. Roxanne struggled out of the power amplifier mask and started toward them.

Then the ship tipped over and she went under, gasping as all the air bubbled out of her lungs.

"Such nastiness," Mince said, smirking at the holographic image of Roxanne flailing underwater.

Steven stared in horror.

"She's the only one who knows how to pilot your little toy, isn't she?" Mince indicated Josie's dazed figure. "And look at that leak. I'd say they've got fifteen, maybe twenty minutes before the whole ship is flooded."

She clicked a remote control and the image vanished. The tectonic plates returned in its place, sliding through the air, shifting and colliding. The whir of machinery filled the two-story lab, louder and more discordant than before.

"So," Mince said, turning to look at Steven, "what you gonna do?"

Steven glanced past the hologram, at his parents. They stood huddled together, backed up against a laboratory sink. The path to them wasn't clear; two large tables stood between him and them.

Mince smiled. She held up her rings, the ones that spelled out DIE, and started polishing their sharp tips. Behind her, the Sha Qi crystal glowed white, powering the deadly machines.

He clenched his fists. There was no solution. If he stayed to protect his parents, his teammates would either drown or be fried by the Dragon. If he left to save Kim and the others, Mince would kill his parents.

He couldn't move. He could barely think. The plate

holograms sliced through the air, faster and faster, mirroring the accelerating activity within the earth itself. The Tigers screamed in his ear: *This is your choice. This is your doom.*

This is the way the cycle ends.

He peered at Mince through the furiously moving holograms.

"I don't know," he said. "I don't know what to do."

"Ha-ha!" she cackled. "The brave Tiger. The chosen one. The great champion of the Zodiacs!"

He looked away. His parents were staring at him. His mother looked worried, expectant, maybe a bit guilty.

His father just glared. Steven's heart sank, and then immediately he felt a surge of anger. *Guess I've disappointed you, Dad. Again.*

"Time's running out," Mince continued. "Check it."

She reached out with both arms and zoomed in on the hologram. A mosaic of plates moved back and forth, left and right, colliding and sliding above and beneath one another. A pair of larger plates crept into view, moving slowly toward each other.

"Those are the big ones," Mince said. "These two plates are the key. Once they collide, the reaction can't be stopped."

Steven didn't answer. He thought of all the people who'd trusted him, who'd followed him up to this crisis point: His teammates. His parents. Maxwell's former agents.

They're all about to die. Because I couldn't cut it. Couldn't break the cycle.

He studied the two large plates. Their movement was slow, almost imperceptible. But they were drawing closer. Another five minutes—at most—and they would touch.

I should have listened to the Tigers. I should never have taken the powers back. Even as the thought occurred to him, though, he knew it was just self-pity. *If I'd followed the Tigers' advice, the Dragon would still have carried out its plans. The earth would still be doomed.*

But I wouldn't have to make this choice!

Visions, voices, memories flashed into his mind. His team, his parents, lying dead at the Dragon's hand. The ancient Zodiacs, hunted to their deaths by riders on horseback. The blasted hole in the desert. The Zodiac wheel, spinning faster and faster in the void.

The Tigers' whisper: *Oblivion.*

The Dragon energy, sparking and flashing in the darkness. His fellow Zodiacs gasping, drowning.

Water falling from the light. *Drip. Drip. Drip.*

The chain-mailed warrior on horseback. *No more Zodiacs. No more.*

The lanky Rat, dying in his arms. *I have always loved you.*

The spinning wheel. The glowing crystal. The crossbow bolt through the heart.

The tectonic plates, creeping closer and closer together.

Jasmine—his own voice, sounding as if it came from the bottom of a deep abyss—*are you gonna forget me?*

And his father—always his father: *What have you*

accomplished with the gifts we gave you? What have you done in your life that is truly worthwhile?

The Tiger pricked up its ears at that one.

We all lived through the cycle, the old Tigers said, *and all of us failed. Now you will fail, too.*

"Shut up," he snarled. He shook off the visions and stared at the hologram. The plates were still converging, closing the gap, slow but steady.

Mince leaned against the table with the crystal on it. Her body language was casual—but that, he knew, was an act. Inside she was coiled, tense, locked in her own private torment.

What had Jasmine said about her? *She wasn't always bad.*

As he took a step forward, Mince turned sharply toward him.

She's tough, Malosi had said, *vicious as a scorpion. But inside, she's just a kid.*

All at once, Steven knew what to do. With an effort of will, he banished all distractions from his mind. His friends in the flooding drill-ship. The volcano rumbling around him. The crystal-driven machines. The slowly converging tectonic plates.

His father, eyeing him from across the room.

Steven walked through the hologram, into the space between the converging plates. Mince tensed and held up her DIE rings.

"One step farther," she said, "and I'll kill you."

Inside, the Tiger roared at the challenge. But Steven didn't move, didn't leap to the attack. He stopped a safe distance from her and raised both hands.

"I'm not going to fight you," he said.

She stood rigid, her fist still raised. He couldn't see her eyes behind her sunglasses, but she seemed less certain.

She's just a kid.

"You've had bad things happen to you," he said. "Haven't you?"

She laughed loudly. "*That's* your play? Psych me out while your pals take a speed-learning course in how to breathe water? No, no, kid. That's not how this game works. You have to *choose*."

"What about *your* choice?" He kept his voice calm, even. "Did anybody ever ask you about that?"

"Nobody who's still around." She jabbed out with the DIE rings, posing like a ninja.

"I asked you before what was going to happen to you. When all this was over."

"And I told you. I'll be right here."

Out of the corner of his eye, he saw the large holographic plates—still inching closer together.

"You said there'd be no people," he said. "That's what you really want, isn't it?"

Her lip quivered.

"People cause you pain," he continued. "Your father—he caused you a lot of pain. Didn't he?"

"Shut up," she muttered.

"That's the lure of the Dragon." He frowned, considering. "I didn't understand it before. I just thought it was evil, inhuman. But it appeals to that part of us that's been hurt, that's terrified to be hurt again. It tells us we can get rid of the hurt forever. That we'll never have to deal with human feelings—with *people*—ever again."

Mince reached up. For a moment he thought she was going to attack him.

But Mince just pulled off her sunglasses, revealing tired, surprisingly light-colored eyes. "What's wrong with not feeling?" she whispered.

"Nothing. If you're an immortal supernatural creature with elk antlers and incinerator breath."

Despite herself, Mince let out a strangled laugh.

"But the rest of us . . ." He shrugged. "We gotta live in the world."

"W-what—" she stuttered, "what do you think you're *doing*?"

He smiled.

"Breaking the cycle."

She stared at him for a long moment. Was that a tear in the corner of her eye?

"Parents," she said. "They screw us up."

"They sure do."

Mince reached into her pocket and pulled out a small remote control. She aimed it at the hologram and pressed a red button. The whirring subsided; the crystal went dark. The two converging plates ground to a halt.

Steven's parents ran to join him. Neither of them tried to hug Steven; he'd never had that sort of relationship with them. His mother eyed Mince with suspicion.

But his father's eyes were fixed on his son. The old man's stare was different now. It took Steven a moment to recognize the expression.

Respect.

It wasn't just his father. Inside, the Tigers also seemed to regard him differently. Almost with awe.

I did it. I did what none of them could do. And I did it by focusing on one young woman . . . not a Zodiac wielder, not an ancient power, not a world-shaking catastrophe. Just a normal person in pain.

Mince clicked off the hologram. When she turned to face them, she looked very unhappy.

"The Dragon's going to notice," she said. "Soon. You better get out of here."

"Thank you," Steven said. Then he remembered: "My mother's air hose . . ."

"There's diving equipment in the *AAAHHHH!*"

Kim appeared in the air, centimeters from Mince's face. Mince stumbled back and fell to the floor. Kim looked around, flailed, and dropped on top of her.

"Kim!" Steven cried.

"Get off me!" Mince cried, swiping out. Kim leaped away, barely avoiding the touch of Mince's rings. Steven ran forward to catch her.

CHAPTER TWENTY-FIVE

Kim coughed, spitting water. She was soaking wet. She stared at him with wide, panicked eyes.

"I 'ported *blind*," she gasped.

"It's okay," he said.

"Never done that before. Didn't know where I was going." She shook her head—a wild, animal motion. "I could have died."

"Steven," Mrs. Lee said.

He looked up. Mince stood holding the remote control again. Her whole demeanor had changed; she seemed once again the vicious predator, the furious creature he'd known before.

"So," she hissed. "All that talk about *living in the world*, about *breaking the cycle*—that was just a trick? To distract me while your girlfriend attacked me?"

Kim coughed again. "Girlfriend?"

"No." Steven took a step toward Mince. "That's not—"

"Stay back!" Mince held up her rings on one hand and gripped the remote control in the other. "I was a fool. A fool to trust you—to trust anybody."

"You *can* trust me," he said. "I meant it. All of it."

"No. Never again." She held up the remote. "No more people." She pressed the button.

Nothing happened. No hologram, no whirring noise. The crystal remained dark.

Mince frowned at the remote. She jabbed at the button again, then a third time.

"It's okay." Steven started forward, his steps slow and measured. "It's over."

She locked eyes with him for a second, then threw the remote control. It struck him in the nose.

"Ow!"

She was already running toward the hatch leading outside. Steven rubbed his nose and started after her.

Kim followed. "Hey," she began, "what's—"

The entire room shook. A huge crack opened in the center of the lab, forcing the floor upward. A lab table toppled and crashed.

Kim lost her footing and reached out. Steven leaped forward, the Tiger manifesting above his head, and caught her.

By the time they landed, Mince was gone. As the tremor subsided, the floor settled back down. The Lees picked their way over to join Steven, stepping carefully.

"Was that the Dragon?" Steven asked.

"I think it was the last explosive charge," Kim said. "Roxanne was about to set it off when I 'ported down here. I was hoping to get you out before—"

A chunk of the ceiling broke loose with a loud crunching noise. Steven hustled the others out of the way as it came crashing down.

"—before, like, *that*," Kim finished.

Steven thought furiously. "How bad is the drill-ship?"

"Not good—it's pretty waterlogged. We couldn't figure out how to fix the hull."

"I can repair the ship," Mrs. Lee said.

CHAPTER TWENTY-FIVE

Steven and Kim turned to her, surprised.

"I watched your Mr. Ox outfit the vessel," Mrs. Lee continued. "I know how to patch the leaks."

"My wife is the engineer in the family," Mr. Lee said. "My talent is for business."

"I have many talents," Mrs. Lee added.

Kim blinked at Steven. "Your folks are full of surprises."

"Yes, they are." He nodded, stunned. "Can you 'port us back up there?"

"One at a time." Kim grimaced. "And only if we can locate the ship. Otherwise we might *poof* back in under two kilometers of water."

"The hologram view," Mr. Lee said.

They scattered, each taking a position at one of Mince's computers. The room shook again; a two-story ladder clattered to the ground.

"All I'm finding is stored Minecraft games," Steven grumbled.

"I have it," his mother said.

The hologram flickered to life in the middle of the room. The drill-ship listed and wobbled, veering dangerously close to the glowing, smoking volcano.

"Where's the Dragon?" Kim asked.

"It must have withdrawn," Steven replied. "Probably thinks the ship is finished."

Kim studied the hologram for a moment. "Okay. I got it." She held out a hand. "Mrs. Lee? I think you're first."

Mrs. Lee hesitated.

"Mom," Steven said. "It's okay."

"Steven," his mother said. "It is not that I don't trust your friend—"

"Oh, I'm kind of more than his friend," Kim said. "Maybe. Not quite his *girlfriend*, though, like the mad-scientist girl said. That's crazy. Well, maybe someday. I talk a lot when I'm nervous, by the way."

Mrs. Lee glanced at her son, then smiled and shook her head. Kim took the older woman's hand, pulled her close, and leaped. With a *poof*, they vanished.

"Oh," Mr. Lee said.

Steven laughed. "Dad, that's the most rattled I've ever seen you."

Mr. Lee grimaced. "If I am to take that ride next," he said, "you may anticipate the joy of seeing me more rattled."

Steven reeled in shock. *Was that a joke? From* Dad*?*

Kim *poofed* back in, breathing hard. Mr. Lee was true to his word; the expression on his face when Kim teleported him away was priceless. Steven watched them go, thinking: *I'll remember that happily for the rest of my life.*

One last time, Kim teleported back in. She staggered toward Steven, dazed from the exertion.

"Just you and me," he said. "Together again."

The room tipped sideways. A sink burst open, spraying water into the chamber. A support beam fell onto the Sha Qi crystal, shattering it in a spray of sparks.

"You and me," she echoed, wrapping her arms around

his waist. "And a half-wrecked ship, a collapsing volcano, and a giant angry monster from before time with enough power to fry the world."

"Think we can handle it?" he asked.

She smiled, tensing her legs to leap.

"Piece of cake."

With a *poof*, they were gone.

CHAPTER TWENTY-SIX

WHEN THEY ARRIVED inside the drill-ship, the water was up to their chests. Kim gasped and went under. Steven hoisted her back up.

"Thanks," she said. "I'll just . . . float here for a minute."

Josie was standing near the pilot's seat, working the few controls that were still above water. There was a bandage on her forehead. She turned and called, "They're aboard!"

On the other side of the cockpit, Roxanne and Mr. Lee held a hard rubber patch against the crack in the hull. Mrs. Lee pushed her husband to one side and pressed a power drill into a corner of the patch. The drill whined sharply.

CHAPTER TWENTY-SIX

"That should do it," Mrs. Lee called. "Try draining it now."

Josie flipped a switch. A hidden compression pump started to hum. Slowly the water level began to drop.

"Anything I can do?" Steven asked.

Mrs. Lee waved him away. Mr. Lee took his hand off the patch and a spout of water erupted into the hatchway, spraying everywhere. Mrs. Lee turned to her husband and let loose a stream of curses in Chinese, too fast for Steven to follow. Grumbling, she stabbed the drill into another corner of the patch.

"Sorry," Mr. Lee said.

Steven watched the drama, his mouth hanging wide open. He'd never seen his father apologize to his mother before. In fact, he'd never seen his father apologize to *any-one* before.

By the time the patch had been secured, the water was below their waists. Kim floated easily down into a chair, exhausted. Teleporting with other people always took a lot out of her.

"That should hold it," Mrs. Lee called. "But I wish to emphasize that the hull is badly damaged. It would be advisable to avoid stressful situations."

Steven laughed. "Mom, which Dragon-hunting mission are *you* on?"

"Holo-projectors should be functioning now," Josie called. "I think I can get an exterior view."

They all gathered by the pilot's console as an overhead

shot of the mountain flickered into view. "Observe," Mr. Lee said. "The volcano's mouth."

"No smoke," Steven said. "The eruption's stopped. Looks like the Dragon's machinery is toast."

"Then we won? The earth is saved—it's party time?" Roxanne mimed playing a guitar. "Maybe even *concert* time?"

A quake shook the ship. Kim stumbled into Steven. Josie muttered something and manipulated the control stick, leveling them out.

" 'Party time'?" Kim frowned at her teammate. "You got a big mouth."

Roxanne shrugged. "It's my power."

"Look," Steven said.

In the hologram, the mountain shook and started to crumble. The mouth collapsed inward, sending bubbles and flecks of ash floating upward.

With a sweep of giant wings, the Dragon burst out of the seabed. It seemed to stretch on for kilometers, across the length of the fallen volcano. Its claws were wider than before, its talons even sharper. Its jaws stretched wide, gaping beneath sparking horns. Energy crackled along its thorny spine.

Holding his breath, Steven leaned closer to the hologram. The Dragon's outlines were blurry, indistinct through the churning water. *It's still growing,* he realized. *It hasn't even reached its full size yet.*

CHAPTER TWENTY-SIX

"It looks different," Roxanne said. "Like it's made of electricity or something."

"That is qi energy," Mr. Lee said. "Amazingly pure."

"Drawn from the stars themselves," Mrs. Lee added. "I've never seen levels like that."

The Dragon's long tail whipped free, ripping a seam through the slope of the volcano. As the creature swooped into the open water, the mountain shuddered and collapsed flat.

"Whoa," Kim said. "Guess there's no point in going back for Mince."

"She wouldn't take our help anyway," Steven replied. "I really thought I reached her, for a minute."

"Bet you she escaped," Roxanne said. "That girl's like a cat."

"I think we've got a more immediate problem." As Josie manipulated the outside view, dark water bubbled across the hologram. "Where'd the Dragon go? That thing is *fast*—"

Mrs. Lee cleared her throat. She pointed at the viewport, eyes wide.

A single enormous eye stared in at them. Its pupil was a crystalline formation, like a glass carving floating in an ocean of red-veined fluid. Huge scales surrounded the eye, each one the size of a satellite dish.

"Um," Roxanne said. The Rooster rose above her. "Last stand?"

Steven clenched his fists. "Guess so."

"Our helmets are buried inside the collapsed volcano," Mrs. Lee pointed out. "We cannot survive unaided at this depth."

"Mom! If you've got a better idea . . ."

He trailed off. The eye was gone; the glow had faded away. The viewport was empty except for the raging, bubbling sea.

Josie was already working the hologram. "There," she said. "It's turned away from us."

Steven and Kim crowded in to look. The Dragon's electric glow was moving incredibly fast. It was headed toward the surface, already barely visible through the dark, rippling water.

"Guess it decided four Zodiacs and two civilians weren't worth its time," Roxanne said.

Steven swallowed, a terrible feeling growing in the pit of his stomach. "How far away is Japan?"

"Roughly sixteen hundred kilometers," Mrs. Lee said, pointing at the receding Dragon, "in exactly that direction."

Josie muttered something and plopped down in the pilot's seat. She turned to look at Steven. "I don't suppose the next thing out of your mouth is gonna be 'Good job, team. Let's head for home'?"

Steven turned away. He was exhausted, waterlogged, and emotionally drained—just like the rest of them. He wanted nothing more than to order that the drill-ship return to

Greenland, and to fight the Dragon another day. But . . .

"There are a hundred and twenty-seven million people in Japan," Mr. Lee said. His voice was unusually gentle.

"Steven?" Kim asked. "What do we do?"

"I want to say it." He frowned. "But it's gonna sound lame."

Roxanne rolled her eyes. "Spit it out, boss."

He turned to Josie, then stared out the viewport and grimaced. The Dragon had already passed out of sight, but the faint glow of its energy lingered across the mountain.

"Josie," he said, "follow that Dragon."

The drill-ship shot through the choppy water. The Dragon's speed was incredible, and it already had a sizable lead on them. Steven rapped his fist on the bulkhead in frustration.

"Come on," he said. "We've gotta catch it!"

The whine of the engines grew louder. The ship began to rattle. Kim braced herself against the wall and clasped Steven's hand. Roxanne sucked in a nervous breath.

"Faster!" he cried.

On the opposite side of the chamber, the hull patch creaked. A small trickle of water ran down the wall.

"If I push it any more," Josie called, "we'll blow apart!"

A sharp noise came from the hull. Steven looked over to see a thin vertical crack, expanding as he watched.

"I do not recommend this," Mrs. Lee said. She and her husband were strapped into the ship's only two crash seats. "The hull's integrity is *extremely* tentative."

"Translation," Roxanne said, "we're about to crack open like an egg."

"Approaching the surface!" Josie yelled. "Hang on!"

There was a noise like a clap of thunder. The ship shuddered as surface tension slammed everyone down onto the floor. The hull groaned, a noise that almost sounded like a human scream.

The ship shot out of the sea like a bullet from a gun. It hung in the air for a moment, engines smoking. Then it bounced down onto the waves, rolled once, and floated.

Water poured into the cockpit. As his parents unstrapped themselves, Steven leaped to his feet and saw the source: the crack along the hull.

"Josie!" he called, pointing at it. "Turn us so that side is facing up!"

"Roger that."

The world tipped on its side. Roxanne, Kim, and the Lees tumbled to the bulkhead, which had suddenly become the floor.

Steven leaped up, grabbed at the crack in the wall, and forced it apart. Above his head, the Tiger roared and flashed. All its senses were alert now, its ancient power lending him strength.

The wall buckled and cracked open. Steven hauled

himself up through the narrow gap. Sunlight shone bright, blinding in contrast to the dim sea depths. He blinked, waiting for his eyes to adjust.

Japan was barely visible, a hazy coastline breaking the line of the water. Still a long way away—but too close, he knew. *Barely a hop across the street for . . .*

"Steven?" Kim called from below. "What do you see?"

Something was wrong. The sun was high; it must be almost noon, Japan time. But some object obscured the bright yellow orb. A thick spiked body with a fan of bat-like wings.

The Dragon dove out of the sky. For the first time, Steven saw the creature clearly. It was pure fury, primal power given corporeal form. It was huge, many times the size it had been under Jasmine's or Maxwell's control. As it drew closer, it seemed to grow even larger, the electric outlines of its wings spreading to cover the sky.

Its jaws gaped wide. Its eyes showed no mercy, no hope, no trace of humanity.

And it was heading straight toward them.

I broke the cycle, he thought. *I beat the curse. But I guess it doesn't matter.*

Looks like I failed, after all.

There was nothing to do, nowhere to hide. No way to save his team or the millions of innocents on the islands of Japan. So the Tiger just stood its ground, reared back its head, and roared.

Steven became aware of a presence at his shoulder. Roxanne stared up at the raging beast.

"Last stand?" she asked.

"This time," he replied, "I'm pretty sure—"

"*kkkkkrackl*—even? Steven, do you read?"

Steven slapped his ear, startled. His earpiece hadn't worked underwater. He'd forgotten he was wearing it. "Duane?"

Roxanne pointed up. *"Look!"*

The Dragon stopped, whirling in midair. Even with Steven's enhanced senses, it took him a moment to make out the reason: a small dot in the distance, flying high—but closing in fast.

"The plane," he said.

"We're almost there," Duane said in Steven's earpiece. "ETA forty, maybe fifty seconds."

The Dragon seemed to pause, as if considering Duane's words. It spat fire at the oncoming plane, but its flame fell short. Then it turned and cast a dangerous-looking glare at the drill-ship.

"Gulp," Roxanne said, enunciating the word carefully.

"Steven," Duane said, "you have to get out of that ship."

"Out!" Steven cried, whirling around.

Roxanne was already leaning back inside the cockpit. "Everybody out!" she yelled. "Now!"

Mrs. Lee climbed up first; Steven gave her a hand, helping her out and into the choppy water. Mr. Lee followed. Josie went last.

"Kim?" Steven called. "Where—"

With a *poof*, she appeared on the outside of the hull. She reached out for Steven, and together they looked up.

The Dragon was circling. It looked like a cat considering whether to eat the mouse on the ground or chase after the fly buzzing above. It whirled, locked eyes with Steven, and opened its jaws.

"Dive!" Steven cried.

He and Kim leaped free, less than a second ahead of the searing burst of flames. Steven struck the water hard and immediately started swimming. He glanced sideways to confirm that Kim was keeping up with him.

Ahead, Josie and Roxanne were treading water. Steven caught sight of his parents and thought: *Good thing they can swim. That's another thing I didn't know about them.*

He looked back. A steady stream of flame reached from the Dragon's mouth to the cracked, battered drill-ship. The hull began to char and melt. Metal dripped down in rivulets, sizzling as it struck the water. Black smoke rose, filling the air with a foul machine-oil smell.

Steven's earpiece crackled again.

"Hang on down there," Malik said. "Let's see if we can distract 'im for you."

The plane screamed down out of the sky, buzzing around the Dragon's head like a mosquito. The Dragon clamped its jaws shut, cutting off the flame barrage, and whirled upward. It shrieked in irritation and coughed fire, three quick bursts blazing through the air.

The Zodiac plane dodged the assault, swooping and zigzagging. It veered sideways, dangerously close to the water, then executed a vertical climb, straight toward the sun. The Dragon followed, still spitting fire.

Malik is one hell of a pilot! Steven thought.

With a screech of tortured engines, the plane reversed course and dove again. The Dragon, momentarily blinded by the sun, continued its upward flight.

"Mom," Steven said, swimming up next to his parents. "You okay?"

She coughed and nodded. "Though I'm glad I did not wear my usual office clothes."

"Bought us a little time," Malik said in Steven's ear.

"Thanks," Steven replied. "I'm glad you're on our side."

"Stand by for a rescue. Boss."

The plane leveled off, turning toward the six floating figures. As it swooped past the smoking drill-ship, the charred vessel burped water and sank below the waves.

"Always liked that ship," Josie said sadly.

A hatch slid open on the underside of the plane. Three figures dove out gracefully: Nicky, Malik, and Snake. Their Zodiac avatars flared as they struck the water and started swimming, moving toward Steven's group with strong, purposeful strokes.

"Geroni-bloody-mo!"

Liam followed out of the hatch, dropping like a rock. He tucked himself into a ball and splashed down hard.

"Vanguard training," Josie said, deadpan. "Some people got it, some don't."

Roxanne laughed and splashed her.

The rescue party fanned out toward the floating Zodiacs. Malik moved easily through the water, reaching out a hand to each of the Lees. Liam lay back and allowed the exhausted Kim to climb onto his stomach.

"You don't dive too good," Kim said, teasing him.

"Nah," Liam replied. "I'm more of a flotation device." He looked like he was lounging in a pool, despite the choppy waves.

Nicky swam over to Josie and Roxanne. "Joze," he said. "This your new BFF?"

"She a'ight. But you'll always be my partner." Josie punched him playfully, then wrinkled her nose. "Wet fur and all."

A shadow fell over the group. Steven looked up to see the plane. It swooped low, hovering over the water as if it were about to land on a runway.

"Tiger?"

He whirled around in the water. Snake floated before him, holding out her hand, her dark hair slicked back. "Rescue time."

He hesitated.

"Don't worry." She smiled in that unnerving way of hers. "This is just Zodiac business."

CHAPTER TWENTY-SIX

Reluctantly, he took her hand, wondering: *How does she always make me feel eight years old?*

The plane slowed to a stop atop the water. One by one, they all climbed onto the wing. Mr. Lee helped his wife up, the two of them coughing and gasping for breath.

Maybe they don't swim as well as they pretend to, Steven thought.

Kim *poofed* onto the wing next to Malik. "If you're here," she asked, "who's flying the plane?"

"Jasmine took the stick," he replied.

"*Jasmine?*" Steven asked. "Is she—"

A roar filled the air, interrupting him. All at once, the assembled Zodiacs turned to see a column of fire, reaching out of the sky to touch the water with a sizzle.

"One bloody guess who that is," Liam said.

Steven frowned. "What's it *doing?*"

The Dragon hovered above, its jaws open wide. But it didn't seem to be aiming at the plane, or at the figures gathered on the wing. It swept its head around, forming a semicircle around them. And everywhere its breath touched, the water *remained on fire.*

"Ah," Roxanne said. "That's, ah . . ."

"Impossible?" Liam asked.

The Dragon's assault continued. It moved in a full circle, its motion steady and unhurried. The fire barrier grew, almost completely surrounding the jet and its passengers. The flames rose at least five meters from the water's surface.

Liam, Roxanne, and Kim gathered around Steven. The

others collected in small groups, watching the mystic fire that seemed to burn seawater itself.

"That," Liam said, "is a *literal*—"

"Don't say it," Kim said.

"A ring of fire," Steven whispered.

The Dragon finished its circle, closing the ring with an extra burst of flame. Then it turned, growling, to regard its enemies.

"Now?" Roxanne asked.

"Third time's a charm," Steven said gravely.

He turned to address the others. Some of them were his friends; some he barely knew. He'd fought against some of them and alongside others. As for his parents, he'd spent most of his life running away from them.

And it's all led to this.

"Zodiacs," he said in his most commanding voice, "*last stand.*"

Jasmine grimaced, grinding her teeth as she watched the holographic display. The Dragon wheeled around in the air, spitting fire down at the sea. The creature was pure fury, unbridled destruction. She knew that better than any of them.

They can't stop it, she thought. *All of us together couldn't put a dent in its hide. Only one thing can.*

She flipped off the hologram and leaped out of the

pilot's chair. As she approached the big table, Duane looked up from his welding torch. "What's going on?"

"You don't want to know."

Carlos shot her a quick worried glance. He had shaved and dressed; he looked weak and shaky but determined. The table was strewn with electronics, tools, and welding equipment.

He held up a hand for Duane to stop. Duane flicked a switch and the torch's flame died.

"How's it coming?" Jasmine asked, trying to conceal the urgency in her voice.

Carlos beckoned to her. He held up the still-smoking object. It was made of bronze, cube-shaped, and roughly the size of a teapot.

"Almost ready," he said.

She took it in her hands. It was warm, its surface slightly tarnished. All six sides of the cube were blank.

A gout of flame, visible through the front windows, seared past the plane. Jasmine tensed, grimaced, and tossed the cube back to Carlos.

"Better hurry," she said.

CHAPTER TWENTY-SEVEN

STEVEN GATHERED the Zodiacs in an arc formation, balanced on the wing of the plane. The Dragon hovered just above its wall of fire, snorting and flapping its enormous wings.

It's in no hurry, he thought. *It knows we're trapped.*

Nicky glanced back at the fuselage. "I, uh, don't s'pose we could just hop inside and fly away?"

Josie gestured at the Dragon. "That thing would burn us out of the sky."

"With barely a thought," Snake added.

The water churned and boiled, rocking the plane. Steven stumbled and almost fell off the wing.

CHAPTER TWENTY-SEVEN

"All right," he said. "Everybody—"

"RAWWWRRRR!"

Nicky sprinted forward, dropped to all fours, and leaped off the wing. He soared into the air, headed straight for the hovering Dragon.

"He keeps doin' that," Liam muttered. He lowered his head and charged.

"No!" Steven cried.

Nicky flew through the air, his sharp claws swiping wildly. Liam followed a few meters behind, the deadly Ram avatar blazing and snorting above him.

"I can't look," Kim said.

The Dragon didn't even move its head. Only its eye swiveled slightly, following Nicky's path. It reached out a single talon and slashed, knocking both Zodiacs out of the air with one blow.

Nicky struck the water—dangerously close to the Dragon's fire barrier. Liam splashed down, went under, and resurfaced spitting water. He pointed at Nicky and yelled back toward the plane: "He's out cold!"

Malik touched Kim's shoulder. "Take me there," he said. She nodded and grabbed his arm. Together they leaped off the wing and *poofed* away.

They reappeared above the water near Nicky, who was drifting toward the fire. Malik dove under and swam toward the unconscious Dog with thick, powerful strokes. He grabbed Nicky under the arms and began dragging him toward the plane.

Kim rode on Liam's back. "You know something?" she asked, pointing at Malik. "He's *heavy*."

Steven registered all that out of the corner of his eye. His attention was focused on the Dragon. It hovered dangerously close, dark clouds of smoke puffing out of the corners of its electrically charged mouth.

The Lees helped haul Nicky back onto the wing. He came to and shook his head, scattering water in all directions. Mr. and Mrs. Lee recoiled.

"Tired of fighting monsters," Nicky muttered groggily. "I want a *real* job."

He's out of action, Steven thought. *This is bad. An unstoppable enemy, no strategy—and right away we're down one man.*

Liam and Kim appeared at his side, both soaking wet. Kim was winded. Liam seemed completely unharmed, as usual.

"We need a delayin' tactic," Liam said.

"Fast," Kim added.

Steven nodded. "Roxanne. Wall of sound?"

She grimaced and inhaled deeply. The Rooster appeared above her head, shrieking and cawing. Roxanne held her breath for a long moment, allowing the Zodiac power to build up.

Then she opened her mouth and let loose a powerful sonic assault. Her head swiveled back and forth, sweeping the sound wall before them. The Dragon growled, eyeing the barrier.

"She can't keep that up for long," Kim said.

CHAPTER TWENTY-SEVEN

"Nope. So we've got to make this count." Steven whirled to address the others. "Nicky had the right idea, but not enough power. Josie, Malik—when the sound barrier drops, you've got to attack the Dragon physically. I'll be with you, and Liam, too. Celine, it's a long shot, but maybe you can distract it with your hypnosis."

He glanced at Roxanne. She was maintaining the sonic barrier, her head moving slowly from side to side. But sweat had broken out on her brow, and her eyes looked desperate.

"Steven?"

He turned, irritated. "Not now, Mom. I just need you to stay back—"

"Your mother," Mr. Lee said sternly, "is attempting to remind you of the weapon we gave you."

He blinked at them. *No clue.*

"In the drill-ship?" Mrs. Lee prodded.

Kim reached a hand into Steven's pocket. As he watched, surprised, she pulled out a small metal cylinder.

"The qi disruptor," he muttered.

"In concert with your assault," Mrs. Lee said, "it may be able to momentarily disrupt the Dragon's form." She sounded like a kindergarten teacher talking to a sleepy five-year-old.

Kim held out the disruptor. Steven glanced at it, then at the Dragon. The creature sniffed at the sound barrier, eyeing the humans beyond.

"Nah," he said to Kim, pushing her hand away. "You keep it."

Roxanne coughed and gasped. In an instant, the barrier was down.

The Dragon growled.

"Go!" Steven cried, sweeping his arm forward.

He ran toward the edge of the wing. *This is the end,* he thought. *The end of the cycle. The Dragon's going to fry us like bacon.*

But at least we'll go down together.

He leaped through the air, the Tiger roaring with power. Josie and Malik followed. Liam rolled himself into a ball and soared behind.

They landed along the Dragon's body, snarling and clawing. Josie touched down on its neck, her Horse avatar whinnying and chomping at the air. Malik landed a powerful punch to the Dragon's wing joint, denting a few scales. Steven almost overshot but grabbed on to the Dragon's powerful tail, braced himself, and tugged hard.

Liam plowed into the Dragon's eye. Eldritch energy, the concentrated power of the Zodiac, blazed all around him, holding him suspended in the air. As the creature cried out in pain, Liam bounced away.

The Dragon glanced toward the plane—where Celine caught its eye. A bright green glow surrounded her; the coiled, hissing Snake whipped back and forth above her body. They locked eyes.

"Fly away," she said. It sounded like a chant. "Fly away and leave this world."

CHAPTER TWENTY-SEVEN

Kim held up the qi disruptor to the Lees. "Like this?" she asked, pointing it at the Dragon. They nodded.

"Fly away," Celine repeated.

Roxanne fired a series of short sound bursts. They struck the Dragon in its belly, jolting it backward in the air.

The creature's tail whipped up, almost shaking Steven loose. He leaped off and landed on its back, between the two crackling wings. The Dragon's skin felt like fire, like raw electric current. He scrambled to keep his balance, recoiling from the touch of its scales.

Josie stood upright on the creature's neck. She surfed from side to side, dodging its sharp horns, punching it repeatedly. Malik clung to a wing, pounding one powerful Ox blow after another into the Dragon's scales. The raging water flowed only a few meters below.

"Spinal tap!" Steven cried, aiming a two-handed punch right at the middle of the creature's back. It howled in pain and whipped its head back and forth. A sharp horn grazed Steven's cheek.

Celine staggered. "Fly . . . away. . . ."

She fell to the surface of the plane's wing, her power depleted. The Snake avatar faded away.

Kim aimed the disruptor with shaking hands. A dark beam burst forth from it, like a shadow against the looming ring of fire. It looked like blackness, the utter absence of light.

When it struck the Dragon, the creature grew stiff. It

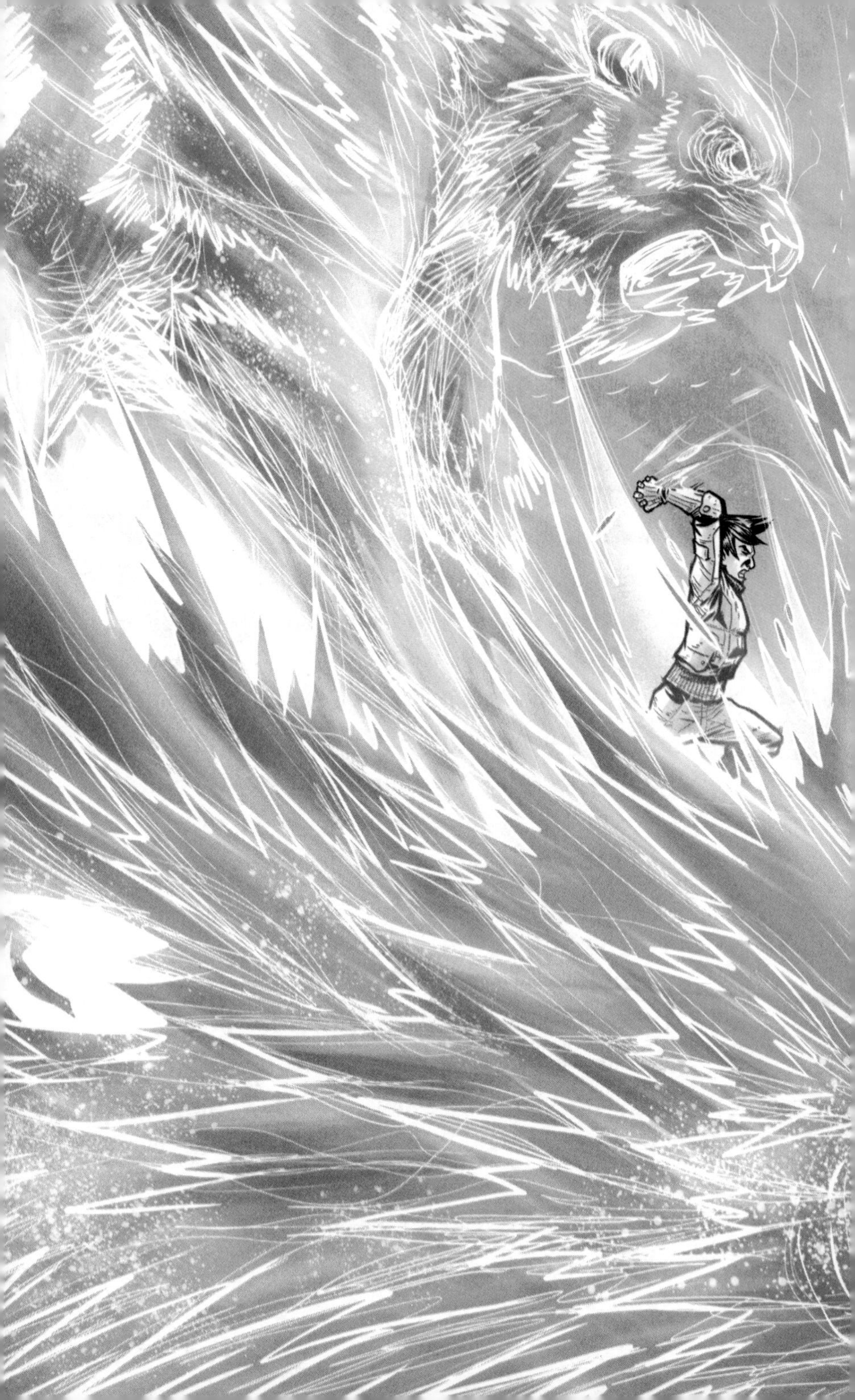

flickered, becoming transparent, intangible. For just a moment, Steven saw through its body to the center of its being. A human figure hovered there, limp, suspended in the air.

That's Maxwell, he realized. *Or his body, anyway. The Dragon's still using it.*

The disruptor beam bored into the Dragon. The creature flickered, vanished for a split second, and cried out. Its massive wings flapped up, then slashed down.

A crackling horn swept Steven off his perch. He lost his grip and tumbled through the air. He caught a quick glimpse of the fire wall, still blazing bright, and then he hit the water.

Malik and Josie swam up next to him. "Knocked us off, too," Malik said.

Josie coughed up water. "Is it gone?"

Liam swam over, pointing. "Not bloody likely."

Steven looked up. The Dragon hovered overhead, larger and more solid than ever. It reared back, blazing with power, and spat fire into the sky.

Kim stepped out to the edge of the plane wing and waved the qi disruptor. "It's out of juice!" She tossed it into the sea.

Nicky and Celine lay dazed on the wing.

Roxanne fired off another volley of sonic bursts, but they were growing weaker. This time the Dragon barely noticed them.

"Mom!" Steven called. "Got any more tricks?"

Mrs. Lee shook her head sadly.

The Dragon wheeled and swept its tail through the air. The ring of fire burned higher, flaring into the sky.

Liam dunked his head and spat water in the Dragon's general direction. "Bloody thing's stronger than ever."

Malik placed a thick hand on Steven's bobbing shoulder. "We did everything we could," he said. "All of us."

"We did." Steven stared upward. "And it wasn't enough."

Duane lowered the screwdriver. "That's the last connection."

"Let me see," Carlos said.

"Will it function as designed?"

"Difficult to say." Carlos held a small analyzing device next to the cube. "Qi balance looks right, but—"

"Wrap it up," Jasmine said, "before I throw you both overboard."

They turned to stare at her across the table.

"Jaz," Carlos began, "the cube's principle is derived from that of the *jiānyù*. But the physical-form containment feature is an entirely new, untested—"

She couldn't stand it any longer. She leaped to her feet, grabbed the cube, and ran. As she flipped open the hatch door, she heard Carlos's feeble protests behind her.

CHAPTER TWENTY-SEVEN

"Now or never, boys!" she cried.

She ran out on the wing and stopped short, assessing the situation. Roxanne and Kim were kneeling near the end of the wing, tending to Celine and Nicky. Mr. and Mrs. Lee stood against the fuselage, watching.

Out in the water, Steven was paddling back toward the plane along with Josie, Malik, and Liam. A wall of fire rose from the sea behind them. And up above . . .

"Hey!" Jasmine called. "DRAGON!"

The great beast paused. It whirled and swooped down, straight toward the plane.

Jasmine held out a hand to Steven, motioning him to stay away. He and the others paused in the water, eyeing the Dragon as it drew closer.

"Jasmine?" Roxanne asked, moving up next to her. "What are you doing?"

"Get back," Jasmine said. "This is my show."

I wish it weren't, she thought. *But it is.*

The Dragon dove low, whipping its tail in the air. *It looks magnificent,* she thought. She'd known the Dragon's power, felt its electric song coursing through her veins. She knew how beautiful it was.

And how deadly.

The Dragon slowed to a hover just above the water. It glanced down at Steven and his teammates, floating near the plane. It spat fire but not directly at them. The flames struck the water, sizzling and hissing. Just a warning, a reminder of the creature's power.

Then it turned and stared straight at Jasmine. Its nose hovered mere centimeters from hers.

Jasmine felt all eyes on her. She knew what they were thinking: the Dragon could fry her with its flame breath anytime it wanted. But she knew it wouldn't.

"Remember me?" she asked. "Your old bud? Your former host?"

The Dragon growled, low and unsure. *It's remembering,* she realized. *It's evolving beyond us, beyond humanity. I'm its last fading link to the human world.*

She held up the cube. "You know what this is?"

The creature hovered, staring at the bronze object. Jasmine stepped forward, almost to the edge of the plane's wing, and thrust the cube forward.

Suddenly, all the Dragon's energy flared at once, like a string of firecrackers igniting across its body. It recoiled, rearing back in midair.

"Yeah," Jasmine said. "You know."

The beast shrank away. Its vast wings flapped, its horns swept through the air. But it seemed weak, unable to move. Its body flickered once again and became transparent. Maxwell's limp body hung like a marionette at the beast's core.

Jasmine closed her eyes and thought a single word: *Go.*

Deep inside her mind, a presence stirred. It soared up, locked in on its destination, and shot forth like an arrow. She felt a tremendous sense of relief, a lightening of her spirit. And there was something else, too: a sound she couldn't make out at first.

Laughter.

Maxwell's essence flashed through the air, into the heart of the Dragon. Its body began to solidify again, but too late. As Maxwell reentered his body, his eyes opened wide. His expression grew dark, angry, dangerous.

The Dragon spat fire. It roared, a desperate howl of pain. The scream seemed to fill the world, but somehow Jasmine heard Maxwell's words over it:

Only I can control the Dragon.

Carlos and Duane emerged from the cockpit. She waved them away, keeping her eyes on the Dragon. *This is my show,* she thought again. *Mine and mine alone.*

The Dragon twitched, its huge wings slicing through the air. It flickered in and out of existence. Each time it returned, it seemed smaller, less powerful. And every time it faded, Maxwell grew stronger.

He raised an arm and pointed at Jasmine.

She nodded, standing her ground. She held up the cube, moving it forward like an offering. Maxwell aimed himself at the cube and started to will his way forward, flying through the air in slow motion.

The Dragon shrieked and wailed. But slowly it began to move along with Maxwell. It struggled, clawed the air, spat fire from its nostrils.

The wind from the creature's wings hammered against

Jasmine. The heat from its mouth was almost unbearable. She closed her eyes and turned away. But she kept her grip on the cube. Nothing else mattered.

As they drew closer to Jasmine, Maxwell and the Dragon seemed to shrink, dwindling in midair. Maxwell spread his arms and pulled the Dragon tight around him. Then he turned and reached out to the cube, as if surrendering to some magnetic pull.

With a final burst of flame, they screamed together and vanished inside the cube.

Jasmine dropped to her knees. The others gathered around her. Steven scrambled up onto the wing, with the other waterlogged team members right behind him.

"Did it work?" Duane asked.

"That was Maxwell," Roxanne said. "I'd know that arrogant laugh anywhere."

Carlos peered over Jasmine's shoulder. The cube pulsed and shook in her hands. It was hot, almost scalding to the touch. And one side now bore a faintly etched image of the Dragon.

"Step back," Steven said. "Give her some room."

Then it was just Steven and Carlos fussing over her, studying the cube in her hands. They helped her to her feet, asking if she was okay—supporting her as they always had.

For the last time, she thought.

Carlos pulled out his analyzer and started to run it over the cube. He paused at a second image, which bore

the likeness of a different Dragon: the thin-taloned creature that had been Maxwell's avatar.

"So he's inside there with it?" Steven asked. "It's over? We've won?"

"Not quite," Jasmine said.

She couldn't keep the sadness out of her voice. Both Steven and Carlos picked up on it immediately.

"Maxwell did as he promised," she continued. "But we can't trust him. He said only he could control the Dragon—but who's gonna control *him*?"

"Jaz," Carlos said, touching her arm, "one problem at a time. We can—"

Jasmine cried out. One side of the cube bulged, as if something was trying to push its way out from inside. The image of the Dragon—the new one, the crackling superbeast—opened its mouth wide, its eyes flaring red. Then it faded, retreating back inside the cube again.

"You see? Maxwell's good, but he's not as good as he thinks he is. He can't contain that thing alone." She took a deep breath. "He's gonna need help."

The realization hit Carlos first. His eyes went wide with panic. Steven was a beat behind, but then he started shaking his head rapidly, almost convulsively.

"No," Carlos said. "Jaz, no. You can't."

"I have to." She shifted the cube to one hand and touched Carlos's cheek with the other. "It's the only way. You know I'm right."

CHAPTER TWENTY-SEVEN

"No!" Carlos's eyes shifted from Jasmine to the cube and back again. "I—I just got you back, Jaz. I can't lose you again!"

"And I love you for that." She felt the tears starting. "I love you forever."

"We'll—Jaz, we'll find another way. Duane and I, we'll—"

"There's no time. You know that."

He moved closer to her, almost whispering in her ear. Steven pulled back, staring at them with wide, desperate eyes.

"You said we had to forgive ourselves," Carlos said. "That means you, too. Not just me."

"Maybe—" Her voice caught. "Maybe forgiving myself isn't enough. Maybe I need to make amends." She leaned in, sobbing on his shoulder. "All these years. All this time, I was too ashamed to admit what I'd done. Now I have the chance to make up for it—to atone for my sins.

"I have to do this."

Carlos said nothing. She heard him crying.

"Be well," she whispered.

Between them, the cube pulsed. She could feel the pressure, the power throbbing within it—the raging beast struggling to escape.

With a great effort, she pulled away from Carlos and cast her eyes over the scene. The ring of fire was already dying down, its flames sizzling away into the calming water. The Dragon was gone from the world, as if it had never been.

On the wing of the plane, Steven stood with the assembled Zodiacs, watching with concern. Kim the Rabbit, Duane the Pig, Roxanne the Rooster. Horse and Dog and the elusive, untrustworthy Snake. Liam the Ram and Malik the powerful Ox.

A real handful, Jasmine thought. *But a good bunch.*

She turned to Steven, forcing a smile. He opened his mouth to say something, but she waved a hand, cutting him off.

"You're in charge now, kid," she said. "Don't screw it up."

She tossed the cube to Carlos and jumped. As she swooped toward the containment unit in Carlos's hands, her body seemed to dwindle in size. For just an instant, Jasmine's old Dragon avatar appeared around her: lithe, wiry, with sharp fangs and deadly claws.

Then, in a flash of fire, she was gone.

EPILOGUE ONE: GREENLAND

STEVEN FOUND CARLOS in the big laboratory complex on the top floor of Zodiac headquarters. The scientist sat all alone in a desk chair, surrounded by computers, workstations, electron microscopes, and discarded clipboards.

Steven cleared his throat. "Gave everybody the day off, huh?"

"I just felt like being alone." Carlos swiveled his chair around. "Well, sort of alone." He held up the containment cube.

Steven walked over and took the cube. It was cool, inert. It hadn't bulged or made a sound since Jasmine entered it, two days before. He turned it over, noting the patterns on the sides. One showed the Uber-Dragon, as they'd begun calling it—the creature that had sought to destroy the human race. Another side bore the image of Maxwell's Dragon.

A third side showed Jasmine's Dragon. Slim, wiry, with short deadly claws.

"Is she really inside this thing?" Steven asked, holding up the cube. "What's going on in there?"

Carlos shrugged. "A world of adventure? A battle without end? An endless, blank void?" He gestured around the lab. "All this equipment, and none of it can tell me. There's no way to know."

Steven stared at the image of Jasmine's Dragon. Then, shaking his head, he handed back the cube.

Carlos held it up to the light, studying the different sides. "Maxwell," he said. "I wish she'd never met him. I wish none of us had."

Steven pulled up a chair. "Do you think he was really trying to sacrifice himself? For the good of mankind?"

"Maybe. Sort of." Carlos frowned. "But at the same time, he wanted to prove he was right all along. That only he could control the power. With Maxwell, it always comes down to ego."

"At least he's gone, too."

Carlos grunted.

EPILOGUE ONE

He looks better, Steven thought. *Still tired, and obviously upset about Jasmine. But his mind seems sharp again. He's back to his old self.*

Somehow, that made Steven think anything was possible.

"She put you in charge," Carlos said.

"Uh, yeah." Steven grimaced. "But you should really be running things. I'm not trying to—"

"No." Carlos looked over the cube, his expression serious. "I'm going to run a battery of tests on this thing, and then I'm going away for a while. I can't just keep the cube here—it's too dangerous."

"Oh," Steven said. "That makes sense."

"Besides, she trusted you." Carlos stared at the cube. "The world is counting on you now."

A dozen lame jokes danced around the edges of Steven's brain. But in the end, he just nodded. "Then I'll try to be worthy." He looked away, uncomfortable. "How, uh, how's the world *doing*, anyway?"

Carlos reached back and activated a screen. A muted newscast came on, showing a pretty blonde woman sitting before a stock image of Tamu Massif and a map of Japan. The headline read DISASTER AVERTED.

"Seismic levels have returned to normal," Carlos said. "I'm in touch with the Hawaii and Catania volcano institutes, but they've downgraded the situation to a wait-and-see."

"Looks like the world dodged a bullet," Steven

replied. "What about all those mind-controlled soldiers at Lystria?"

"Reviewing the reports from Malik's team, I'd say they only got a mild dose of the Dragon's mind-altering power. With the creature gone and the Lystria complex destroyed, they've returned to their normal state."

"Meaning they're a small army of confused mercenaries with no boss and no special powers." Steven nodded. "I think we can handle them."

"Of that," Carlos replied, "I have no doubt."

On the screen, the newscast zoomed in on the underwater volcano. A pile of rubble laid still, all that remained of Tamu Massif. No quakes shook the ocean floor.

And yet . . .

"There's one thing I don't understand," Steven said. "At the end, Mince tried to reactivate the volcano machinery. But the tech didn't work. Why?"

"Maybe all that Dragon energy shorted it out." Carlos frowned. "Or possibly it was the explosives from the drill-ship."

"Yeah. But . . . she was always so meticulous. Had every angle covered."

"Hell, maybe the circuitry got flooded with seawater." Carlos held up the bronze cube. "Some things, we may never know."

Carlos paused, as if considering his own words. He stood up and crossed to a high table. He set down the cube and donned a pair of reading glasses. Then he picked up a small analyzer, thumbing it to life.

Suddenly, Steven felt like an intruder.

"Well," he said. "I better go say good-bye to my parents."

"Oh, they left early this morning."

"What?"

Typical, he thought. *They couldn't even say good-bye. And I actually thought we were getting somewhere. . . .*

"They dropped off a few analysis tools that may prove useful. Oh, and they left this for you."

Without looking up, Carlos tossed a small metal object over his shoulder. Steven almost fumbled the catch. It was a flash drive.

When he looked back, Carlos was running the analyzer over the impassive metal cube. "I'll get her back," he said, almost too quietly for Steven to hear. "She never gave up on me; I won't give up on her."

Steven turned away, clutching the flash drive.

"I know you won't," he said.

The classroom two floors below was also empty. Steven didn't even turn on the lights. He took a seat, drew in a deep breath, and plugged the flash drive into a computer.

His father's face filled the screen. Mr. Lee looked the same as always: perfectly groomed, stern, disapproving.

"Steven," Mr. Lee said, "as you know by now, we

have already departed. Events dictated this change in our schedule."

Events, Steven thought. *Events like your need to avoid dealing with your son.*

"The destruction of Lystria has left a power vacuum in Maxwell's business operations," Mr. Lee continued. "I—we—intend to fill that vacuum."

Steven frowned. That was an unpleasant thought.

"Malosi will continue to assist us," Mr. Lee said. "He is already at work on several new projects that . . . well, you will hear of them shortly."

Malosi! Perfect, Dad. Why don't you just disown me and get it over with?

"Right now, however, I wanted to tell you something. And I thought it was best said this way, rather than face to face."

Of course.

"We have not always been easy on you, Steven. As your mother has said, that is because of our high hopes, our belief that you can become something greater than you are. As parents, it is both our right and our obligation to promote that growth through whatever means we deem best."

Steven turned away, rolling his eyes. *Is this an apology? Or an excuse?*

"I told you I believed you had accomplished nothing. With your gifts, your privileges, your great power." Mr. Lee's voice changed, dropped sharply in pitch. "I was wrong."

EPILOGUE ONE

Steven whirled back to face the screen.

"When you reached out to that girl . . . that strange, cruel girl inside the volcano . . . you made a great leap. She had tried to kill you, menaced your mother and me, committed hideous crimes against the world. And yet you tried to save her."

"I . . ." Steven spoke, his mouth dry. "I failed, though. I *didn't* save Mince."

"You tried," his father repeated, as if he'd heard Steven's words. "That is what matters. For one moment, you broke through her lifetime of pain and anguish. You also delayed her plans long enough for your friends to arrive and stop the Dragon."

On the screen, Mr. Lee paused. Steven felt uncomfortable, as if the two of them were actually in the same room, having an awkward conversation.

"In that moment," Mr. Lee continued, "I was very, very proud of you."

Steven blinked, stunned.

"Your mother says to stay warm." The screen went blank.

He couldn't speak, couldn't even move. He just sat in the dark, drinking in the silence.

Another cycle broken, he thought.

Kim appeared with a *poof*, scaring the hell out of him. He nearly fell off his chair.

"There you are!" She reached out and yanked him to his feet. "Come on. We're late!"

Before he could protest, she was dragging him into the hall. For someone so physically small, Kim was disturbingly strong when she set her mind to something.

"Hey," he said, struggling to keep up as she strode down the hall. "How's your dad?"

"Huh? Oh, he's doing better." She kept moving. "They probably don't need to stay here much longer."

"Then . . . did you mean what you said?" He hesitated. "In the volcano?"

"What? Which volcano?"

"The *first* volcano." He held out a hand to stop her. "You said we'd go away together. To see the wild animals."

She stopped, puzzled. Then she saw the earnest expression in his eyes, and she burst out laughing. Before he knew what was happening, she jumped up and kissed him on the lips. It was a quick peck, over in less than a second. But it meant something.

"Of course. Of course we will!" She punched him in the arm. "But right now we're late for—oh, come *on*. . . ."

She grabbed hold of him and leaped into the air. They disappeared with a *poof*.

Steven stumbled, disoriented, as they *poofed* into the training room—which had been completely transformed. Festive lights hung from the high ceiling, bathing the room in multicolored patterns. People milled around: civilians, Zodiacs, even a few formerly mind-controlled Vanguard soldiers invited by Malik and Josie.

EPILOGUE ONE

"Look!" Kim cried.

On the far side of the room, a stage had been constructed. Roxanne paced back and forth across it. She wore tight jeans and a black T-shirt with the Zodiac logo on it, a guitar strap slung over her shoulder. Behind her, another guitarist, a bass player, and a drummer laid down a powerful electric sound.

"That's her old band," Steven said, astonished. *"Les Poules."*

"Victoryyyyy," Roxanne sang, projecting into the microphone with every fiber of her being, *"over the forces of . . ."*

"What's this song about?" Steven yelled, struggling to be heard over the music.

"Saving the whales, probably!" Kim was practically jumping up and down with excitement. "Isn't this cool?"

"Oi!" Liam pushed his way through the crowd, holding out three plastic cups. "You two kids care for a nonalcoholic beverage?"

Steven took a cup and frowned. The liquid in it was bright blue. "What is this?"

"I call it Dragon Punch," Liam replied. "Looks nasty, but it goes down pretty fast."

Kim downed hers in one gulp. "Take that, Dragon!"

Steven laughed.

"Everybody's here!" Liam said. "Rox even gave Nicky and Josie jobs as roadies!"

He pointed to the stage. Nicky, in full Dog form, had

hefted a huge amplifier onto his back and was lugging it from one side of the stage to the other.

"He said he wanted a job!" Steven said.

"I offered to play percussion!" Liam said. "Bloody Rooster turned me down. Blasted me into a wall with her power, in fact."

The song ended with a flourish. The room erupted in applause. Steven saw Malik in the audience, talking with Mags, Billy, and Dafari. Onstage, Josie helped Nicky rearrange the drum set.

Celine, the enigmatic Snake, stood alone across the room. She caught Steven's eye and raised her cup in a silent toast. Then she smiled and turned back toward the stage.

"Thank you!" Roxanne cried. Her amplified voice echoed through the room. "And now I'd like to play a very special number. . . . It's dedicated to all my teammates." She pointed the microphone out into the audience. "Especially Mr. *Steven Lee*."

A spotlight played across the room and picked out Steven. He cringed in mock terror.

The lights dimmed. The band launched into a new song: a softer, slower piece. Roxanne's eyes seemed to light up with a deep, warm confidence. She grabbed the microphone and leaned forward.

"Justice," she sang. *"There must be justice in this worrrrrrld. . . ."*

Kim clapped her hands.

Liam frowned. "What's so special about this one?"

"I know," Steven said. "It's the song she was playing when Jasmine and I first met her."

Duane approached, tapping on a tablet computer. "Madness," he muttered. "I cannot make this work. . . ."

"Duane!" Liam clapped him on the back. "Put down the Zodiac business for one night, man!"

"This isn't Zodiac business." Duane looked up. "I'm planning Roxanne's tour schedule."

"She's going on tour?" Steven asked.

"She wants to do three shows a night." Duane clicked the tablet off in disgust. "Impossible!"

"With justiiiiiice," Roxanne sang, *"all is possible. . . ."*

Steven reached over and took Kim's hand. She squeezed his hand and moved closer to him. He leaned down to speak into her ear.

"The last time Roxanne played this song," he said, gesturing up at the stage, "her power started a riot."

"She's learned to control it," Kim replied. "Maybe she can be a hero and lead a normal life, too."

"Yeah," he said. "Maybe we all can."

The song segued into a long instrumental bridge. Liam moved in closer to Kim and Steven. "I hear you two are takin' a break," he said. "What's next?"

Kim and Steven exchanged blank looks.

"After that," Duane elaborated. "What do we do now? The team, I mean?"

Steven looked out over the sea of people. Zodiacs and Vanguards; scientists and soldiers; powered people and civilians. All dancing, laughing, celebrating the victory they'd fought so hard to win.

The cycle, he thought. *It's finally broken.*

"Anything," he said, squeezing Kim's hand tight. "We can do anything we want."

EPILOGUE TWO: LYSTRIA

MONKEY SAT, DEJECTED, munching on his last banana. His long toes gripped one of the metal arms that had once stretched above the Lystria complex; now it was just a jagged strut hanging precariously from the remains of a control tower. The central building had completely collapsed into the abyss.

Smoke rose from the deep hole, thick and foul-smelling. Monkey lifted a long finger, following the gray trail as it flowed up into the sky. "It won't go out," he muttered.

"Maybe it's the fires beneath the earth," said someone with a lilting voice. "The ones our dear departed Dragon tried to harness."

Monkey rolled his eyes. He looked toward the edge of the abyss, knowing what he'd see. A short hooded figure scuttled along the metallic strut, headed toward him.

Rat.

"On the other hand," Rat continued, "maybe it's the souls of Lystria's dead. They're finally free of Maxwell."

"Shut up," Monkey said. But he could barely work up enough energy for an argument.

"Sorry," Rat said, a smirk creeping over his face. "I shouldn't have mentioned Maxwell."

"He was a great man," Monkey muttered. "And now he's gone."

"Yeah . . . well . . ." Rat reached into his coat. "I had a little to do with that."

He pulled out a ragged circuit board with a few wires hanging loose. Monkey stared at it and shook his head in irritation. "What's that?"

"Main control board for the Tamu Massif installation," Rat said. "Took a bit of doing. But no matter how sophisticated the tech, all it takes is one Rat to muck up the works." He mimed a vicious chewing motion.

Monkey looked closer. The circuit board had visible bite marks on it.

He looked at Rat, astonished. "Why? Why would you betray Maxwell?"

"He wasn't Maxwell. Not anymore."

Monkey turned away, but Rat scuttled over next to

him. The strut dipped slightly under their combined weight.

"Come on," Rat said. "This is exciting! Maxwell's gone; the cycle has been broken. We can do anything we want."

"I just want him back."

"There's technology here that I've never even *seen* before." Rat pointed down at the remains of the complex. "Now it's all ours."

Monkey looked down. Little men dressed like Rat bustled all around the edges of the hole, pulling out equipment and salvaging pieces of the damaged machines. One of them pried a computer screen free of a fallen piece of control tower, squealed in delight, and vanished into the shadows with his prize.

Ratlings, Rat called the men. Monkey didn't like them. They gave him the creeps.

"Evil never dies, you know," Rat continued. "Take you, for instance. Maxwell *created* you, in a way, by altering your mind to make you loyal to him. Now he's gone. If you wanted, you could replace him."

"I don't wanna replace him," Monkey grumbled.

He tossed his banana peel into the hole. It disappeared in the smoke.

"Wait a minute," he said, turning sharply to Rat. "Do *you* wanna take Maxwell's place? To run Vanguard?"

"Honestly? I haven't decided."

Monkey shook his head. That was the trouble with

talking to Rat; all you got was riddles. You never knew which side he was really on.

Monkey looked down again, into the burning hole in the desert. He wished he could be like the smoke, rising into the sky. Free to fly, free to go wherever he wanted.

Rat was staring at him.

"Let me ask you a question," Rat said. "Something your precious Maxwell would never have thought to ask."

Monkey threw up his long arms. "What?"

Rat's beady eyes seemed to bore into him. Those eyes weren't cruel, though. They seemed to burn with a strange, urgent curiosity.

"What do *you* want?"

END BOOK THREE